C000246947

About the author

Susan Parry began writing when she was a university professor at Imperial College. Her work included forensic studies and archaeological investigations that form the basis for her writing. She lives with her husband in Swaledale, where the views from her house provide inspiration.

website: www.susanparry.co.uk
facebook/instagram: susanparryauthor
twitter: @susan_parry

THE YORKSHIRE DALES MYSTERY SERIES

FROZEN GROUND

A YORKSHIRE DALES MYSTERY

SUSAN PARRY

Viridian Publishing

This edition first published in the United Kingdom in 2013 by
Viridian Publishing

Reprinted in 2021

Viridian Publishing
PO Box 594
Dorking
Surrey
RH4 9HU

www.viridian-publishing.co.uk
e-mail: enquiries@viridian-publishing.co.uk

ISBN 978-0-9567891-2-9

For Elspeth

Chapter 1

'Couldn't you have waited until morning, Gran?' Len muttered as he struggled out of bed. Cursing, he pulled an old work shirt over his vest, tightened the belt on his jeans and knelt down in the dust to fumble under the bed for his boots. With a quick look round the caravan he grabbed his jacket, patting the pockets for his keys.

The icy wind cut through him as he locked up and struggled with the door of the truck. It took several minutes of scraping before there was a reasonable area of clear windscreen. Impatient to be off, he jumped in, revved the engine, slammed it into first and left the field in a cloud of blue smoke.

As soon as there was a signal, he called his sister.

'It's Gran, she's getting worse.'

'I know, our Daryl called me. He says it won't be long… I wish I could be there.'

'Don't worry, I'm on my way.'

'Be careful, now. We've got ice…'

Len threw the phone on the seat beside him; there would be no signal again until he reached Sedbergh. Turning up the music, he put his foot down, knowing every twist and turn of the road. Not that it was a difficult journey, at four in the morning the lanes were empty except for the occasional rabbit.

He went through the empty streets of Hawes at speed, enjoying the opportunity to behave a little irresponsibly. The road was fairly straight once he'd left the town behind and, although white with snow, it was passable. He pictured his grandmother the way she'd been on his last visit – hardly conscious, drifting in and out of sleep. He had to concentrate as he approached Garsdale; the road wound this way and that, and twice he nearly lost control on a bend.

The wind was blowing the snow straight at him, slowing the truck. He pressed the accelerator harder, took the bend too fast and immediately slammed on the brakes, swerving to avoid a large vehicle parked at the side of the road. He'd been so preoccupied he'd almost gone straight into the back of it. There was a rush of adrenalin as he tried the brake pedal again then pulled helplessly at the steering wheel, but he was on an inevitable trajectory towards the wall on the other side of the road. Another repair job, he thought, as the sound of metal scraping along the stones reached a crescendo. The road was rushing towards him as the truck flipped onto its side and came to a gradual halt. Len was left dangling, suspended by the seat belt and wondering where the air bag was, before slipping into unconsciousness.

Daryl's huge frame was hovering awkwardly at the end of the bed when Len drifted back from a series of alarming nightmares into the warm, bright environment of the ward.

'You were supposed to come as a visitor, man,' he joked, looking down at him with a grin. There was weariness in his face that belied the light-heartedness.

It took a few seconds for Len to gather his thoughts. 'How's Gran?' he asked, struggling to get up.

His brother held up a hand to stop him. 'I think you'll find that difficult – you've hit your head and broken your arm.'

The throbbing pain eased a little as he lay back down on the pillow.

'She's comfortable.' Daryl looked anxious. 'That's what they said – comfortable.' He waved the carrier bag he was holding. 'I said I'd take these things of hers back to the home, for Eileen to wash.' He hesitated, rubbing his ear, a nervous gesture familiar to Len. 'The police want to speak to you, mate. They need a statement. I told them it would've been the ice… but they've got to hear it from you.'

A nurse appeared pushing a small trolley.

'I'd better be going,' Daryl said. 'I'll be back this evening.'

'See you later.' Len lifted his arm in an attempt to wave then thought better of it.

'Later.' A brief forced smile and Daryl was gone. Len watched him disappear through the double doors before turning his gaze to the other patients. Most were propped up, with visitors seated beside them; two at the end of the ward were obscured by curtains. He closed his eyes to concentrate on what had happened. When he opened them again, a young police officer was standing beside his bed.

'Len Meehan?' the policeman asked.

'Aye.' He struggled to sit up but fell back exhausted by the effort. 'Sorry, I was asleep.'

'I'm Jamie… PC Jamie Reed.' He rummaged in his top pocket and produced a pencil.

'You've come about the crash?' Len asked.

'Yes, sir. It won't take long.' He pulled up a chair and carefully opened his notebook. After writing down the address of Len's caravan, he asked, 'The accident. How did it happen?'

'It was icy. When I swerved to avoid another vehicle, I lost control.'

'What time was this, sir? You weren't found until six this morning.'

'Daryl rang me. It was about four o'clock. My grandmother, she's not well. She's in hospital.'

'Here in Lancaster Infirmary?'

Len saw the irony. 'Well, I got here then.'

'And what exactly caused you to turn the truck over?'

'I told you, there was a big van or something parked in the road.'

'Did it have its lights on?'

'No, that's why I didn't see it.'

'There was no sign of it when the motorist found you. Are you sure?'

'Does it matter? I didn't hit it.' He was beginning to tire of the interminable questions. His head was going fuzzy.

'I don't know, sir, at this stage. It depends on whether you are found to have been driving without due care and attention. I don't imagine you'd be done for dangerous driving.'

'Great.'

'I'll be visiting the location to find out if a vehicle *was* left in the road but I need to ask you, sir, had you been drinking?'

'No! No, I had not.' He closed his eyes, hoping the copper would take the hint.

He heard the notebook snap shut.

'Your insurance is in order, we checked that; repairing a stone wall can be expensive – it's a craftsman's job.'

'You don't need to tell me – it's what I do for a living.' He opened his eyes again.

The constable laughed. 'In that case you'll be able to save a few quid.' He stood up and put his notebook away. 'Once you're fit enough of course.'

Len slept, interrupted only by the tea trolley and the smell of dinner. Soon after he'd finished eating, Daryl arrived carrying a large sports bag.

'Eileen sent some pyjamas and an old dressing gown from the home.' He pulled out a blue towelling robe and a red creased bundle, shoving them in the locker beside Len's bed. 'She says the old man doesn't need them now.'

'You want me to wear a dead man's pyjamas?'

His brother ignored him. 'Is there anything else you need?'

'A bottle of whisky would be good.'

Daryl laughed.

'I'm serious,' Len told him. 'I'm gasping for a drink.'

'They wouldn't let you, would they? I mean with the medicine and stuff?'

Len sighed. 'How's Gran then?'

'Just the same. She's away with the fairies, doesn't know who I am. You're best out of it, mate.'

'It's not fair on you though.'

'I'll survive.' He slumped down in the chair, staring at the floor.

Len must have dozed in the silence between them because when he woke his brother was gone. Visitors were leaving the ward and Len felt surprisingly melancholy and alone. The medication trolley came round; the shift changed and just after the ward lights had dimmed Daryl reappeared at his bedside.

'They said I could come in…' he began.

Len could tell he was shaken.

'Is it Gran?'

'Yes.' He lowered himself onto the edge of the bed. 'Just now. I was there.'

It was the first time Len had seen his big brother cry.

PC Jamie Reed stepped gingerly out of his patrol car into the muddy yard. The arrangements for the visit had been inconclusive so he was hoping that now was a suitable time, between milking and the farmer's tea. A middle-aged woman in an apron answered the door. She was not unlike his mother.

'Hello young man, come in.'

The door opened directly onto the kitchen and he couldn't help but notice the array of pies and cakes laid out on the table.

'Excuse the mess. I've been baking for the WI stall. Sit yourself down. I'll call Tom.'

He could hear her summoning her husband with an urgent hushed tone. A man's voice told her not to fuss. She returned followed by a tall man with black greasy hair, drying his hands on a grubby looking towel. His wife grabbed it from him and busied herself making a pot of tea.

'So what's this all about, then? Did my brother-in-law send you?' He scowled across at Jamie suspiciously.

'Take no notice of him,' she said. 'My brother, Mike, he's in charge at Kirkby Stephen, that's all.'

'Sergeant Crossland?'

'Aye, that's right, lad. But that's not why you're here, is it?' asked the man, easing himself into a chair at the table.

'You heard about the accident down on the main road?' asked Jamie.

'Oh aye, made a right mess of the wall along there.' He took a thick slice of bread and butter, tearing a large mouthful off and chewing it angrily.

'Is it yours?'

'Not mine. Have you got the fellow who did it?'

'Yes, he's in hospital with a broken arm.'

'Car a right-off?' He took another slice of bread.

'Yes, I think so.'

'It's a dangerous corner and it were icy last night. Poor bugger.' He sounded unsympathetic despite what he said.

'He says he swerved to avoid a large vehicle parked on the side. Would that be yours?'

He looked up. 'Last night? No. Why would I be there at night?'

'Is there anyone else who would be parked down there in the early hours of the morning?'

'No. I'd know if there were anything.'

'To be honest, sir, I'm beginning to wonder if there was a vehicle at all. I reckon he was driving too fast and it's just an excuse.'

The farmer's wife placed a mug of tea in front of Jamie, and a large piece of fruit cake.

'Does he look like he needs building up, Margaret? I tell thee, lad, she'll not let you go until you've eaten every scrap!' He appeared to be joking but there was an irritation in his voice that suggested he would be glad to see him gone.

The sky had turned a thick grey by the time Jamie left the

cosy farmhouse and ventured into the freezing wind. There were light flakes of snow in the air and he drove more cautiously than usual, particularly when he reached the bend where the crash had happened. Slowing right down, he surveyed the road ahead. There was a stretch between the corner and the place where the wall had been hit. The truck would have cleared the corner before it swerved. Whatever had happened, he could see no point in pursuing the poor guy in hospital over what was probably just an accident in bad weather. But it wasn't his call, he'd do the report and it would be up to his superiors to make the decision.

By the time Jamie arrived at the station, the snow was falling in large flakes. The yard was devoid of tracks and his own car stood with a layer of white at least a centimetre thick. The boss is still here then, he thought as he walked carefully round to the front of the building.

'Ah, young James. How did you get on, lad?'

He described his interview at the hospital as briefly as he could.

'So Meehan is saying that there was a vehicle parked without lights on the road, causing him to swerve and lose control of his truck?'

'Yes, sir.'

'D'you think he's telling the truth?'

'The owner of the farm says he didn't have a vehicle out there overnight.'

'Is he reliable, d'you think?'

'It were Mr Drysdale, sir. I think he's a relative?'

'Tom? Is that where it happened?' He laughed. 'I think we can assume he's telling the truth. Indeed, why would he leave a vehicle in the road? It's not an obvious thing to do unless it had become immobile – in which case it would still be there now.'

'The driver swears it were there, sir.'

'We only have his word. I suggest you write up your report and we'll pass it on. You'd best be quick, the snow's getting right heavy.'

It took Jamie an hour to write the short report required by his senior officer. He'd always been slow at compiling his thoughts and in this particular case he felt muddled, finally accepting that all he could do was repeat what the driver and the farmer had said. By the time he closed the file, several more centimetres of snow had fallen and cars were sliding down the road outside.

'Are you done, lad?' The boss was switching off the light in his office and pulling on a large anorak. 'Best be getting home before it gets worse. By the way, there's been a general warning gone out about sheep rustlers in the area. There was a theft in Lancashire last night. I hope there's not a call out tonight for our sakes!'

'No, sir.' Privately Jamie thought it would be a bit of excitement he'd be happy to get out of bed for.

'Well, keep your eyes open for any strange vehicles when you're out and about.'

'Yes, sir.'

It took Jamie considerable time to clear his car and the interior was freezing cold. The route home was slippery and slow, particularly when he turned off the main road and crawled along the lane towards the farm. The sight of the open gate into the yard reminded him of the need to be vigilant; after all, it would be easy to entice hungry sheep into a wagon with a bit of fodder this weather.

His parents had been worrying about him, anxious that

he would make it home in time for tea. Mum had kept his pie and chips warm in the oven and she fussed over him until he'd finished eating. It was then he remembered to tell his father about the warning.

'There's been some sheep taken in Lancashire, did you know?'

'Aye, so I heard. Nigh on fifty near Preston. They've got a nerve, I'll say that. They just drove up wi' a trailer, piled 'em in and went off again. No sign of 'em.'

'A trailer? How do they know?'

'Left tracks. A sixteen-footer they reckon.'

'You'd think someone would have seen something.'

His mother had brought in coffee. 'How many people d'you see at night on your travels?'

'True enough Rita. There won't be many folk about tonight, that's for sure.'

'All the more reason for them to be on the prowl,' suggested Jamie.

'Coffee?' his mother asked, as she poured a cup without waiting for a reply.

'Can you stick it in a flask for me, Mum?'

'You're not going out tonight?'

Jamie shrugged his shoulders.

'But you're working tomorrow. And there are a couple of inches of snow out there. Bob, tell him not to be so daft.'

'Is it to do with them sheep thefts?' his father asked.

'Yes. We've been asked to be extra vigilant.' It was the truth, he thought.

'Well, the overtime will be useful, son. But you'd best take the Land Rover. It looks like the snow's settling in for the night. And take my shooting jacket – it'll be warmer than that waterproof of yours.'

When Jamie left the house, the snow covering the yard was about ten centimetres thick. The icy wind was freezing the ground and his hands were almost numb by the time he'd cleared the windscreen. It was not much better inside the vehicle when he started the engine and pulled out onto the lane.

He was driving on pristine snow and visibility was poor as the headlights picked up the falling flakes. The Land Rover slewed its way to the main road, where at least there were some tracks, indicating it was passable. He guessed the A66 would be closed by now and hoped there wouldn't be a call out – there would be trouble if he was out of contact when they tried to reach him. Progress was slow on the empty road and it was nearly ten o' clock when he reached Sedbergh and turned down into Garsdale.

The snow persisted and the wind was sweeping it into drifts at the side of the road. Jamie had been driving on the farm for years and was used to poor conditions but he was struggling to keep the Land Rover on course, at times slowing down to a crawl to take the corners. He was beginning to think that no-one in their right mind would be out in such weather. But he was certain the sighting of a large vehicle the previous night had been sheep rustlers disturbed by the truck crashing into the wall. If he was going to steal livestock he would also choose this time of year, when the animals were cold and hungry and it would only take the shake of a bag of food for them to come running.

When he reached the damaged wall he drove on another few metres until he found the entrance to the next field. It was just round the corner from where the large vehicle had been seen. The snow was so deep it would be difficult to get into the field and he gave up the idea of hiding behind the stone wall. Moving further down the road, he turned onto the track to the Drysdale's farm and left the Land Rover parked out of sight. Unfortunately this meant he was unable to see the road but he was sure he would spot the lights of any vehicle that passed.

Once the engine was off and the lights out, the residual heat soon eked away. Jamie poured a coffee, grasping the cup for warmth and sipped it gratefully. He found the cake and biscuits his mother had thoughtfully provided but soon they were gone and he was left sitting in the cold and dark thinking it had been a bad idea to come out. Nevertheless it would be difficult to return home without having appeared to have done a full shift, so he pulled the collar of his jacket up and huddled down for warmth.

It took a few seconds to remember where he was when he first woke. Realising he'd been roused by a sound from behind him, he sat up slowly, forcing himself awake. Before he could turn round there was an icy draught as the car door was flung open and he was blinded by the light from a torch being directed in his face.

Chapter 2

Brian Maynard pulled on his long woollen socks and wellingtons before taking his old Barbour from the peg in the lobby.

'I won't be long!' he shouted to his wife as he reached for his cap and called the dogs.

Wild Boar Fell rose magnificently in the distance, completely covered in fresh snow. His hands were numb with cold as he struggled to open the barn door against the deep white drift. This is going to be a long job, he thought. The dogs, anxious to be off, yelped and whined until he'd finished loading up the hay. The quad bike was sparkling with frost and the sacking he used on the seat crackled under his weight.

'Come on, you two, let's be having you.'

Brian let the brake off, the bike rolled slowly out of the yard and down the snow-covered track towards the road as the collies jumped obediently onto the back. At first they travelled quietly on the layer of snow that had fallen overnight, but at the bottom of the lane the surface cracked noisily where it had frozen into peaks and troughs. He moved slowly until he reached the field where his first flock was grazing. Leaving the engine running he walked over to the gate with a bag of pellets, expecting to see the ewes running down towards him. But the field was silent and empty. The dogs ran round sniffing and yelping while Brian cursed. Someone had left the gate open and he'd have to spend the morning finding them. The most annoying part was that the gate had been forcibly opened, pushing back the snow into a pile by the wall. He could see where the sheep had left tracks in the snow but whether the boot prints were his or someone else's he couldn't tell.

'It's no good,' he moaned when he returned to the farm for breakfast, cold and miserable. 'There's no sign of 'em.'

'They can't have gone far, can they?' Angela had her back to him and was frying bacon on the Rayburn.

He didn't answer. Now he would have to wait for a phone call to tell him where they'd got to.

'What about the ones in the field further along the road?' she asked as they sat at the kitchen table.

'They're fine.'

'So how many are missing?'

'Twenty-four. I'll ring the police; they might've had a call. I don't want them causing an accident in the ice. Then I'll have another look round.'

The dogs were pleased to be out again, jumping eagerly onto the bike as he set off. He planned to secure the gate with twine, even if there was nothing left to protect. He'd expected a call by now, sheep don't just disappear unless... well, he wasn't going to contemplate that possibility just yet.

The collies cavorted excitedly in the snow and disappeared from sight while he struggled to tie the twine with cold hands. There was no sign when he called and in the end he was forced to climb the gate he'd just secured and walk up the field to find them, whistling at intervals. The sight that met him when he reached the brow of the hill would stay with him for ever. The grotesque form of a motionless sheep prostrate in the crimson snow. The dogs, frozen by the anger in his voice, crept away from the body. He recognised one of his best ewes and bent down to examine it then stepped back in horror. He called his dogs to look for any more but she was the only one left in the field.

Shaken, Brian walked slowly back to the bike. The dogs, seeming to sense his mood, followed on foot and crept into their sleeping quarters where they stayed for the remainder of the day.

'They've been stolen right enough,' Brian announced when he got through to the police station. 'There's a dead 'un been left in the field. She's been finished off with a shotgun. There'll be no lambs from her come spring.'

'I'll get someone to you as soon as I can – we're a bit short-staffed this morning I'm afraid, Mr Maynard. And I'll contact the Wildlife Officer.'

'Come on Jamie, where are you?' Sergeant Crossland muttered to himself as he put the phone down and searched under a pile of paper for the sheet with the Wildlife Officers' contact details.

The sergeant tried two numbers before he received a response.

'Harry Clark.' The voice at the other end was bright and friendly.

'Sergeant Crossland here. I was told to get in touch with you.'

'Yes?'

Harry was used to calls out of the blue, particularly at the weekend. A dead badger. An injured bird. Even livestock on the motorway. But he'd not been contacted about lost sheep before.

'You say they were stolen last night?'

'So he says. One's been shot and left behind dead. I'm sending one of my constables out, as soon as he comes in, to get the facts, but they told me I had to let you know as well.'

'Fair enough. If you give me the address...'

Jamie's car was the only vehicle in the yard when Bob Reed looked out to check the weather. He stood at the window for a moment scratching his head before going into his son's bedroom.

'He's not back yet, Rita!' he called.

Although he hadn't been in the force very long, Jamie often had to work nights and at first Bob wasn't concerned, even though his son's shift should have finished an hour ago. But the boy knew he would want his Land Rover to start work on the farm.

When the eight o'clock news began on the radio, Bob and Rita looked at each other.

'He'd better bring it back soon – I'll be needing it this morning.'

'Can't you ring the station, Bob?'

'If they're out working they'll not be there, love.' But he could see she was fretting and he wanted to get out to the fields. 'All right, I'll do it anyway.'

He got through immediately and was about to ask to speak to his son when the sergeant interrupted. 'Are you ringing in for Jamie? It's thick here – I expect it's worse with you. Tell him not to worry if he's going to be late.

We'll manage until he gets here.'

'He's not here. I was calling to find out where he's gone.'

It took a little while for Bob to understand that Jamie had not been on duty the previous night.

'Perhaps he's visiting his young lady,' the sergeant joked, but Bob knew his son wouldn't let his mother worry unnecessarily, whatever the reason.

'I need the Land Rover,' he complained, but it wasn't the vehicle he was really concerned about.

'Don't you worry Mr Reed, we'll get to the bottom of it.' He laughed loudly. 'After all, that's what we're here for, isn't it?'

It was too soon to formally report Jamie Reed missing but Bob could tell that the sergeant was disturbed. He knew that Jamie was a dependable boy. He took the registration number of the Land Rover but said there wasn't much else that could be done at the moment. Bob didn't tell the sergeant how concerned he really felt: people could die of hyperthermia in this weather and he was afraid for his son.

When he related what had passed between him and Sergeant Crossland, Rita insisted they telephone Shelley, Jamie's girlfriend.

'He may be right, Bob,' she insisted. 'He might have dropped in to see her and got caught by the snow.'

Grudgingly Bob called her number, before realising she was probably travelling to work. Sure enough it went to voicemail and he waited for her cheery message to finish before simply asking her to call him as soon as she could.

Harry watched the CSI team carrying the body of the ewe away for necropsy, which, as he'd informed them, was the official term for the postmortem examination of an animal. It was obvious how it had been killed but they might at least get some lead shot as evidence. He'd had little chance to examine the body but that was fine – the training course had not equipped him for dealing with sheep and he was nervous that he'd look foolish. He'd covered badger-baiting, raptor-poisoning and egg theft among other things but the nearest he'd been to this was deer poaching.

'Your first experience of sheep rustling is it?' A kindly officer from Cumbria Constabulary, who had introduced himself as Graham Patterson, was asking. He'd accompanied the body to the vehicle but was now back beside him, panting slightly with the exertion of climbing up the field.

'Yes, sir.'

'You'll get used to it. These types, they don't look after the animals. They could at least have the decency to treat them well before they go to slaughter.'

'Where d'you think they'll have taken them?' Harry asked, thinking they might be shipping them abroad.

'A dodgy abattoir somewhere. There are plenty of bent people around, particularly now times are harder. D'you know how many animals were taken last year?'

'Quite a lot.'

'Over sixty thousand.'

'Never! Do they ever get them back?'

'Aye, there were some fifty-five pregnant ewes taken from Preston last year. Got them back and charged three men – the case is due at Preston Crown Court.'

'At least they caught the culprits then.'

Graham didn't answer but prodded the snow with his toe. Finally he looked up. 'There were fifteen hundred sheep taken down in Lincolnshire. They made an arrest but they've not got the sheep.'

'Fifteen hundred?' repeated Harry, 'That makes this seem small-fry.'

'Still a big problem for the farmer concerned.'

'Let's hope they find them this time then,' suggested Harry.

'They? What d'you mean *they*, lad? We're the wildlife experts. It's down to us.'

Harry felt ill-prepared for the task and it must have shown because Graham patted him on the shoulder. 'Don't worry, lad, we'll have some help. I'm in touch with the National Wildlife Crime Unit and they'll give us some support in contacting other regions if we need to.'

He turned to walk down to the gate and Harry followed. The numerous pairs of boots trudging up and down the field had formed a slippery track that made progress difficult. When they reached the gate the men exchanged mobile numbers with the promise that any news would be passed on. Harry had been assured that Cumbria would keep him posted but the feeling was that the thieves would have used the M6 to get away from the area. If that was the case then all Harry had left to do was get back to Harrogate to write up his report.

As he prepared to drive off, Graham stopped him and indicated to him to wind down his window.

'Are you busy tomorrow?' he asked.

'No. I mean I don't know. Why?'

'Just a thought. We could speak to a few of the locals, find out if anyone saw or heard anything last night. It's too late now but if we make an early start…'

'What time?'

'I'll meet you here at, say, ten – after all it is a Sunday.'

The main roads were passable and Harry made good progress, reaching the flat before dark. He turned up the heating and left his jacket on until the place was warm. He was hoping for a message from Mills – she'd promised to ring when she knew what she was doing at the weekend but so far there'd been nothing. He'd left a message on her mobile but there had been no response and her land line just went to voicemail. He quickly sent a text then turned on the television. He found a lasagne in the freezer and stuck it in the microwave, opened a can of beer and waited for her call.

Rita Reed looked small and frail hunched in her chair by the window. The cat jumped off her lap when Bob came in and walked round his feet as he made for the teapot. It was warm – just.

'I'll make some more, it must be cold,' his wife said, pulling herself out of the chair.

She didn't look at him as she held the kettle under the tap then placed it on the Aga. Her face looked pale under the glare of the fluorescent light. Bob couldn't bring himself to ask if there had been any news. He felt guilty for sleeping while she held her overnight vigil. She'd tell him if the police had been in contact.

'I just wish there was something we could do.' Rita's voice was so soft he hardly caught what she'd said.

'Why don't you get some sleep?'

'No, it'll be light in a couple of hours. I need to be doing something to help but I can't ring round at this time.'

'Is there anyone we can text or e-mail? There must be places on the internet where people put information.'

Rita's body straightened almost imperceptibly. 'You're right. I'll go and post something on a noticeboard or whatever...'

She disappeared into the study leaving Bob to make the tea. When he took her a cup, she had become alive again and was anxious to show him a site giving advice to families in their situation.

'I know it's different for us because we know he hasn't run off and the police will do everything to find him but it suggests things we can try...'

'Like what?'

'Making posters, circulating his description. I thought I'd make a flyer – I've got that nice photo from Duncan's wedding.'

'Good idea.' He tried to mirror her enthusiasm.

Bob had his own view of what had happened and feared that his son was lying frozen out on the fells or in a river having foolishly got lost in the blizzard. It was only time before they would find his Land Rover abandoned on the side of the road on the tops, somewhere remote over in Garsdale or Mallerstang. At least he could be proud that his son had been doing his duty as a police officer – even if it was in an informal capacity.

As soon as it was light Rita persuaded him to go out looking for the Land Rover. She had to stay, in case the police called and she was still working on the leaflet, but she wanted him out there doing something constructive. So, reluctantly, he took the car and set off through Kirkby Stephen to Mallerstang.

Wild Boar Fell was as imposing as ever in a covering of white and, as Bob drove, the sun appeared to cast bright shafts across its flanks. Normally his heart would lighten at the sight but this morning the loneliness of the scene reminded him of what a small fragile being his son would be out on its slopes.

He didn't need a map to search, there were few farms and fewer roads crossing the isolated dale. He knew it was pointless and pulled up on the side of the road opposite the ruins of Pendragon Castle. A strange Land Rover parked overnight would soon be reported, particularly after sheep being taken so close to home. Farmers hereabouts would be on full alert – if anyone had seen his vehicle or his son they would have reported it by now. He hit the steering wheel in frustration, allowing himself to be wretched – but only for a few seconds – then anger replaced despair. The police had done nothing, refusing to launch search parties until they knew where he'd been seen last. The sergeant had assured him they'd set every possible means of finding Jamie but nothing was happening and it was driving them both mad. He pulled himself together and continued on to the Moorcock Inn, where he turned right to Sedbergh. When he arrived, the town was just waking up and he parked the car to walk through the melting slush in search of a coffee.

It was difficult to hear Rita's strangely tense and shaky voice against the rattling of crockery and the radio playing bland music in the background. There was no news but he told her he'd get home as soon as he could.

'Ask the newsagents if they'll take some of the leaflets,' she said.

He didn't want to. 'When they're ready, love.'

'I've been thinking we should talk to the papers.'

'You mean the Herald?'

'That and others. There's the Gazette as well but I was

thinking the national papers. It says on the net that we should advertise as widely as possible and if that means the radio and national…'

'OK, all right. Wait until I get back, there'll be time for that later. The line's not good.'

He understood why she was doing it – anything to keep occupied, to feel useful.

As soon as he was on the road again, speeding home, he felt better. Perhaps there would be some news. He'd go and see Sergeant Crossland later, make sure the police were doing everything they could. Maybe it was a big misunderstanding and Jamie would be there when he got back.

But there was no need for him to go to the police station: Sergeant Crossland was in the kitchen talking to Rita and Shelley when he reached the farm.

'… so we'll keep you informed regularly and let you know if there are any developments.' He drained his cup and placed it carefully in the saucer before moving his large frame out of the chair and into a standing position.

'We're very grateful, aren't we Bob?'

'Yes, we know you'll be doing everything you can.'

'I was telling your wife, we've got every patrol in the region looking out for your vehicle and the number has been reported to ANPR – the automatic number plate recognition system. If it's on the road it'll be spotted sooner or later.'

It won't be on the road though, will it? Bob thought, but he just smiled and thanked the sergeant again as he showed him out. Once they were outside, he caught the man's sleeve.

'When will they start searching the fells? He can't survive

long in this weather.'

'I'm sorry, Mr Reed, but until we know where to look, our hands are tied.'

'Can't you get a search helicopter?'

'I'll see what I can do,' he replied, looking down at his arm.

Bob released his grip and watched him go before returning indoors. Rita was on the phone in the study and when she returned she looked flushed with excitement.

'The Cumberland and Westmorland Herald and the Westmorland Gazette are going to run a story this week; I've sent them the nice photo of Jamie in his uniform – I thought it was best. Shelley doesn't mind being interviewed if it helps find Jamie – do you?'

The girl looked pale and drawn. Her usual smile was gone and her large eyes were red-rimmed.

'I'll do anything, Rita, you know that.'

They sat round the table in silence for a while until Bob could bear it no longer.

'Would you like me to run you home, pet?'

'No, it's all right – I'm in the car. I should be going. Mum and Dad asked me to get home for lunch.'

'Are you sure you're all right to drive?'

'Yes. I'm sure.'

She put on her jacket and picked up her bag before smiling awkwardly and making for the door. She pulled it gently behind her as she left and the house fell silent.

Now it was real. And Rita must have felt the same because when he put his arm round her, she just crumpled and he held her tightly while she wailed like a baby.

Chapter 3

'This was a good idea,' remarked Harry as he took the pint glass from Graham's hand.

It was only a few minutes after twelve but the tables were beginning to fill up slowly in the "The Black Bull Inn".

'They said they'd do us a quick soup. I've ordered them – is that all right?'

Harry nodded and pulled the table towards him as Graham eased himself onto the bench opposite.

'Sorry there's not been much of interest this morning, Harry, but it's not surprising; there were few people about on Friday night. Not much traffic on the roads.'

'Particularly with the weather being so bad,' offered Harry.

'Aye, you're not wrong there, lad.'

Harry listened to his stories of tracking down deer poachers around Keswick until their food arrived. It didn't take Graham long to finish his soup and he stood up as he drained his glass. Reluctantly, Harry left what remained in his bowl and finished his beer.

'We'd best be off, there's not many hours of light left and there's someone I particularly want us to see. And leave your car here, it's a difficult track over the fell.'

Harry hung on to the handle above his shoulder as the Land Rover proceeded slowly across a snow-covered track. The first part of the journey up the lane had been easy but once they left the road it was slow going. Harry had no idea where they were and wondered aloud how Graham knew where the track went, but he was assured he'd "been to see this particular fox in his lair many times".

Puzzled, Harry said no more but waited to see what would happen. They appeared to be travelling in open countryside, a white landscape devoid of trees, fences or animals, but suddenly the land dipped in front of them and a small settlement came into view. A typical dales longhouse surrounded by tumbledown shed and barns. As they descended to the farm, Harry could detect old agricultural vehicles haphazardly dotting the yard under a layer of snow.

'Who lives here?' asked Harry.

'I call him "The Fox". He's a recluse, doesn't go out much – except at night.'

'You mean he's a poacher?'

'Oh, yes.'

'Does he have a name, I mean a proper name?'

'Probably, I've never had the pleasure of having to record it officially.'

As they left the vehicle and walked the last few hundred metres towards the gate, three border collies began barking. The noise had obviously alerted the owner, who appeared dressed in an odd assortment of clothing. His trousers, tucked into wellington boots, were so dirty it was impossible to discern the colour; a grubby vest was just visible under a striped pullover, and to top it all he was wearing a knitted bobble hat that was unravelling over one ear.

'What d'you want?' he snapped.

'Just a word about some missing sheep, mate,' answered Graham – amiably enough, Harry thought.

'I know you.' The Fox was addressing Graham. 'But who's this 'un?'

'He's with me, old fella. Can we come in?' Graham winked at Harry.

'Certainly not. You're not coming in 'ere.'

'It's very cold out here.'

'Then you'd best be about yer business.' The old man turned to go back inside.

'I'm looking for some sheep that's been taken from a farm hereabouts,' Graham called after him.

The man turned. 'I've not lost any sheep, thank 'ee.'

'Brian Maynard over towards Sedbergh.'

'Oh aye.'

'Wondered if you'd had any taken?'

'Me?' The old man looked surprised. 'I don't keep no sheep.'

'Would you know of anyone looking to buy some meat, no questions asked?'

He looked hurt. 'Me? Why would I know 'bout that?'

'Because you know where to get shot of venison, don't you.' It was more of a comment than a question.

'That's different, eh?' The old boy smirked. 'That's them rich buggers' meat – mutton's different.'

'So you can't help us?'

'No.' He turned his back and Graham indicated to Harry that they should leave. They were halfway to the gate when The Fox called to them.

'Hey, wait. You could try 'em up at the old hall!'

'The old hall?'

But he had disappeared inside. Harry waited while his colleague hammered on the door but there was no response.

'Slippery character,' Graham muttered. 'Never know if he's serious or not.'

Back in the Land Rover he pulled out a map and spread it out across the steering wheel.

'The only hall I know of round here is Wharton Hall — it's a ruin but it's on a working farm.'

'He did say the *old* hall,' said Harry.

'Blast the old git.' Graham folded the map with a flourish. 'He's probably trying to send us on a wild goose chase anyway.' He looked at his watch. 'How long does it take you to get home, lad?'

'Hour and a half.'

'We'll have to call it a day soon then. I'll take you back to your car but we'll make a trip down Mallerstang on the way in case we spot any more old halls, eh?'

Harry nodded obediently and secured his seat belt. There was no point in arguing since he didn't know the area and had no idea where he was anyway. He kept a close eye on the gateways, hoping to spot a sign carrying the word "Hall" but there were few signs of any kind and he soon concluded that Mallerstang was one of the most isolated places he'd ever visited.

Soon they were turning round to retrace their route. Before he recognised the surroundings, they were back at the pub where Harry had left his car and Graham was suggesting that they drop into the police station in Kirkby Stephen to let Sergeant Crossland know what progress they'd made. Harry picked up his car and followed the

Land Rover into the small town, parking alongside it.

'This way, lad. He'll be interested to meet you.'

The two men greeted each other as friends and the sergeant shook Harry's hand vigorously.

'Is Graham looking after you, son?' he asked. 'You listen to him, mind, he knows all there is to know about wildlife crime in these parts.'

They spent a short time discussing what they'd been up to in the previous hours.

'...so nothing much to report so far, Mike.'

'Early days, Graham, early days.'

'Harry here's got to get going – he lives over in Harrogate, would you believe?'

The sergeant looked surprised. 'Are you coming back again, lad? It's a long way to commute.'

Harry shrugged his shoulders. He'd been wondering how his work in Cumbria would be formalised.

'I'm seeing about getting Harry seconded for a few weeks,' confided Graham.

'He'll need somewhere to stay,' warned the sergeant. 'But I could do with someone to help out...'

Harry felt uncomfortable at being spoken about as if he wasn't there and removed himself to study a notice relating to open access arrangements on the moors.

Soon Graham was standing beside him.

'There you are, lad, a perfect arrangement. Mike here needs a PC and you need to be over here. They can put you up locally – it'll save you travelling every day.'

Harry did his best to look pleased.

'Mike's sister has a B&B down at t'other end of Mallerstang,' he continued. She only takes visitors in the summer months so she can look after you in style. It's a small farm by all accounts. I'm sure you'll be well looked after.'

'I didn't think you'd be out of hospital so soon, Nina.' Mills gave the tiny new-born back to his mother. 'Have you chosen names yet?'

Nina smiled. 'Bit of a moot point, isn't it Nige?'

'Not finalised, like.' He grinned, rocking the other infant in his arms.

'I told him, Mills, I draw the line at naming my boys after footballers!'

'It was just an idea.'

'Don't you have any names that run in the family?' suggested Mills.

'Like Trevor, you mean?' Nina replied. 'Nige has a favourite uncle called Trevor.'

'Rosie wants to call them Thomson and Thompson like in "Tintin",' said Nige, 'Don't you?'

The little girl nodded.

'He's been putting ideas in her head,' Nina said, yawning.

'Go for a rest, love. They're both asleep and it'll be time for another feed before we know it,' said Nige. 'You go and lie down now. We'll manage.'

'OK.' Nina lowered her baby son onto the sofa and put out a hand. 'Come on Rosie, we'll go and have a little rest, shall we?' The toddler followed obediently.

'I'll put the kettle on,' offered Nige, placing the baby's twin beside him on the sofa. 'You don't mind if I put the telly on quietly, do you? I just wanted to see the game. Wales are playing Ireland this afternoon.'

Mills knew better than to try to have a conversation with Nige while the rugby was on. She picked up the book of boy's names lying on the floor and amused herself thinking of suggestions for the twins. As the match was getting towards the end, one of the babies started whimpering. Nige immediately picked him up and rocked him gently, looking up and cocking his ear as if to hear whether Nina was awake. Soon both babies were stirring and footsteps sounded on the stairs. Mother and daughter appeared looking sleepy and the routine of feeding and changing began. Mills noticed that the babies now had Nige's full attention despite the rugby match continuing on the television.

Rosie wanted to show her the doll's house that she'd been given just before the birth of her baby brothers. Taking her hand, the little girl led Mills over to it and insisted they rearranged the furniture together.

'The babies can't do anything for themselves yet,' she said. 'Daddy and I are going to have to look after them when Mummy goes back to work.'

'And when do you have to go back, Nina?' asked Mills when the twins were changed and lying on their parent's knees.

'The force only gives me three months paid leave and I had to stop work after Christmas when I was too big to carry on. So I'm due back around Easter.'

'Is that when you're going to take your sabbatical, Nige?'

'Yes, there's no point in her being away any longer when she won't be earning. I can get paid paternity leave for three months if Nina is back at work, until they are old enough to go to the university crèche.'

'It'll be hard work, looking after two babies and Rosie,' Mills suggested.

There was a pause while he watched an important

decision by the referee.

'Not easy looking after three little ones, Nige,' Nina repeated.

'No.' His eyes still glued to the screen. 'But I've thought it through and, with careful planning, I'll be able to cope.'

'And are you still looking forward to taking over from Nige at the university, Mills?' Nina asked, leaning her baby against her shoulder and rubbing its back.

'I think so. It'll be fun to do some research again, if I get time.'

'You should do. Jake will share some of the teaching and the summer term's not hard,' said Nige.

'So when do you stop work exactly?' Mills was anxious to know how soon she could get back into academic life. Her time at the forensic laboratory had been good and they still gave her bits of work to do in between but she was hoping that the university job would give her a step up to something more permanent. She was nearly twenty-six and it was time her career was going somewhere.

'I'm on leave from April but if you want to start before that I'll be able to take time off to give Nina a hand.'

'That's a brilliant idea!' Nina said. 'Can you really do that, Nige?'

'I don't see why not.' His eyes were back on the match.

Nina handed Mills one of her tiny offspring and reached for the book of children's names. 'Got any ideas?' she asked Mills. 'We're still arguing over them.'

'I was looking at the Welsh names,' Mills suggested. 'I was thinking with Nige being from there…'

She was interrupted by a roar as the Welsh side scored.

'Well, we hadn't really thought about that.' Nina flicked through the book, stopping to study a page here and there.

'What sort of names would they be?'

'Tomos, Owen, Bryn, Arwel, Trevor...'

'No!' Nina shrank in mock horror.

The match was over – Wales had won and Nige, was jubilant. 'Aled, Tavis, Gethin, Ryan, Toby, Huw!' he called.

'Are these more of your relatives, Nige?' Nina asked.

'No – they're in the Welsh team!'

'Well some of them sound interesting. Did you say Owen, Mills?'

'Yes and Tomos.'

Nina flicked to the back of the book then searched for a particular page. 'Tomos means twin, apparently. That's rather appropriate.'

It was getting dark and Mills began gathering her things together.

'It's been lovely to see the babies,' she said, 'but I'll leave you in peace now.'

'Are you sure you want to drive in this snow? You're welcome to stay another night, you know that.' Nina looked tired.

Mills didn't want to outstay her welcome. She said her goodbyes, telling them to remain in the warm and stepped outside, shutting the door behind her. The wind was blowing large white flakes down the street and the Mini was almost completely covered in a layer of snow that came away in thick slices as she cleared the windscreen. Cars driving slowly down the middle of the road hardly made a sound as they glided past. Thank goodness it has a good heater, she thought as she started the engine and pulled gingerly out onto the icy road. Sheets of snow slid down across the bonnet as she travelled round the corner.

The main road was quiet and the surface was slushier so

progress was better until she reached Swaledale where fresh snow formed a layer about two centimetres thick. Mills had driven the Mini in worse conditions and knew its limitations so she was taking it more slowly and carefully with each corner. Her heart was pounding as she turned off the "A" road towards Reeth. She passed an abandoned car at the side of the road and ahead one had gone into a wall, destroying a section of stonework. Soon her Mini joined it at the side of the road as the tyres began spinning on the icy tarmac. There was an eerie silence when she turned off the engine - it was dark and she felt very alone.

Chapter 4

Seven-thirty, eight o'clock and no-one had passed in either direction. No way was Mills leaving the car to walk out into the night; she'd have to stay there until morning. It would be fine, she decided without conviction, as she locked herself in. Convinced it was unwise to keep the radio on or run down the battery on her phone, despite the lack of signal, she sat in silence considering her situation. Feeling cold and hungry, she started counting to a thousand and had reached three hundred and fifty-seven when she saw a pair of headlights coming towards her. Before she'd decided whether to jump out and stop the vehicle, it slowed and pulled over. A man jumped down from the large pick-up truck and climbed into the abandoned car; soon the engine was roaring and it edged forward a few metres. Mills could hear the back wheels spinning on ice followed by cursing as the driver emerged and shouted to his companion.

To her relief she recognised the second man in the truck. He'd done some work for her grandmother at the cottage in the past. His name was Derek or Darren, she couldn't remember.

'Hi!' she shouted as she stepped gingerly onto the icy

road.

Both men were startled by her sudden appearance, laughing at the way they'd reacted.

'Hi! I'm Mills Sanderson. I live in Mossy Bank.'

A torch blinded her and she automatically put her hand to her face.

'Sorry, love. Didn't realise you were in there. D'you want some help?'

Before she could reply the other man intervened. 'We can't help her, Daryl. We've got to get mine back to Reeth first.'

'It'll be safe here, love. We'll see you home. You can fetch your car in the morning.'

Mills grabbed her rucksack, locked the car and climbed into the warm truck. She sat quietly as they manoeuvred it round until they could hitch the other car up. Once Daryl was back in the driver's seat, she began thanking him again but he just shook his head, concentrating on the road. The windscreen wipers were working hard against the build-up of large white flakes and the way ahead was hardly visible in the sheet of falling snow.

'No problem,' he finally replied once they were safely down into Reeth. Daryl stopped the truck, indicating for her to stay put, and jumped out to help his friend unhitch his car. When he reappeared he was brushing snow off his jacket.

'So where is it you live?' he asked.

Despite her protestations he insisted on taking her home.

'But it's mad. I don't want you to get stuck. I can stay here – I'm sure there'll be room in one of the pubs.' She picked up her bag and opened the door.

'Look, I'm going to Muker. I can at least drop you off at

the turning to Ivelet.'

She agreed reluctantly and he started the engine, revving to get the truck moving again. It seemed as if the snow was easing a little and visibility was definitely improving. A car appeared and passed them slowly, going the other way.

'That's a good sign,' said Daryl. 'Looks like we'll get through OK.'

Now he had relaxed, they made polite conversation and Mills learned that her rescuer was a joiner who was working on a house in Reeth. The owner of the property had spun off the road earlier in the day on his way back from Richmond and had sought his help.

As they approached the junction at Ivelet Bridge, Mills told him to drop her off and continue on the main road.

'There's no way you'll get up the hill and I'd hate for you to get stuck when you've got this far.'

'You'd better take this then.' He leaned across, handing her a torch.

She jumped down, thanking him again and slammed the heavy door closed, waiting for him to move away before crossing the road. She walked carefully on the compressed snow, anxious not to fall on its slippery surface. It was easier in the untouched snow once she was off the main road, although she wouldn't have got far without the torch. Everything came alive when it entered its beam, glistening with a momentary beauty before reverting to its ordinariness again as the light passed. The water dripping down the high bank had frozen, sparkling like a jewel-encrusted wall. It illuminated the tracks of a fox crossing the lane but those were the only signs of life she detected on her journey home.

Mossy Bank was almost invisible. There were lights in

one or two of the cottages but many, like hers, were in darkness. She rummaged in her bag for the keys and closed the door behind her with a sigh of relief. It was nearly ten o'clock and she was exhausted. A warm bath and some hot chocolate was all she needed before collapsing into bed.

The phone rang as she reached the top of the stairs and she hesitated before deciding to ignore it. As she ran the bath water she could hear it was Harry leaving a message. She sighed as she turned off the taps and crept downstairs again, where the answer machine light indicated she'd had three calls.

Mills, I've been trying to get hold of you all day. Where are you? Ring me when you get this. What have you been doing?

The other messages were in a similar vein and she became irritated while she waited for him to pick up.

'It's me,' she said, hoping she sounded suitably aggravated.

'Mills, are you all right? I didn't know where you were. Where have you been?' He sounded anxious.

'I went over to see Nina and the twins.'

'Really?'

She'd noticed how he became suspicious when she hadn't been in touch for a while.

'I told you she might be bringing them home this weekend.'

'I don't think you did. You might have rung.'

She could tell he was cross but he would never admit it. Mills was tired and shivery. She wanted to get into a hot bath and didn't have time for politeness.

'Sorry.' Mills knew she didn't sound it.

'What are you doing tomorrow? I could come over later.'

Her answer was terse. 'I'm going to the lab tomorrow.'

'Great, come round after. I'm going to be based in Kirkby Stephen for a week or two – I can tell you all about it. You'll see it on the news,' he continued, 'There were cameras and the farmer was being interviewed while we were there.'

Mills sighed. 'Look, I'll call you tomorrow evening.'

'Are you sure you're OK? Is there something wrong? Are you ill?'

'No, I'm fine. I'm just very tired. I've only just got back.'

There was a silence that went on too long. It was Harry who spoke first

'Right then. I'll wait for you to ring.'

Mills could tell he was upset but she hadn't the energy to put things right.

Tom waited impatiently for Margaret's programme to finish before turning over to the ITV news. His wife went out to make tea. He was nearly asleep and barely listened to the politics and overseas news that dominated the topics every night.

Margaret came in with the drinks and perched on the edge of her chair. 'Poor girl looks frozen.'

The first item of local news featured a woman reporter wrapped in a scarf with coat collar up round her ears. She was standing in the snow outside a police station.

'A young police constable has gone missing from Kirkby Stephen over the weekend. Apparently he was not working on police business at the time but was out late in the bad weather conditions on Saturday night. The public are requested to keep a look out for a green Land Rover...'

They were showing a photograph of the young man in police uniform, beaming with pride.

'That's the lad that came to see us about the accident on Saturday,' she exclaimed, jumping up.

'So it is.'

'D'you think it's anything to do with why he was here, Tom?'

'No.' He held up his hand to silence her as the next item came on. 'That's Brian Maynard!'

The farmer was being interviewed, standing in the middle of an empty field that was covered in snow.

'How many sheep were taken?' the reporter was asking.

'Twenty-three, all with lamb.'

'You must be devastated.'

'Well, yes. It's not pleasant to be robbed but to lose your animals...'

'I understand that one of the ewes was shot.'

'Yes.' He looked angry. 'They left one of them dead. It's inhumane.'

'The poor man,' said Margaret. 'Imagine.'

Tom had imagined it. When the policeman had told him about the vehicle parked down the road the other night he imagined it all too well. 'He'll get the insurance,' he said and switched off the television.

Bob sat tensely waiting for the local reports to follow the main television news at ten. Rita was immobile at the other end of the sofa but he knew what she was waiting for. The papers had been in touch for her to e-mail more photographs of Jamie. And could they have one of him with his girlfriend? Bob had put a stop to that straight away; he didn't want Shelley dragged into it. The poor girl was holding it together for their sake but he could see she was stressed out. He couldn't face the prospect of watching them discuss his son on television and went to settle the dogs for the night.

By the time he carried a hot drink in to her, she was back on e-mail.

'You should get some rest tonight, love,' he said.

'I will. Promise.' She gave him a wan smile. 'I just wanted to let the others know it was on the news. I'll be up soon.'

He put the guard in front of the fire and fiddled about with the few remaining logs.

'You missed the bit about the sheep rustlers, as they called them.' She sounded exhausted.

'Oh, aye?'

'They took twenty-three ewes from a farm down near the bottom of Mallerstang.'

'Mallerstang? Really?' Bob went to the cupboard to fetch the ordnance survey map, spreading it out on the table. 'What farm was it?'

'I don't know. I wasn't listening really.'

'Did you see the farmer?'

His wife sighed. 'The man they interviewed was about our age I'd say. D'you mind if I take this up?' she asked, carrying the mug to the door.

'No you'd best get some rest.' Who knows what we might have to face in the morning, he thought. 'Don't turn off the computer though. I'll be up in a minute.'

It didn't take long to find the article on the local news website. The farmer's name was Brian Maynard. The photograph was blurred but Bob was certain he'd seen him at the Kirkby Stephen auction mart.

'Poor sod,' he said to himself. He could imagine what he was going through. Then he laughed bitterly at the irony – twenty-three sheep could be replaced but if Jamie didn't come back…

Sergeant Mike Crossland was in the office earlier than usual. He'd asked Jamie's father to e-mail photographs of his son so he could send them directly to the Missing Persons Bureau online. Before, it had always seemed appropriate to wait the seventy-two hours before making a report to the bureau, but when it's so obvious that they haven't disappeared intentionally, then the sooner the better. He'd already registered Jamie as missing but he needed photographs and soon he would be asking the family for dental records. He'd spare them that for now though.

When he opened his e-mail, a new message from Bob Reed was waiting. Three pictures were attached. He stopped at the one of the young lad bursting with pride in his smart new uniform. A lump formed in Mike's throat and he closed the file quickly, transferring the photographs to the MPB.

Now for the job he promised he would do next. He pulled out the report that the young man had been working on before he disappeared, in the hope it might indicate what, if anything, Jamie had been sufficiently interested in following up that made him go out in a near blizzard. He almost broke down again at the sight of Jamie's spidery handwriting at the bottom of the typed page – but it had to be done. It was a straightforward traffic accident with nothing controversial except for the existence or non-existence of the vehicle parked at the side of the road. Mike couldn't see how that could be connected with Jamie's disappearance and closed the file, disappointed and irritated that it told him nothing he didn't already know.

He spent the rest of the morning making calls, hoping that colleagues had heard something or had a sighting of the missing Land Rover. His enquiries were futile.

Mills was up early to catch her neighbour, knowing she went shopping in Richmond every Monday without fail. However, Muriel was still at home, worried about the conditions on the road.

'It'll be fine now,' Mills promised her. 'The sun's out, look. The snow will be nearly gone by the time we get there.'

Reluctantly the older woman went back inside to collect her coat, leaving Mills on the doorstep. She hoped that she was right – she wanted to get the Mini home in one piece.

Muriel's four-wheel drive estate was no problem on the hardened snow and they sailed through Reeth without incident. It was not the first time that Mills had expressed the wish that her stepmother had given her a more appropriate car.

'I know I should be grateful, Muriel, but a Mini is just not the best vehicle for getting round the Dales.'

'True. Now where is it you left it?'

'Just where the road forks off to Richmond.'

Soon they were pulling up at the junction, where her car was covered in a thick layer of snow. Mills thought she recognised the truck parked beside it from the extra lights on the roof bar and was not surprised to see Daryl moving around beside it. She thanked her neighbour for the lift, jumped out and walked over to see what he was doing.

'Hi! You look busy!' she said.

As he straightened up she could see he was in the middle of repairing the wall where it had been hit the night before.

'Hello there. Have you come to get your car? I was going to ring, to see if you wanted any help.'

'No, I mean thanks, I'm fine. I got a lift with my neighbour.' She looked at the wall. 'That's a really nice job you're doing.'

'Bit rushed but I've got to get back – my brother's in hospital and I've got to organise my gran's funeral.'

Mills didn't know what to say. 'Well it looks very professional.'

'I should hope so – it's one of my day jobs, among all the other things. I help my brother. He's the professional.'

Mills watched him go back to his work then started trying to clear the frozen snow from her Mini. After a while he came over to see how she was getting on and offered to help, going to his truck to produce de-icer and a second scraper. Mills had to admit that without his help to free the door lock and start the car, she probably would not have retrieved the Mini at all that day.

'Are you off to work?' he asked when she was finally sitting in the driver's seat with the engine running.

She explained that she was going to the forensic lab to help with some analyses.

'Wow,' he said. 'You must tell me all about it some time.'

He closed the door gently before she could think of a suitable reply, leaving her wondering if he really meant it or was just being polite. As she carefully turned the car in the road, she glanced surreptitiously in the rear-view mirror and saw that he was watching her leave.

The main roads were surprisingly clear of snow and she made good time to Harrogate. Before she'd even removed her coat, Brenda had appeared, asking her to come into the office.

'I want you to attend this conference. We've got to keep up to date with the techniques and this purports to be at the cutting edge of forensics.'

Mills studied the paper that Brenda had thrust into her hand. 'But this is next week!'

'I know but they said you can still register, so I've booked you in.' She beamed at Mills.

It was typical of Brenda to go ahead without consultation but Mills couldn't be cross with her – it was a fabulous opportunity to hear researchers in the field talking about their work. Her boss had ambitions for the laboratory and was working hard to make it world class, although she was the first to admit it would take a while.

'Thank you, Brenda. It sounds like a really good opportunity.'

'You're not teaching or anything are you? The only thing is…' she continued without waiting for an answer, 'the accommodation at the conference hotel is fully booked, with it being so late. You'll have to find somewhere nearby – although the cost of hotels in London…'

'That's not a problem, Brenda. I can stay with my Dad,' Mills offered without thinking.

'Good, that's settled then. It means we've got to get busy now to get all the work done before you go. I've had a call from Newby Wiske. They have a cold case they want to try us out on.' Brenda indicated for Mills to sit. 'It's a series of burglaries from the early nineteen-eighties. They want us to do DNA, fingerprints and fibres.'

'Why now?' asked Mills.

'DNA techniques weren't being used routinely back then so they want to see if they can help now. All the methodologies have improved and some serious cases are being reviewed.'

'Serious?'

'I know – but these burglaries were nasty – violence for the sake of it. An old lady dying of a heart attack, another terrified to leave her house for the rest of her life.'

'I see.'

'So if you could register the samples and get the analyses going.' She handed Mills a large cardboard box. 'Off you go!'

She carried the samples into "Receipts" and began carefully unpacking the evidence bags, one by one. Each sample had to be logged on the computer, chain of custody forms completed and the work allocated to the relevant section. She'd been working quietly alone for about an hour when the door opened.

'Hi Mills, Is it all right to come in?'

'No!' She jumped up and ushered Harry back outside.

'Sorry, I didn't realise…'

Mills hadn't meant to be so brusque – the samples were sealed so it wasn't contamination that worried her – but he wasn't supposed to wander about on his own. What if one of the junior staff had seen him?

She pushed him into the tearoom and closed the door.

'Sorry, I didn't know I wasn't meant to…'

'It's, OK, really. What do you want?'

'Well, that's nice. Don't I get a kiss?'

'Not here, no.' Mills didn't know why she was so irritated by his behaviour.

'What about lunch?'

Mills looked at her watch. It wasn't even eleven. 'Not yet.'

'I've got to go to Kirkby Stephen this afternoon. The

sergeant wants to show me where I'll be staying.'

'I must finish booking in these samples, sorry.'

'But I won't see you for at least a week, Mills.'

'I'm going to a conference in London, so I'll be busy too, sorry.'

'Right then. I'll see you when I see you. Keep in touch.' He leaned forward and pecked her on the cheek, then left.

Mills guessed he'd finally got the message.

Chapter 5

'Heard any more from the police?' Daryl asked.

His brother was sitting up in bed, looking more like his old self. His arm was in plaster but the dressing had been removed from his head.

'No, thank goodness. I'm hoping that'll be the end of it.'

'I asked the nurse when you would be getting out.'

'And?'

'They wouldn't say. It depends on the results of the scan on your head but she agreed it would probably be in time for Gran's funeral anyway. That's Friday week.'

'How's it going?'

'All right. I've booked the crematorium and the vicar and everything.'

'What about after?'

'Eileen said she'd organise something back at the home.'

'That's nice. Will many of them be coming to the funeral?'

'I doubt it.'

'When are Mum and her toy boy getting in?'

'They said there'd be no point in coming before next week, now it's all organised.'

'But they *are* coming?'

'Yep, the flight's booked from Palma on Tuesday.'

'You'd better warn them to bring some warm clothes.'

'Aye, it's still cold outside but the snow's melting fast. I was out this morning repairing a wall that got damaged last night by the guy from Reeth. He slid off the road from Richmond and I had to rescue him – and a young lass from Mossy Bank too.'

'Oh aye? Who's that then?'

'Not sure. I think she's renting the cottage that belongs to the old lady who moved to Harrogate.'

'A looker is she?'

'She is an attractive young lady, as it happens. I saw her again this morning when I was walling.'

'And when will you have time to fix the wall *I* demolished? It's best done as soon as you can.'

'OK, OK. I'll get it done this week. You forget I was at the Registrar's office today and the Funeral Director's. By the way we have to think about the service for Gran. There's no panic but we need to choose hymns and readings.'

'Won't Mum do that?'

'What do you think?'

'Call me Margaret, pet. And thank you, I'm glad you enjoyed it. It's nice to see a young lad that appreciates his food.'

Harry sat back, replete. He had to admit, Margaret was an excellent cook.

'So, you're starting work tomorrow?' she asked.

'Yes, I'm meeting the Cumbrian Wildlife Officer in Kirkby Stephen and we're visiting a few of his contacts that might know of any illegal slaughterhouses.'

'And this is because of the sheep that were stolen on Friday night?' Margaret carried the plates to the dishwasher.

'Yes, but there have been other incidents in the past few weeks.'

Tom Drysdale spoke for the first time since the meal began. 'They were asking about a vehicle down below here. A young lad was here asking damn fool questions.' He scowled at Harry.

'He was that colleague of yours,' explained Margaret. 'He's the one that's gone missing. Jamie Reed. We saw it on the news. The one that disappeared in the bad weather at the weekend.'

Harry hadn't heard about Jamie Reed but it explained why they were short-handed at Kirkby Stephen. He listened with interest, determined to ask Sergeant Crossland about it when he saw him in the morning.

Tom Drysdale said nothing while his wife recounted what she'd heard on the news.

'I don't know what Mike were thinking, sending that lad down here snooping about. What made him think we'd know owt about sheep taken from a farm miles away?' he grumbled.

'It was because of the accident,' Margaret responded. 'He thought there might have been a vehicle down on the road.'

'As if I would leave my trailer down there!' the farmer muttered angrily.

'Don't be silly, Tom. That young policeman didn't think it was *your* vehicle.' She straightened her apron. 'Now, Harry, love, would you like a bit more pie?'

Harry extracted himself from the kitchen with the excuse

that he had some work to do. It was true that he wanted to go onto the internet to see if there were local abattoirs worth investigating but to be honest he just wanted to watch a bit of telly online. He sat down on the single bed and turned on his iPad, only to find there was no signal. It hadn't occurred to him. He wandered back into the kitchen, where Margaret was tidying up.

'Do you have broadband here?' he asked. 'I don't seem to be able to get a signal.'

'Do we have broadband, Tom?'

'You mean the internet?' her husband asked.

'Yes,' said Harry. 'And I can't get a mobile signal.'

'There's no signal here, lad. We don't use the internet. Wouldn't know how.'

'He won't have it,' added Margaret.

Harry shrugged. 'Is there a telly?'

'Of course, in the sitting room. You go and help yourself.'

Harry found his way through the hall into the sitting room. It was obviously set aside for visitors, with tourist information leaflets on the coffee table and a large old television in the corner. The fire was set with coal and logs but there was no other form of heating. He switched the television on and watched absently for a while but reception was poor and he was beginning to feel really cold. Turning off the lights he wandered back to the cosy kitchen.

'I think I'll be off,' he announced.

'Are you going to bed already?' asked Margaret. 'Goodnight, then.'

Harry lay on the hard bed wishing he was back in his flat. A week of evenings with no connection to the outside world was not what he'd expected.

The full English breakfast next morning made up for the tepid shower and instant coffee. Harry left the farm at eight, planning to spend time on the internet catching up with his e-mails – hoping there might be a message from Mills. The roads were clear of snow and there were only patches of white on the fields and hilltops. It was very different to his usual journey to work that morning. Not another soul in sight as he joined the main road to Kirkby Stephen and, until he reached the outskirts of the town, he passed only one vehicle going in the opposite direction. Sergeant Crossland greeted him eagerly, ushering him into a tiny office and offering him a seat behind a cluttered desk in the corner.

'You'll be fine here,' he said, moving a few papers aside in an ineffectual attempt to clear a space for him.

'Is this someone's desk?' Harry asked, wondering if it belonged to the missing constable. 'Should I move the papers?'

'No lad, leave them be. He'll be back soon I expect.'

'I'll just make a pile of them then.'

His temporary boss wandered off, looking distracted, without responding.

Harry logged himself onto the computer and searched for the name "Jamie Reed". The local papers had reported he was missing, but little else. The Force had put out a search for the vehicle but nothing had been sighted so far. Harry studied the photograph that had been placed on the Region website. Jamie Reed was about his age; he looked younger in the picture – it had been taken at the passing out ceremony so was probably a few years old. There was no apparent reason why he'd gone out that night and no trace of him or the green Land Rover since.

'Hey up, lad!' It was Graham Patterson looking red-cheeked and jovial, his large frame filling the doorway. 'Ready?'

'Yes.' Harry logged off and climbed out from behind the desk.

'Made yourself at home, I see,' remarked Graham. 'Digs all right?'

Harry was conscious that his sergeant could hear. 'Really nice place and the food's good.'

'Champion.'

Harry followed Graham out to his car.

'I thought we'd start by visiting a local abattoir,' Graham said as they took the road towards Sedbergh. 'There's a guy in Wharfedale who has a small slaughterhouse on his farm – for his own use and other local farmers.'

'Are they allowed to do that?'

'Of course. It's all highly regulated and probably a damn sight better supervised than the big set-ups. This one is a prime example of the high standards that can be achieved.'

'So why are we going there?'

'To see if they've been approached by any strangers about doing a bit of slaughtering and butchering on an *ad hoc* basis.'

Harry leaned back, enjoying the drive. They'd been climbing for a while but now they were over the tops and were travelling downhill alongside a small river. They passed through several attractive villages and plenty of pubs that caught Harry's eye, before turning off the main road down narrow lanes, finally coming to a halt outside a group of farm buildings. It looked to Harry like a typical dales farm except for a very large new barn to the rear. Harry noticed there was a farm shop advertising lamb, beef and pork.

'He's got a butcher's shop!'

'Aye, cutting out the middleman,' commented Graham. 'Happen he'll be slaughtering, butchering and selling his own stock – and meat from his farming colleagues in the area.'

As they left the car, a lean, athletic-looking man emerged from the barn, waving them into the building.

'You'll find everything in order,' the farmer said, looking at them anxiously. 'We had the Food Standards Agency here only last month.'

Harry looked round, amazed by the gleaming steelwork inside the barn.

'No problem,' replied Graham, 'I'm sure it is. As I said on the phone, we're just checking out places where there might have been illegal slaughtering.'

The man's face was a picture of indignation. He looked as if he would explode and as he drew breath Graham held up a conciliatory hand.

'No offence meant, sir. We thought you might've heard something or even been approached yourself. Any unusual request is what we're after.'

The farmer appeared to calm down and stroked his chin for a while. 'Can't recall owt unusual. I've only a few customers like and they're all well known to me – been coming here for years. They're all local farmers who want a bit of their own meat for themselves, or their friends. Some supply local shops; they like to know the history, if you see my meaning.'

Harry was intrigued by the small scale of the business.

'Are there many of you in the Dales?' he asked. 'I mean abattoirs like this.'

'No lad. There's one or two others but there's not enough business to support much more than that.'

Graham gave the farmer a card, asking him to get in touch if he heard anything that might be relevant and thanked him for his time.

'D'you think there might be other places like this that he doesn't know about?' Harry asked as they set off back down the lane.

'If there are, they'd have to comply with the health regulations.'

'If they do.'

'Aye, that's what bothers me. If the people that are taking livestock are slaughtering them in unhygienic conditions, who knows what might happen. Folks are always keen to get a bargain, no questions asked. It's a disaster waiting to happen.'

Harry had already learnt that Graham enjoyed his food, so wasn't surprised when he suggested stopping in Grassington for a bite to eat in the café there. Harry took the opportunity of the break to find out more about Jamie Reed.

'There's not much to know, lad,' Graham informed him between mouthfuls of meat pie. 'He was on duty on Friday and went off at the end of his shift as usual. He lives with his mum and dad, and he told them he had to work that night. The weather were pretty poor so his Dad told him to take the farm Land Rover. And that was the last they saw of him.' He wiped his mouth on the back of his hand and took a swig of tea.

'Doesn't anyone know where he was going?'

'No.' He finished his tea in several large gulps, placing the mug down firmly on the table. 'Right, we'd best be off. I've got another job on this afternoon.'

As they drove back, Graham explained he needed to get to Carlisle to speak to a man about suspected badger baiting. 'You can come if you like,' he offered.

Harry declined politely. 'I ought to catch up with some paperwork.' It wasn't exactly a lie. He wanted to go through the files on Jamie Reed's desk, partly to make some space but he was also intrigued to find out what made the PC go out on his own that night, without speaking to his sergeant first.

As soon as he was back at the station, he checked his phone for messages but there was nothing from Mills. He grabbed an empty cardboard box from a pile of rubbish waiting to be collected and carried it through to the office. Sergeant Crossland followed him to see what he was doing and Harry explained tactfully that he was tidying up the papers ready for when Jamie returned. Alone again he settled down to read through each document. Most of the papers were routine circulars that could have been put in the bin but Harry carefully preserved them in the order he came across them, tucking the box under the desk. Finally he was left with a single file marked RTA 4/2/12 which he'd left until last, sensing it was the most important since it carried the date Jamie had disappeared.

Settling back in his chair, Harry read and re-read the report carefully, concentrating on the final conclusions and actions. He could find nothing in it to cause Jamie to rush out that night. The car had crashed in the early morning and it occurred to him that the PC might have wanted to check the conditions on the road at that precise time. It seemed unlikely. He needed to know the outcome of the case.

'Would you like a cuppa, Sarge?' he called but there was no answer and when he put his head round the door he found the other office empty. A cigarette packet on the desk suggested he had gone outside for a smoke and Harry found him in the car park.

'I'm making a brew,' he offered.

'Aye, lad. Good idea!' Sergeant Crossland stamped on what was left of his cigarette and followed him inside. He stood in the small kitchen while Harry poured boiling water onto the teabags and poked at them with a teaspoon.

'Sarge, I was tidying my desk and I couldn't help noticing that PC Reed was in the middle of a case.' He didn't look up as he squeezed the teabags and dropped them into the bin.

'Aye, the RTA.'

'I could finish off the details if you'd like me to. Maybe have another chat with the guy in the car.'

The older man seemed to understand what Harry was doing and nodded.

He offered him the milk. 'Can I ask something, Sarge?'

'Yes lad?'

'About Jamie Reed.'

'What about him?'

'What's being done to find him?'

'They're looking for the vehicle but there's nowt to go on. If you find anything...'

'Yes, sir. That's what I thought... since I'm here...'

'The RTA, Harry. You know it were just down the road from Old Hall Farm – my sister Margaret's place?'

'I noticed that, sir. I saw the names in the report. I can

talk to them about it, if you like. See if they remember anything.'

'Anything, lad. Just now there's nowt to go on – bugger all.'

Chapter 6

Mills studied the evidence bags lined up on the bench in front of her. The dates ranged over five years, starting in nineteen-seventy-six when the attacker had broken into a house wearing a handkerchief over his nose and mouth. The woman who had disturbed him was knocked over and beaten round the head but she'd managed to pull off the handkerchief in the struggle before he ran away. Could they look for DNA on it? In seventy-eight a similar scenario occurred. This time the assailants wore balaclavas and gloves, leaving no evidence in the house, despite a vicious attack. However, a cordless screwdriver was found outside that might carry evidence – but it was a long shot; attempts made at the time to collect prints were unsuccessful. The final bag, dated nineteen-eighty-one, apparently contained a single hair, not much to go on but there was a good chance it belonged to the assailant.

Mills knew what the laboratory was capable of and allocated the tests accordingly: DNA first on the hair; a check on the handkerchief for body fluids and DNA if found; fingerprint tests on the screwdriver and DNA if possible.

When everything had been recorded she took the forms

into Brenda for confirmation.

'I don't know why you bother me with this,' she exclaimed, without moving her gaze from the computer monitor. 'I know you'll do it all properly.'

'But I have to,' Mills pointed out, 'It's a requirement that you authorise it.'

'A lot of nonsense.'

Mills had to laugh. Her boss would never understand the need to work to a proper system. She guessed Brenda was not the sort of person to keep her CDs in alphabetical order.

'Keep the work moving, Mills' Brenda said. Now she was looking up and there was a serious edge to her voice. 'It's important we get this job right. If we do, there'll be more and we need everything we can get. It's open season at the moment with the FSS closing – we need to be seen as the main attraction up here now, it's a critical time.'

No pressure then, thought Mills as she nodded and set off to the laboratory. She was already familiar with the procedures for DNA analysis but she needed to better understand the process for obtaining fingerprints if she was going to write a coherent report. Glyn, the laboratory manager, was working in his office, a lamp on his desk the only illumination in the gloom of the late afternoon. He looked up when she went in brandishing the evidence bags.

'Looks like more work.' He smiled, despite the remark.

'I've got a screwdriver found over thirty years ago. They want DNA but they've also asked us to look for fingerprints.'

'We'll do the prints first – we can only get DNA from a print anyway.'

He took the bag and examined it carefully. 'You didn't

say it had a battery. Now we're in with a chance!'

'What d'you mean?'

'Generally a burglar will wear gloves to handle any tools, but they often forget to be so careful with what's inside. With a bit of luck he'll have fingered the batteries without thinking to wear gloves when he put them in the screwdriver.'

'Wouldn't they have looked for fingerprints thirty years ago though?'

'Of course, but the methods are much better now. If dusting doesn't show anything, we can use the superglue.'

'Superglue?'

He motioned to her to follow him into the laboratory, switching on the fluorescent lights before stopping in front of a small transparent box.

'This is it.' He took a small tube from a drawer and held it out to her. 'See, ordinary superglue. Just a drop or two on there...' He pointed to the small dish inside a box. 'When the glue vaporises it discloses any prints, even if they've been invisible to the eye.'

As they walked back to his office, Glyn asked what else she was carrying.

'A hair for Donna to look at for DNA and a handkerchief for anything we can get from it basically.'

'Fine, give them to Donna for the DNA while I get the prints done on this one.'

As she left, Mills had a thought. 'If you do have to use the superglue, may I come and see how it works?'

Glyn nodded.

Mills made her way back down the corridor to find Donna but it was obvious she was hard at work in the laboratory and any discussions would have to wait.

'Mills!' Brenda was waiting by her office door. 'Come in, quickly. I've just spoken to the woman in London who's organising the conference – she rang to ask if we wanted any advertising space. They've had a cancellation so it's very reasonable. I said we'd take it since you'll be there anyway.' She was beaming. 'Wasn't that lucky?'

'What sort of space?'

'Oh just a table really but we can tart it up – some posters to highlight our capabilities. You'll know what to do, I'm sure.'

The phone rang before Mills could answer and Brenda returned to her desk to take the call. Mills sighed and waited but when it became clear it would not be a short conversation, she went back to see when Donna would be free to talk.

It was well past six when she finally put on her coat and picked up her bag but the light was still on in Brenda's office.

'I'm off now,' she called.

'OK.' Her boss sounded distracted.

'I'm taking the brochure home. I thought I might drop into uni tomorrow to see if I can get a poster done.'

There were incoherent murmurings from behind the door. Mills knew it was best not to interrupt Brenda when she was working and left the building. Her Mini was the only vehicle in the badly lit car park, except for Brenda's new Toyota. This was not unusual and now she was in no hurry to get back home, where she would have to face more phone messages and e-mails from Harry asking her to contact him.

However, when she walked into the cottage, she was relieved to see there was no flashing light on the answer machine. She took off her coat and picked up the phone to make an important call and, as usual, Fiona answered.

'Mills! How lovely to hear your voice. I've been meaning to ring. I mean your father keeps saying…'

'Hello Fi. How's the baby? How's Dad?'

'We're all fine, Mills. It's been so hectic here. It seems ages since we saw you at Christmas. We must…'

'That's why I'm ringing. I'm coming down to London next week for a conference and I need somewhere to stay. I thought …'

'Of course, darling, you *must* stay here. Hugh will be so pleased and Flora will love to see her big step-sister!'

Mills ignored the reference to her relationship with the baby and asked if her father was around.

'You know Hugh, darling,' Fiona said, 'always busy. He's at Rotary tonight. Shall I get him to call you when he gets in?'

'No, don't worry. Just tell him I'm coming down on Sunday.'

'Is that this weekend?'

'This Sunday – I'll be busy getting organised before that.'

They made polite conversation for a while until Mills felt she could reasonably ring off. She had little in common with her father's wife and, although their relationship was more amicable now, frankly they had little to talk about. Christmas had been difficult but that was her fault for taking Harry with her. He obviously felt completely out of his depth with Fiona and her Sloane Ranger friends – and who could blame him – but he needn't have been so churlish about it. His reaction to her, admittedly bizarre, family had contributed to the deterioration in their relationship as far as she was concerned, although he hadn't yet noticed, apparently.

Harry braked as he reached the place where Len Meehan had demolished the drystone wall. He could see in the headlights that it had been quite a collision. On the other side of the road, a little further on, was the entrance to a field, Mr Drysdale's by all accounts, where there might have been another vehicle parked. A vehicle that the farmer had seemed quite keen to convince him wasn't there. He put the engine back into gear and drove the last few hundred metres to the entrance to the farm, turning up the track and into the yard.

The Drysdales were seated at the kitchen table listening to the radio. When she saw him, Margaret jumped up and busied herself at the tea tray.

'We didn't know what time to expect you,' she gently admonished him.

'Sorry – I should've said.' He seated himself at the table.

'Had a good day?' Tom Drysdale asked. 'Got the bastards yet?'

'Tom!' exclaimed Margaret, looking genuinely shocked.

'No, I'm afraid not. Graham thinks we probably won't.'

'Really? Well I'm not surprised; they'll be long gone now.'

'Why's that, Mr Drysdale?' Harry asked.

'Why not? They come from Lancashire, don't they?'

'We don't know,' replied Harry. 'Do we?'

'They were close enough when they took those twenty-three ewes,' Margaret said, putting a cup of tea in front of Harry.

'Yes, and the young lad that went missing thought they'd been down this road,' Tom replied sarcastically.

Margaret shook her head. 'No he didn't. All he said was the lad in the car *thought* he saw a vehicle.'

'That's true,' interjected Harry, hoping to get Tom's opinion. 'He said in his statement that there was a vehicle parked by your field gate.'

'P'raps they was after *my* sheep then,' he said sullenly.

'You're daft, Tom Drysdale,' his wife said. 'There's no proof there was anyone there. The driver could've been making it up as an excuse for his bad driving. He's worrying about nowt, isn't he?' She looked to Harry for confirmation.

'I don't know to be honest. He *might* have been telling the truth.'

Tom Drysdale was looking quite red-faced. 'Maybe I should be keeping a watch at night. I don't want to be losing my ewes so close to lambing.'

'Don't be so ridiculous.' His wife flapped her tea towel in his direction and stood up, pushing the chair away. 'Your tea will be ready in half an hour – and I hope you like rabbit, Harry.'

He smiled. He didn't think he'd ever tasted it.

'I'll feed the dogs,' Tom said, getting up from the table.

Harry thought he detected a small nod, a signal for him to accompany him.

'I'll give you a hand if you like,' he offered.

'Aye, if you like.'

Harry followed him into the yard, where the collies were kept in the barn. Their barking suggested they knew what time it was. Harry watched him tip food from a sack into three bowls and place them on the ground in a row. As soon as he opened the barn door, three dogs flew out: two black and white and a merle. Each went directly to a different dish. Harry couldn't see how they decided which to choose but Tom explained that he always put them in the same places and they knew which was their own.

'They're lazy animals, no damn good wi' the sheep. I'd get rid of that old 'un.' He pointed at the merle. 'But Margaret won't let me. She'd have it in the house if she had her way.'

Tom lit a cigarette while they watched the dogs feeding. It didn't take long before they wandered away from the empty bowls. The old dog came over and sat at Harry's feet. He bent down to stroke her matted back.

'You're wasting your time looking for those thieves round here,' Tom said. 'They'll be down in Lancashire, like I said.'

'How do we know that?'

'I keep my ear to the ground.'

Harry hesitated. He felt the farmer was trying too hard to refute any connection between his farm and the theft of the sheep.

'You will tell me if you hear anything, won't you?' he asked.

The man nodded before calling the dogs back into the barn. Two disappeared obediently but the one at Harry's feet refused to budge. Tom grabbed it by the scruff of the neck and threw it into the barn, swearing under his breath, before slamming the door. He threw his cigarette on the ground and went back to the house without a word. Harry followed. Margaret turned from the sink to give them an inquisitive look but nothing was said.

*

When Harry left for work the next morning, there was activity down on the road. A truck parked by the field gate first caught his eye as he made his way down the farm track. He turned slowly onto the main road and stopped behind the vehicle. Across the road a young man dressed in a hooded jacket was standing beside the drystone wall. Harry turned off the engine, stepped out into the cold air and wandered over to speak to him.

'How do,' the man said.

'Hi. How's it going?'

'All right, as long as I can get this finished before the snow comes,' the man replied, looking up at the sky.

Harry could see he was repairing the damage to the wall.

'It's looking good,' he said.

'Aye, it's coming on.'

'Is this your land?' Harry asked, assuming the man was repairing his own wall.

'I wish. No, I'm just putting back what my little brother destroyed.'

'It was your brother who hit the wall? How is he?'

'Not so bad. He bashed his head so they're keeping an eye on him 'cos they think there might be a bleed. Otherwise it's just a broken arm.'

'What was he doing out at *that* time of night?' Harry asked, knowing he should have produced his warrant card by now.

'Funnily enough he was on his way to the hospital. Our Gran were in a bad way. He was trying to get to see her before…'

'I'm sorry.'

'No need.' He turned away, picking up a stone to continue his work.

It was too late to explain that he was a police officer now. 'Is your brother still in hospital?'

'Aye. I reckon he'll be there a while yet.'

'Right then.'

He left awkwardly and went back to the car. Instead of turning right to Kirkby Stephen he took the road to the motorway and Lancaster Infirmary. The boss would understand that it was important to speak to Len Meehan.

When he arrived at the entrance to the ward, he felt less confident. Everyone was preoccupied and it took a while to attract someone's attention. When he told the staff nurse that he was a police officer, she directed him to a chair in the corridor, explaining that the consultant was on his rounds and nothing could interrupt that. Ten minutes passed before a group of young men and women swarmed down the corridor with an older man at their centre. They swished by in a sea of white coats and disappeared into the ward, leaving Harry waiting patiently for them to emerge again some twenty minutes later. He crept quietly over and peered through the glass in the door.

'You can go in now,' a voice behind him called.

He looked round to see the nurse leaning over the desk.

'He's in the right-hand corner.'

The ward held eight beds, two tidy rows of four, each containing a man of indeterminate age. The patients lay neatly under tucked-in bedspreads with white sheets folded over in identical fashion. One of the men was calling for a nurse but the rest lay uncomplaining as if grateful for the peace at last.

'Mr Meehan!' Harry called softly.

The man was lying like a soldier at attention, his arms straight by his sides. His eyes were slightly open but he didn't seem to be awake. Harry called again, this time louder, and the eyes shot open and the man lifted his head slightly.

'Hello, sorry, I must've dozed off,' he said, struggling to move under the tight bedclothes.

Harry had been rehearsing what to say while he was waiting outside. 'Hello Mr Meehan, I'm a police officer. My name is PC Clark. I've taken over your case from PC Reed.'

'Hello.' The man raised an arm in a weak wave. Harry noticed his other arm was in a long plaster.

'I'm afraid I'll have to go over some of the points again – I hope you don't mind?'

'Fire away. I've got nowt else to do this morning.' He was smiling.

Harry asked the questions in Jamie's report and Meehan gave the same responses as before. When he came to the question of the vehicle parked on the road, Harry asked him to think back.

'Was there anything about the vehicle that you remember?'

'It's funny that,' answered the man becoming more animated, 'because the longer I'm in here the clearer it all becomes. He asked me before to describe it and I couldn't but now I've got this weird feeling it was a trailer.'

'A trailer?'

'Yeah. The sort of trailer you move livestock around in. What's the name?' He screwed up his face.

Harry waited patiently.

'Ifor Williams, that's it. Ifor Williams. They're everywhere aren't they?'

'So how big was this trailer?'

'Not big. Just the usual size –the sort for moving a

handful of sheep I suppose.'

Harry was busy making notes. 'So was there a car with it?'

'I don't know. I keep thinking but I still can't see it. But if it were gone next morning, there must have been, eh?'

Now was the time for Harry to test Meehan's story. 'If I told you that you would be more likely to be done for dangerous or careless driving if you swerved to avoid a parked vehicle than if you just skidded on ice, would you still think there was a trailer parked there?'

Meehan was confused by the question, asking Harry to repeat it several times but finally he understood.

'So if I say there was no trailer, I'm less likely to be prosecuted?'

'That's a suggestion,' Harry wished he hadn't proposed such a complicated scenario.

Still looking puzzled, Len Meehan shook his head. 'I can't change what happened, can I? If it means I'm prosecuted, then so be it.'

'So the trailer was definitely there.'

'Yes.' He was looking weary.

Harry asked how he was doing.

'My head gets fuzzy. They're doing tests.'

Harry wished him well and took his leave as the man's eyes began to flutter, finally closing as sleep overcame him.

Chapter 7

'I've spoken to Len Meehan and he definitely saw a vehicle that night,' Harry told his boss when he reached the station. 'A farm trailer – the sort used for transporting sheep.'

'Keep it down, lad,' Sergeant Crossland instructed, pointing towards the closed door to his own office. 'Bob Reed has come in to see how the investigation into Jamie's disappearance is progressing. He heard about the helicopter search. I'm just getting him a drink.'

'I'll do it, Sarge,' offered Harry.

When he carried the tray into the office, Sergeant Crossland introduced Mr Reed to him as Jamie's father.

'The sergeant here tells me you're helping out.' Reed's voice was slow but betrayed no emotion.

'Yes, sir. I've come to assist the wildlife officer – because of the sheep rustling,' he explained.

'I meant helping out with the search for my son.'

Harry looked at the sergeant, who gave him an almost imperceptible nod.

'Yes, sir. I've been looking over Jamie's cases and following up his investigations.'

'Do what you can, son,' the man begged. 'There's

nothing we can do. Nothing. You do what you can.' He straightened up in his chair and cleared his throat.

'If you want to come to the house… to look at his room… anything that will help… Just tell me.' His voice wavered. He pulled out a handkerchief, blowing his nose noisily.

Crossland stood up. 'We'll do everything we can, Bob. And Harry here will come down to see if he can find anything that might help us, won't you Harry?'

'Of course, sir.'

As soon as Jamie's father had gone, Harry told his sergeant about his visit to see Len Meehan.

'So you're certain he saw a trailer parked in the road that night? But it was gone before anyone arrived at the scene of the crash?'

'Yes, sir.'

'You do realise that means whoever drove it away left Mr Meehan trapped in his car and badly injured?'

'I suppose it does.'

'It's a serious accusation to make.'

'Yes, sir.'

'We'll ask for CCTV to be checked in case it's picked up as it leaves the area. They won't be happy though – they've only just finished running it for a sighting of the Land Rover young Jamie was driving.'

'Any luck?'

'No. Seems to me it must still be in the area, somewhere. It's as if he's disappeared completely.' He rubbed his chin absent-mindedly. 'Look, why don't you take up Bob's offer and go down to his place. Have a look around – see if there's anything of Jamie's that might suggest where he went on Saturday night. Carlisle CID don't want to start a detailed investigation yet – not until we know what happened to the vehicle.'

'What about Graham? He was talking about visiting some markets.'

'Don't worry, I'll tell him you're out on important work, if he comes in.'

So Harry picked up his car keys and set off, wondering anxiously how Jamie's family would react to his intrusion, despite Bob Reed's invitation to search his son's belongings.

When he reached the farm, he found he'd arrived before Bob. This left him feeling even more awkward as he stood on the doorstep explaining to Rita Reed the reason for his visit. She nodded and opened the door wider, allowing him to enter and wipe his boots energetically on the doormat before climbing the stairs to a small bedroom at the back of the house. It had the air of a room that had never quite managed to complete the evolution into adulthood. Walls and furniture had been painted but there was a sense that underneath were the original trappings of a child's bedroom. The candlewick bedspread was threadbare and the worn rug had once carried a picture that was now obscured.

In contrast, the desk by the window was covered in paraphernalia associated with a modern computer. Harry, feeling more comfortable with the familiar hardware, seated himself on the swivel chair and turned the computer on, hoping it wouldn't be password-protected. But of course it was and he wasn't stupid enough to try to log in. He poked around in the desk drawers but there was little of interest among the leaflets, guarantees, receipts and scribbled notes. He closed the drawers quietly as he heard footsteps on the stairs.

'I thought you might like a coffee.' Mrs Reed came in with a tray, putting it on the bed. 'I'm sorry if I seemed a bit... well... off-hand, earlier,' she said. 'I was, you know... surprised, I suppose. Bob said he'd ask but...'

'He thought it might help,' Harry offered.

'Do you take sugar?' She'd turned her back as she went towards the tray. Her voice was high pitched and she audibly took a deep breath. 'Milk?'

'Just milk please.'

He watched her move her hand quickly across her face before turning back with the mug.

'There you are. Sorry, I didn't catch your name?'

'Harry... Harry Clark... PC Clark.'

'May I call you Harry?'

'Yes.'

'I think my husband thought that there might be something on his computer – an e-mail or some sort of message. We're not very computer literate I'm afraid.'

'Do you know the password for his computer?'

'No. we don't.' She paused. '*We* don't but I suppose Shelley might.'

'Shelley?'

'His girlfriend. Would you like me to call her? She'll do anything to help, she's such a good girl.'

Mrs Reed went off to call the girlfriend while Jamie drank the weak instant coffee, thinking how good a proper cappuccino would be.

Finally he heard steps coming back upstairs. Mrs Reed arrived flushed and out of breath.

'Shelley511. It's the date they started going out.'

'Brilliant.' He typed the password and up came the desktop.

Mrs Reed stood watching as he scanned Jamie's documents. After a few minutes he told her politely it would take some time and she withdrew, asking him to call if he needed anything. He wanted to find out what social media sites Jamie used but it didn't seem right to be intruding. Facebook was easy – the password had been remembered so he was in immediately. There were the usual conversations, none since last week of course, and nothing out of the ordinary. His e-mail account was the same: just mundane interactions with friends and on-line shopping sites. Harry checked his watch – he'd been up there over half an hour. Just a bit longer, he promised, and opened Jamie's Twitter account. Harry smiled at the lad's username: PendragonCop. He described himself as *a copper with a strong sense of justice – like the knights of the round table.* When Harry called up Jamie's previous tweets, he was surprised to find how assertively they came over: *Sheep rustlers had better look out! We will hunt you down & bring you to justice.* The previous one was a warning to the public: *Be vigilant! Protect your stock & prevent these villains from achieving their evil goal.* Further back, his messages had been aimed at thieves stripping lead from church roofs and vehicle thefts but clearly the topic that had been on Jamie's mind most recently was the spate of sheep thefts. When he checked who Jamie was following on Twitter, he found that many were in the police force, either in this country or in the United States. The stream of messages continued despite Jamie's absence and his direct messages included a series of calls for him to answer, dominated by Shelley, his girlfriend. The latest one simply said *Speak to me, Jamie, wherever you are.* It was sent on the Monday after his disappearance. Reluctantly he closed down the various sites and logged off the computer. Downstairs he commented to Rita Reed about her son's dedication to the police force and she agreed that it was "his life".

'Does the name "Pendragon" mean anything to you, Mrs Reed?'

'D'you mean the castle in Mallerstang? It's named after Uther Pendragon – King Arthur's father.'

'Like Arthur and the Knights of the Round Table?'

'That's it. I don't know a lot about it but you can see the castle if you go down towards Outhgill. Jamie would be able to tell you more about it – he did a project when he was at school... or his girlfriend, Shelley. They were at the same school.'

I might just do that, he thought. 'Do you think he went out on police business last Saturday night, Mrs Reed?'

She nodded vigorously. 'Oh yes. He wouldn't have been doing anything else in such bad weather – and taking his father's Land Rover.'

The back door opened and Bob Reed came in, brushing snow off his cap. Harry spent a few minutes explaining what he'd been doing and at Bob's request, he called the station to ask if he should bring the computer back with him.

'What for, lad?' asked Sergeant Crossland. 'Jamie's only missing, it's not a serious crime investigation... not yet, anyhow. CID will tell us if they need anything. One thing you can ask Mr Reed though – how much fuel was in his Land Rover?'

Harry relayed the query.

'Not a lot, lad. I always fill it up on a Monday when I take Rita to the market in Kirkby Stephen. I reckon there wouldn't be more than a quarter of a tank left... enough for fifty, maybe sixty miles.'

As he drove back to Kirkby Stephen, Harry realised he'd begun to form a picture of the young colleague he'd never met: an enthusiastic local lad, keen to demonstrate his abilities to his seniors, with an idea in his head that needed investigation – that wouldn't wait until morning. All Harry needed to know was why Jamie had gone out into the snow that night – and why he didn't come back.

'There's been a young lady by the name of Shelley…' Mike Crossland began when Harry arrived back at the station.

'Jamie's girlfriend?'

'Aye. She said she wanted to have a word.'

'Where does she live?'

The sergeant held up a hand. 'Hold your horses. She's at work until six but she can come down to see you this evening. I've given her directions. I've told my sister and she thinks she knows her from the hairdresser's where she works.'

Harry took the opportunity to catch up on his personal e-mails and was rewarded with one from Mills. It was in response to his suggestion that she came over to Garsdale at the weekend – just to see the place. He had proposed a pub lunch "for old time's sake" hoping he could persuade her to continue their relationship. Her exact words were: *I could come over on Saturday for lunch. I won't have much time but it would be interesting to see Pendragon Castle.* He suggested they meet at "The Black Bull" in Nateby.

Mills had spent the morning at home working on a layout for three posters highlighting the capabilities of Yardley Forensics. She was anxious to present the laboratory as well as she could, but without help from Brenda she was feeling a little out of her depth. When she thought she'd done enough, she saved the files on a memory stick and drove to the university to print out a first draft in full size.

If she was forced to choose, Mills would have had to admit that she felt more comfortable at the University of North Yorkshire than at any of the other places she'd worked. As soon as she stepped into the lift she was back where her heart was. The departmental office staff knew her well and she was soon able to offload the printing of the posters onto them, excusing herself to find Nige. He was in his office surrounded by marking, but was more than happy to make time for a coffee in the cafeteria while Mills caught up on news of the twins. As she left he reminded her that she'd be welcome any time to take over his classes, allowing him to give Nina a break from child-care duties.

The Head of Department was in the outer office when she went back to retrieve her posters.

'Hello, Mills. I've been looking at these.' He indicated the brightly coloured sheets of A3 that had come from the printer. 'Very interesting.'

She waited for him to continue, unsure whether he was referring to the content or the fact she was using university facilities to publicise the laboratory.

'Do you do much forensic work yourself?' he continued.

'I do some of it,' she offered. 'I can do the analysis of paints and glass. I can do hair samples. That sort of thing.'

'What about the tests mentioned here.' He pointed to the poster. 'DNA and fingerprinting.'

'I know how they are done but I'm not authorised to carry them out.'

'So you could talk knowledgeably about forensics?'

She guessed so.

The Head went back into his office and Mills rolled up the posters to carry them home. As she waited for the administrator to work out the charge, the Head of Department re-appeared carrying a leaflet.

'Mills, this is a draft of our new Forensic Science course. It started last term.' He thrust it into her hand. 'Have a look and let me know what you could contribute. We're desperately short of lectures on analytical procedures – anything you could do to help. I'd really appreciate it.'

She looked at the leaflet as he returned to his office.

The administrator caught her eye. 'It's a good opportunity,' she whispered. 'I know for a fact they're increasing staff by at least two posts next academic year.'

Mills smiled politely at her, took the posters and put the invoice in her bag with the leaflet. To be honest, she didn't know whether she could do it or, more importantly, whether she wanted to.

Margaret Drysdale was ready with his tea when Harry arrived back at the farm.

'I thought you'd like it early, since that girl is coming to see you.'

She began serving out the meal at once and he noticed there were only two places set.

'Is Tom not eating?' Harry enquired.

'He'll be back later. Had to see someone about some work, he said.'

Harry ate quickly to avoid the series of questions about his life in Harrogate. Margaret was probably only being polite but it was quite an inquisition and he was glad to leave the table to change into more casual attire in readiness for his visitor.

He had a mental picture of Shelley from the messages she'd sent Jamie, so he was surprised when she arrived to find she was quite mature with an air of confidence that he'd not expected. She was also more attractive than Harry had envisaged.

'Rita told me you were looking at Jamie's computer so I thought it would be good to speak to you about what's happening.'

Margaret had suggested they use the guest sitting room, bringing them coffee. Harry noticed she'd also put a plate of homemade biscuits on the tray.

'Shall I pour?' Shelley suggested, seating herself on the sofa and picking up the pot before Harry could answer.

He took a biscuit and sat in the armchair.

'So,' she said briskly, handing him a cup, 'what are they doing about finding him?'

It wasn't a conversation he was trained for. He hadn't done "family liaison" – it would be years before he could do such a course.

'I… it's… the trouble…' he stuttered. 'You should speak to Sergeant Crossland.'

'I did,' she said. 'He said they wouldn't be able to do anything until they find the Land Rover. What if they never find it?'

Harry poured milk into his cup and took a sip. He could think of nothing to say that would help.

'Did you find anything this morning when you went to his house, Harry?'

She was looking at him with large blue eyes, her blonde hair falling round her face in long strands. He wanted to help her, to say something to comfort her.

'Not really, no. But I have been looking at his current investigation. That may help.'

'What's that, then?'

'A possible attempted sheep theft.'

'Really?'

'Does it ring any bells?'

She laughed almost scornfully. 'No. Sheep? I don't think so. He was covering like serious assaults, drug rings, bank raids, that sort of thing.'

'Sheep rustling can be big money,' Harry suggested but Shelley appeared unimpressed. 'Is that what he told you?' he asked. 'Was that what he said he was investigating – drug rings?'

'He couldn't talk about them, obviously but when it was in the papers he'd tell me about it.'

'Shelley, do you know why he called himself "PendragonCop" on Twitter?'

She smiled. 'It was his idea. He liked to think of himself as a modern-day knight fighting crime so he used the name of Arthur's father because of the castle.'

'Is there anything that you think might give a clue to where he's gone?'

Her lips were pressed tight for a while. Harry assumed she was thinking but she pulled a tissue from her sleeve and put it to her eyes, making a kind of squawk.

'I'm sorry,' she said, when she'd recovered. 'I... have... no... idea... why...' She paused to regain control. 'It was my day off on Sunday but he was supposed to be working, so we said we'd go to the pub in the evening.'

She started crying again and, without thinking, Harry went over and seated himself beside her. He put his arm round her shoulders and she leaned against him.

'Please find him, Harry,' she sobbed.

They were in the same position when the door handle turned a few minutes later and Margaret appeared.

'I… I wondered if you wanted any more… coffee?' she asked as they leapt apart.

Before Harry could answer, she was gone again, pulling the door firmly shut behind her.

Chapter 8

Waking early, Harry decided he would have to clear the air with the Drysdales at breakfast. He'd avoided them on the previous night and gone straight to his room after Shelley had left, but he'd known he would have to face them in the morning.

'Poor Shelley was in a state last night,' he began.

'Aye,' Margaret replied, placing a plate of bacon and egg in front of him. 'I could see.'

'It must have looked... well... a bit...'

'I'm sure I don't know what it looked like, Harry.' She glanced across at Tom, adding, 'It's none of our business.'

'I didn't want you to think...'

'Don't worry lad, we don't think – do we, Tom?' she said, giving her husband a look that indicated he should agree.

She turned back to the stove repeating, under her breath, that it was none of her business.

'Did she have anything useful to say?' It was the first time Tom had shown any interest in the PC's disappearance, Harry noted.

'Not really. She was too upset. I think she just wanted reassurance that everything is being done to find him.'

'Poor young thing,' Margaret remarked to no-one in

particular, before leaving the kitchen.

'I think what she means to say,' began Tom, 'is that you have to be careful of young impressionable girls like Shelley.'

'I know. In fact I think she had an inflated idea of what Jamie did as a police officer.'

'Is that right?'

'He was looking for sheep rustlers, that's what he was doing that night, I'm certain.'

'Really?'

'Yes. I think whatever happened to him is connected to that. And I mean to find out.'

The old man looked concerned but remained silent as he finished his breakfast.

'Have you heard any more on the grapevine?' Harry asked him as he poured himself another cup of tea.

'About what?'

'The rustlers. You were sure they came from Lancashire. I wondered if you'd heard anything else?'

'No.' He got up from the table and put on his cap and jacket. 'Must be getting on.' He slammed the door behind him.

Harry was disappointed. He was convinced Len Meehan had seen a vehicle parked on the road and he was sure Tom Drysdale knew more than he was letting on. Had he detected a certain edginess when he'd raised the subject this morning?

At the station, Sergeant Crossland was keen to let Harry know that CID were doing everything they could to find Jamie.

'So what are they doing now?'

'They'll be searching obvious places, making enquiries, talking to his parents and the girlfriend. Oh and they're doing a detailed scan for the vehicle using ANPR and CCTV at the motorway service stations.'

Harry thought of Shelley, sobbing in his arms and sighed. 'Well, let's hope they have more luck than I did.'

He was relieved when Graham arrived, with a list of abattoirs to visit in Lancashire.

'Why Lancashire?' asked Harry.

'Because, lad, the snow that night meant the A66 was closed. With the roads being so bad across the Dales and the Lakes, and into Scotland, I reckon the thieves would more likely be heading south on the M6. Hurry up; we've got a lot to cover today.'

When Harry saw how rapidly they reached the motorway from Kirkby Stephen, he agreed that Lancashire was a good bet. Graham had planned a tight schedule of visits including Lancaster, Preston, Clitheroe, Burnley and Colne. They spoke to the managers of the slaughterhouses, some of whom were most helpful and others who were suspicious of a visit from the police. None of the places they visited seemed a likely repository for stolen livestock but the more helpful managers did suggest one or two smaller organisations that were less scrupulous in their dealings. One man in particular spent considerable time complaining to them about the unlicensed abattoirs that were springing up as the result of the increased value of meat generally and halal meat in particular.

When Graham asked him for specific details the man was less helpful.

'I'm not giving you owt that can be tracked back to me. I've got my family to consider.'

Graham pressed him to speak out but Harry could see the man was really nervous for his safety.

'Well at least give us a hint of where it is. Are we still in Lancashire?'

'Aye, but I'm saying nowt else.'

As they left, Graham muttered that he would have to give evidence if it came to court, whether he was scared for his family or not.

'So we know there's an illegal abattoir in Lancashire — that's a start, I suppose,' Harry suggested when they were driving back to the motorway.

Graham laughed. 'I think we knew that, didn't we? The problem is finding it. We may have to go undercover.'

Harry wasn't sure he'd heard correctly. 'Sorry?'

'Undercover. Pose as punters. Have you not had to do that before?'

'I thought that was for CID.'

'We can't let them have all the fun, can we lad?'

Harry wasn't sure whether he was right or not but he was certainly up for it.

'These unlicensed slaughterhouses are nothing like the places we've visited today,' Graham explained as he pulled out to overtake a lorry in the middle lane. 'It'll be someone's farm... in a barn. Quite possibly killing the animals by cutting their throats and letting them bleed to death for halal or kosher meat. Some think it's barbaric but it's not supposed to be inhumane if it's done in accordance with the correct procedures.'

'Really?' It sounded cruel to Harry.

'Yes. And you've got to keep a cool head if you're going to help me catch them. OK?'

'Right.'

'There's been a couple of cases over your way – one about ten years ago and another a bit later on.'

'Before my time then…'

'Farmers using their barns for meat going to Asian restaurants. Dreadful conditions – filthy, no concern for BSE or foot and mouth. Terrifying.'

'Did they steal sheep?'

'In some cases. It was mainly sheep and cattle, I think.'

'I'm glad I had my beef sandwich before you told me that.'

Graham laughed. 'Don't you worry about that, lad. My missus only uses the best and that came from a local farm – I like to know where my food comes from!'

They drove in silence while Harry thought about the scenario Graham had described. An abattoir on a farm would be difficult to find whether it was in Yorkshire, Cumbria or Lancashire. Setting a trap sounded exciting but there was one problem.

'If the sheep are being stolen for halal meat…'

'I didn't say that, son.'

'But you said…'

'I said the previous cases pointed that way.'

'OK, so how do we pass ourselves off as being interested in buying stolen sheep or lamb or whatever it is?'

'We might own a restaurant or maybe supply one,' Graham suggested. 'There's plenty of ways. These guys are greedy – they don't generally care what happens to it once they've sold it.'

'I suppose we could be interested in supplying halal meat for our own restaurant?'

'Exactly – there's a high demand now.'

They were leaving the motorway and heading for the

rounded silhouettes of the Howgills. Graham turned on the headlights and they made their way along the last few miles in near darkness. Harry's thoughts turned to Jamie Reed, missing, probably dead, his body lying in a ditch somewhere not so far away, and then poor Shelley. He wanted to tell Graham about her but it didn't seem appropriate. He waited until they reached the station before saying that he'd met her.

'Poor kid,' was all Graham said before bidding him goodnight.

Harry couldn't get her out of his mind as he drove back to the farm. It would be another long evening with the choice between listening to Margaret droning on about something trivial that had happened that day or sitting in the cold lounge struggling to watch the antique television. What did people do round here on a Friday night, he asked himself.

The kitchen was warm and the hot tea was welcome but after supper Harry felt he could stand it no longer and rang Shelley.

'I wondered if you'd like me to come over. I could let you know how the investigation is progressing.'

She sounded pleased. She was very grateful. Her Mum and Dad had gone out but she would really like him to visit.

'About eight then, Shelley, I'll look forward to it.'

To her surprise, "The Black Bull" was busy when Mills arrived, even for a Saturday. As she stood at the bar she looked around fruitlessly for a table.

'Don't worry,' the woman behind the bar said as she emptied a bottle of juice into a tall glass for her, 'they'll all be gone soon – the Cumbrian Mountain Express is coming. The pub will be empty before one o'clock.'

She explained to Mills that the steam train would be coming up Mallerstang and stopping at Kirkby Stephen around one-forty. Most of the customers were train spotters and photographers, keen to get a glimpse and some pictures of the famous locomotive. Mills asked three elderly gentlemen if there was space at their table, which clearly could seat six, and squeezed in. They all were white haired but with different degrees of baldness. Inevitably she fell into conversation with them about the impending arrival of the train, which she learnt was travelling from London that morning to return after reaching Carlisle.

'So will you be seeing it at Kirkby Stephen?' she enquired politely.

'Oh no,' they replied almost in unison.

'Nay, we're going to Aisgill viaduct to take photographs,' the baldest of the group explained. 'It's the highest railway summit in England.'

'Over a thousand feet,' added his friend. He looked at his watch and declared they should be leaving. Already the pub was becoming emptier and soon Mills was alone. She took out her map and was searching for the viaduct when Harry joined her. He looked at her glass, asked if she wanted another and, when she declined, went to the bar to fetch a drink for himself.

'Do you know where Aisgill viaduct is?' she asked him when he returned.

'Yes, I just passed it to get here. Is there something happening down there? There are quite a few cars parked on the road.'

'There's a steam train coming at half-past one. I wondered whether there's time to eat.' She looked at her watch – it was half past twelve.

Harry grabbed a menu from the bar and they ordered straight away. Until then it had been easy to converse but now, as they sipped their drinks and waited, Mills couldn't think what to say.

'How are you getting on over here?' she asked eventually.

'Oh, you know. It's OK, I suppose.'

Mills asked him about his digs, and what the police station was like. Harry was becoming more animated when their soup arrived.

'It sounds quite an interesting investigation – the sheep rustling,' said Mills.

'It is, but it's not the only one. There's this other thing with the officer disappearing in the middle of the night. No-one seems to be getting any closer to finding where he's gone.'

Mills listened and then began asking questions. They'd finished their soup and Harry suddenly noticed the time. 'It's one o'clock – hadn't we better go?'

Neither of them was mad about trains but they agreed there was something about a steam engine that could not be ignored. They went in Harry's car, leaving the Mini by the pub and Mills sat back to enjoy the drive. Harry pointed out Pendragon Castle as they sped past and he assured her they would stop on the way back. It was easy to tell when they were approaching the viaduct by the scattering of sightseers on the route. They parked at the side of the road and sat, not wanting to leave the warmth of the car.

'I was looking at the map,' began Mills, spreading the ordnance survey sheet out on her lap. 'We could go up towards the summit of Wild Boar Fell. One of

Wainwright's walks starts from here.'

'Have you seen the snow up there?' Harry asked, pointing unnecessarily.

'We're dressed for it. We don't have to go to the top.'

'OK but let's wait until the train's gone.'

'We're not going to see much down here anyway. We'll have to leave the car and walk up to the viaduct if you want to get a picture.'

'There's a bridge a bit further on. Why don't we go down and see if there's some space to park off the road.'

They drove a short distance until the road crossed the railway line, where a man with a tripod was perched precariously on the bridge. Beyond him, a single car was parked on a small lay-by. They pulled up behind it and stopped.

'Shall we get out?' Harry asked.

'Is it time yet?' Mills could feel the wind buffeting the car.

'Five minutes.'

'Let's wait then.'

When the sight of a plume of black smoke announced the train's arrival, they were taken unawares and only just jumped out in time to see it go past. Mills, who was hugely impressed by the steam locomotive, was surprised at Harry's apparent lack of enthusiasm. The driver looked out from the magnificent gleaming engine and passengers waved from the old carriages.

'Well, that's it then,' Harry commented as they stood watching the empty line in the direction the train had gone. 'What was this walk you suggested?'

Initially the sight of the train had distracted her but now she could feel the ice-cold blast cutting through her jacket.

Mills wished she hadn't mentioned the walk but, on the other hand, how else would they spend the next few hours?

'There's a path that goes up through the viaduct,' she shouted against the persistent wind.

'You mean we've got to go back again?' Harry asked.

'Well – there is a track from here.' She looked up from the map. Across the road from the car was a small area which had been quarried. She pointed to the farm gate. 'We go through there, between the quarry and the bridge.'

'If you know where you're going,' Harry remarked with a shrug.

They trudged back to the car to don hats and gloves before setting off along the road. Mills was battling to fold the map in the strong wind as the photographer returned to his vehicle, laden with equipment.

'Wasn't that fantastic!' he remarked.

Mills agreed and Harry muttered something under his breath that sounded like '...if that's what turns you on.'

A thin layer of snow still covered the ground on the other side of the gate. They walked in a generally northerly direction, as Mills had remembered from the description she'd read.

'Why didn't you bring the instructions,' moaned Harry.

'Because it was in a book, I didn't want to get it wet.'

The snow under foot became thicker as they progressed up the slope and soon there was no sign of a track, just clean white snow forming drifts, causing them to suddenly sink up to their knees. At one point Mills found herself almost waist deep. Unaware, Harry marched on ahead, ignoring her calls, leaving her to struggle out as best she could. After a long, long silence he staggered, righted himself and turned to wait for her to catch up.

'Where's the map?' he demanded.

She handed it to him, waiting while he studied it – turning it round from time to time.

'They've marked mine shafts here,' he announced and began to express concern over the danger of falling down an old shaft.

Soon the snow was deeper, forming drifts that meant progress slowed to a halt.

'This is stupid.' Harry turned back with a face set in frustration.

'If we keep going up we should avoid the pits,' Mills countered.

'No way. I'm going back down. It was a daft idea to come in the first place.'

He began slipping and sliding his way back down in the direction of the car. Mills was tempted to go on but was not convinced he would wait for her to return. So, reluctantly, she folded the map, shoved it in her pocket and followed. Flakes of snow were falling and by the time they reached the gate it was settling. It was only three-thirty but already the skies were grey and soon it would be dusk.

'Good we decided to come back,' offered Mills, hoping to restore communications now Harry was back on *terra firma*.

There was no answer. He unlocked the car and climbed in. Mills spent time removing her hat, coat and gloves before sliding into the passenger seat. They sat in silence for a while.

'That Land Rover won't be able to get back out if it snows much harder,' remarked Mills, idly.

'Land Rover? What Land Rover?'

'The green one parked under the arch – down there

below the railway line.'

Harry rubbed the condensation from his window and stared out. He opened the door, climbed out and marched down towards the line. Mills watched from the car as he stood peering at the vehicle. Eventually he brushed the snow from the number plate and stepped back. After a pause he pulled at the rear door before disappearing beneath the arch.

Unable to retain her curiosity any longer, Mills put her coat back on and followed, slipping as she ran down the slope to the arch. Harry had obviously managed to open the driver's door and was sitting inside the vehicle. Mills went round to the passenger door, opening it gingerly.

'Don't touch that!' shouted Harry. 'You've not got gloves on, you stupid woman!'

Mills stepped back, responding instinctively to the reprimand, banging the door on the brick wall and nearly losing her balance.

'What's the matter with it?' she asked.

'It could be a crime scene. We've been looking for this vehicle for a week now.'

'Should we call someone?' She struggled to retrieve her mobile from her pocket.

'No, don't!' Harry ordered. 'I'll handle it.' He was still looking around. 'You go and wait in the car. I won't be long.'

Mills was tempted to call the police anyway. Surely he's not supposed to be inside the vehicle fiddling about, she thought. She stood in the falling snow for a while until she was so cold and wet that she gave in and sat in the car. Ten or fifteen minutes later Harry was back. He appeared to be carrying something but she couldn't see what it was and he put it in the boot before joining her in the car.

'Did you find something?' she asked.

There was no response.

'Do you need to go to the police station in Kirkby Stephen?'

'Yes, I'll drop you at the pub on the way.'

He turned the CD player on. It was old stuff… stuff he liked. He knew she didn't but he didn't seem to care. At Nateby she climbed out and said goodbye. Harry seemed preoccupied but that suited her. She cleared the layer of snow from the windscreen and set off back over the tops, hoping the snow wasn't settling on the road. Why she'd thought it was a good idea to see him, she had no idea. It was over and good riddance. She needed to concentrate on the coming week and her conference.

Back outside the pub, Harry waited until the Mini had disappeared from view before turning the car round and setting off towards Hawes. He had a sense of excitement that he rarely experienced. It would be a good hour and a half before he would reach his flat in Harrogate. He slowed as he passed over the railway line, stopping to view the Land Rover once more. In the light of the headlights he could see it was already covered in a thin layer of snow; he smiled, reassured that no-one else would know it was there – yet.

Chapter 9

Fiona appeared delighted to see her. She opened the door wide, baby Flora tucked under her arm, and gave Mills a kiss on both cheeks.

'Darling,' she said, 'come in, come in.'

She kicked the door shut with her stiletto heel, ushering her down the hall and into the spacious living area. Mills stopped abruptly, once again slightly terrified at her first glimpse of London spread out so far below them.

'Put your bags in here,' Fiona ordered, opening the door to the spare bedroom, 'then come and have a cup of tea. You must be dying for one after that long train journey.'

Mills dumped her rucksack and briefcase on the bed, leaning the poster holder against the wall. She tried not to look at the full-length window that stretched along the entire wall.

Back in the main room, they drank tea and Mills nibbled delicate chocolate biscuits, noting that Fiona did not.

'Hugh will be back soon – I sent him to the deli to fetch some bits for supper.' She smiled across at Mills. 'He's such an angel at the weekends. We see so little of him during the week, don't we Flora?' She jiggled the baby on her knee for a while then offered her to Mills. 'Here, say hello to baby sister while I go and change.'

By the time her father had returned with the shopping, Mills was sitting with Flora fast asleep on her knee.

'Don't get up,' he said softly with a wave. 'Take advantage of the peace and quiet.' He dumped the shopping in the kitchen then disappeared to the bedroom, returning with a grin. 'She's spark out.'

So they were able to chat for a while: her father asking about work and the conference, Mills telling him about the opening at the university for teaching in forensics.

'And what about Harry?' Fiona had woken and was standing by the bedroom door. 'Is he still on the scene?'

'No.'

'That's a shame,' offered her father. 'He seemed a nice lad.'

'Nice?' Fiona came into the room. 'He struck me as a miserable sort of guy. Not very talkative. Bit sullen.'

Hugh raised his eyebrows at Mills and she grinned back.

'Well, he's not around anymore,' said Mills, hoping to shut her up.

'So who is it now? Shall we expect a Valentine's card on Tuesday?'

Fiona could be so irritating, thought Mills. 'There's no-one. I'm too busy, anyway.'

She was saved further interrogation by Flora waking up, signalling the end of adult conversation. The rest of the evening was dictated by the needs of the tiny tot, even down to when they ate their evening meal. Mills was glad to retire soon afterwards, with the excuse that the meeting started early next morning and she had to get her stand ready before the programme began.

*

The conference was being held at a large venue in Piccadilly. She'd grown up in the south and knew London well but the number of people travelling by tube surprised her. Arriving at the meeting by eight-thirty, she found the reception desk unattended. She was scanning the rows of badges trying to read the names of delegates upside-down when a posh voice asked if they could be of help.

The receptionist insisted on taking her to the table that was to house her "exhibition". On either side were very professional stands, belonging to large organisations. Some had pieces of equipment displayed on tables in front of beautifully designed screens bearing advertisements. Mills unpacked her three posters and stared at the plain board behind her.

'Don't worry,' offered the receptionist. 'By the time you've got those pinned up, you won't see the bare cork.'

The table in front of the board was at least covered in a baize cloth. She unpacked the leaflets from her briefcase and spread them in piles, trying to make them look attractive. More exhibitors had arrived and the room was looking busier. One or two people said hello, walking past slowly to see what her stand was about.

When she'd done all that she could to her own display, Mills wandered round the others, reading the boards, picking up the odd business card. She was taking this opportunity seriously, not wishing to miss any chance of making new contacts to enhance Brenda's company.

There was coffee at nine o'clock in the next room, so Mills brought a cup back to her stand and there she sat until it was time for the programme to begin. This morning the talks were focussing on new analytical tools but first there was an invited lecture by a professor on the latest technologies and their impact on detection of crimes. She settled down in the conference hall with paper and pen at the ready – she was going to make sure she missed nothing. The morning went surprisingly quickly.

'I couldn't help noticing that you were making notes during my presentation.'

Mills turned to see who was behind her in the lunch queue. It was the invited speaker who had talked about novel technologies. To be honest, thought Mills, it hadn't been that inspiring and half the time she was doodling.

'I'm reporting back on the conference to my boss at Yardley Forensics,' she admitted.

'I see,' he said, peering down at her name badge. 'Mills, that's an unusual name.'

'It's short for Millicent but…'

'Millicent,' he repeated.

There was an awkward pause. 'Actually it's Madeline Millicent but I prefer my middle name.'

'Better than being called Mad I suppose.'

She could feel her face burning. He seemed young for a professor: late thirties or early forties, no older, but he was rather patronising. To her relief further conversation was halted by the need to concentrate on choice of hot or cold buffet lunch. Once her plate was loaded – with salad because she was eating out with Dad and Fiona that evening – she had to stand alone since she knew no-one in the room. Consequently the professor soon caught her up and this time he had a colleague in tow. They stood in a semi-circle while she tussled with her salad; it was a poor choice because she couldn't cut it up and had to stuff quite large lettuce leaves in at once. She ate as fast as she could then apologised, saying that she had to go to her stand. She left, hoping they were not visiting the exhibition that lunchtime.

It was a relief to have somewhere to hide until the start of the afternoon session. This time the talks were fascinating: detailed descriptions of ground-breaking techniques that had been used to solve really difficult cases. Some were far too sophisticated for Harrogate but some were not and by the end of the day she felt very enthusiastic about what the laboratory might eventually achieve. She paid particular attention to the advances in DNA testing so she could tell Glyn all about it when she got back.

As she was fetching her things from the cloakroom she bumped into the professor again.

'Did you enjoy the afternoon session?' he asked.

She enthused about the talks while she struggled to get her arm in the sleeve.

'Let me help you,' he said, holding the coat as if it was a designer garment.

'Thank you.'

'I wondered if you had any plans for eating tonight? There's a crowd of us going out later.'

She explained that she already had a previous engagement, hoping she sounded suitably sophisticated.

'Perhaps tomorrow?'

'Yes, maybe.' She made for the door before he could develop the arrangement further.

Sitting on the tube back to Canary Wharf, Mills considered what to do about Harry. Various parts of the afternoon talks had reminded her of how secretive he'd been about their discovery. He'd said he was going back to the police station, so presumably he reported finding the missing Land Rover. If he had, would they need a statement from her? She decided to give Nina a call when she got back to the apartment.

'Nige? It's Mills. How are you?'

Nige always knew that when Mills rang it would be to chat to Nina. He called her immediately, making small talk until she appeared on the end of the line.

'Hi Mills, I thought you were in London?'

'I am. I just wanted to ask a favour, although I know you're not really back at work.'

'What is it? What have you been up to now – or is it forensic stuff? I'm not sure I can...'

'No, it's not forensics, Nina.'

She explained how she'd spotted the Land Rover and how Harry had examined it. She tactfully said that Harry had reported it but she wasn't sure if they'd need a statement from her. 'It's a bit awkward, Nina, with Harry and I not being together anymore.'

'Honestly Mills, sometimes...'

'Will you find out for me, please?'

'OK, I'll ask Hazel to check it out. I won't be able to get back until later tomorrow though.'

'That would be great, thanks Nina.'

'How's the family?'

Mills knew by her tone that Nina meant Fiona.

'Not too bad... yet.'

There was a call from the sitting room. 'Are you ready? The baby-sitter's here!'

'I've got to go, Nina. I'm being dragged out for a meal.'

'Lucky you!'

'I'll speak to you tomorrow.'

*

The following day passed quickly; people began to mingle in the breaks and Mills was kept busy explaining what Yardley Forensics could offer. The afternoon programme went on until six, when a drinks reception was to be held, funded by a group of the larger exhibitors. By now Mills recognised a few faces and was able to pass the time chatting to other delegates in the same position – new to the game and knowing no-one. She would have been happy to continue speaking with the two girls from Manchester when she felt a tap on her shoulder.

'We're going off to eat now, you'd better hurry.'

It was the professor. He took her arm and Mills allowed herself to be steered to the cloakroom. It was too late to politely refuse the invitation – he was helping her on with her coat. Soon she was being introduced to his colleagues as they fought their way along the pavement against the flow of commuters. Mills persuaded herself that this was an excellent opportunity to raise her profile in their community and tried to participate in the conversation. But soon she sat back, defeated, as the group discussed the day's presentations and examined the speakers' reputations – yes – forensically. The restaurant was full of couples celebrating Valentine's Day and her group seemed incongruous among the red balloons and heart shaped menus. She was beginning to feel awkward in their company and finally decided that she didn't really like the professor and his cronies. She was just pleased that he kept her glass topped up throughout the meal.

When it was time to settle up, she pulled out her purse to put her share of the bill on the table with the others but Greg, as she discovered he liked to be called, told her to put it away.

'My treat,' he said with a grin.

He insisted on walking with her in the direction of the tube station, taking her arm as they reached it.

'I thought we might go on for another drink,' he suggested with a smirk. 'Just the two of us. Since it's Valentine's Day.'

'Oh no,' Mills hoped her voice didn't betray her panic. 'I'm quite tired... it's been a long day.'

'Well, my hotel's just a bit further along here. We could have a quiet nightcap there, if you like.'

'Honestly, I must go,' she mumbled, turning away, and made for the stairs down into the warmth of the underground without looking back.

Fiona was already in bed when she reached the apartment. Her father was watching the television with the sound turned down. He put his forefinger to his pursed lips, indicating that Mills should be quiet.

'They're both asleep,' he whispered. 'Flora's only just gone down.'

It was difficult to hear the news and they sat in silence for a while as Mills strained to follow the reports. When the London news had finished, her father reached for the remote and pressed the off button.

'Good day?'

'Yep, very good.' She told him about some of the more interesting presentations while he listened attentively. After a while she excused herself and went to her room to check her mobile. Nina had left a text: *No report on LR call me.* It was too late to ring so she sent a text and began to get ready for bed. She was cleaning her teeth in the opulent en-suite when she heard loud music and raced to answer her phone before it woke everyone in the apartment block.

There were never any formalities when Mills asked Nina for help.

'What d'you mean "no report", Nina?'

'What I said. No-one has reported a sighting of the Land Rover – Hazel specifically asked Cumbria for an update. There's been nothing yet.'

The wine had slowed down her reactions and Mills tried to think clearly. She didn't want to get Harry into trouble but if he really hadn't told anyone about finding the Land Rover, somebody should.

'Nina? Are you still there?'

'Of course. Are you going to tell me what this is all about?'

'Can I just give you details of where to find it?'

'The Land Rover? You know where it is?'

Mills explained the location – just before the railway bridge, under the arch. 'Please don't ask any more, Nina. Not now. Just tell Hazel where to find it. I'll explain when I get back from London, I promise.'

She climbed into bed, switched off the lamp and tried to concentrate on what to do, but the next thing she knew it was morning and Fiona was shouting for her to get up – it was nearly time to go.

Graham was waiting when Harry reached Kirkby Stephen police station on Wednesday morning.

'I was beginning to think you'd been avoiding me, lad.'

'No, of course not. I've been busy... you know... the other investigation.'

'How's it going? No sign of the young officer I suppose?'

'No.'

'Well, I've got something you can get your teeth into.' He laughed loudly. 'There's a butcher in Preston who reckons he was offered some dodgy meat.'

'D'you know him?'

'No but I've got a mate in Lancashire HQ. He's been keeping his ear to the ground for me.' He tapped his nose as he moved towards the door. 'Come on, lad, we've not got all day. We need to visit old Foxy in his lair again.'

Harry was more familiar with the area now and was able to recognise where they left the road and turned onto a rough track. The snow had almost gone and he could see they were crossing fields on a barely visible route, heading towards the farm where The Fox lived.

This time Graham was less polite. He hammered on the door and as soon as the old man opened it to make a small gap, he heaved against it, almost falling into the cluttered hallway. Harry followed, looking as stern as he could. The Fox didn't seem so intimidating in his lair, which was dark and cluttered. Harry tripped as he followed his colleague through the hall into a tiny room where a fire was blazing in the hearth. An old dog jumped off the only arm chair as they entered and ran past them whining.

'What you want?'

His piercing eyes contrasted with his wrinkled leathery skin. Harry thought he'd be seventy, maybe eighty, but he couldn't really tell.

'I reckon you know more about the sheep stolen from down Sedbergh way than you're letting on.'

'Why d'you say that, then?' His yellow teeth were crooked and there were several missing.

'Because someone saw you in Preston Market Hall talking to a stall holder.'

'Not against the law.'

'The owner sells meat.'

'I have to buy me dinner, don't I?'

'He says you were offering him a cheap supply of lamb.'

'Rubbish.'

'He's willing to swear to it in court.'

The man shuffled in his seat, staring at the fire. 'He's got nowt on me.'

Graham turned to Harry. 'Would you like to fetch my file from the car, lad?'

'File?'

'On the back seat.'

It was cold outside with a wind that cut across the field from the east. Harry opened the back door of the car but the seat was empty. He searched around but there was no file. He slammed the door, turning to go back to the farmhouse but Graham was already on his way.

'I couldn't find it,' Harry said as they climbed into their seats.

'Happen I left it at home, lad.' He sounded tense.

Harry waited until they were back on the road before asking, 'Did he tell you anything else?'

'Oh aye. I know who I need to speak to now.'

He turned south but after Sedbergh Harry lost his bearings. They'd driven for about thirty minutes, he reckoned, when they stopped at a farm track. Graham turned off the engine and took out the keys.

'Stay here.'

'Where are you going?'

'To see a man about some sheep, lad.'

Harry watched the big man gradually disappearing down the track. There was a faded sign on the open gate indicating the name – "Mildroke Farm" and he could see buildings in the distance, partly hidden by a small wood. A flock of crows rose from the trees and flew around before settling again.

When Graham was no longer in sight, Harry followed. He disliked being left out of the investigation; he wanted to see what his colleague was up to. As the track curved round to the right, he suddenly had a clear view of the farm buildings. Graham was walking through a gate and soon disappeared from sight again. Suddenly there was a loud cry, followed by shouting. A dog started barking – no, more than one. Graham reappeared; he was being pushed and shoved backwards by an angry man in overalls.

'Get off my land and don't come back! You've no business on my property! Out now or I'll call the police!' He pushed at a shock of straw-coloured hair as it blew across his face.

Harry ran forward, to provide support, but Graham threw him a look, with a surreptitious shake of the head, that shut him up.

'We don't want no police,' said Graham calmly. 'I heard you might have something we're looking for, that's all.'

'Well I don't, so clear off.'

Graham held up his hands in submission. 'OK, OK. No harm done. We're off.'

With that he turned, pulling Harry with him. 'Keep walking,' he said under his breath.

They moved quickly back to the car.

'I expected *you* to stay here,' he said when they reached the gate.

'I expected *you* to tell me what's going on,' muttered Harry.

'I would've told you, if he'd co-operated but as it goes, he's not going to.'

He said no more and they set off back to the station without another word. As they took the road through Mallerstang and approached the railway line, Harry tried to maintain a calm exterior, determined not to look in the direction of the arch where the Land Rover remained hidden. But suddenly, when he thought they were clear, Graham slammed his foot on the brake.

'Hey up,' said Graham, 'there's summat going on over there!'

Two police cars were parked at the side of the road; men in uniform were milling about. Harry looked round cautiously. There was no doubting what he saw – they'd discovered where the Land Rover was hidden. Now everyone would be searching for Jamie Reed and he'd lost the opportunity to show he was CID material.

Chapter 10

The conference dinner was to be held on the Wednesday evening, so the delegates had a free afternoon. Mills noticed there was a David Hockney exhibition almost next door to where the conference was being held and had decided to spend her afternoon there. However, Fiona had other plans.

'If you're free this afternoon we can have a real girly time. We'll go to the salon and I'll treat you to a new hairstyle,' she said as Mills gobbled down a bowl of cereal.

Fiona took a handful of hair and inspected it. 'As I thought – split ends! When did you last have it conditioned?'

Mills would not admit that it was never conditioned. She'd had it cut last year some time and now tended to tie it back in a ponytail rather than think about it.

'I'd really like to see the exhibition, Fiona.'

'No problem, we'll go another time. How about Saturday?'

'I told you, I'm going back Friday night.'

'No, no you can't. I promised Hugh we'd have supper together before you go.'

'I'll be here tomorrow night. We can have a family meal

then. I must get back by Saturday morning – I've got things to do,' she lied.

'In that case you're coming to the salon this afternoon. They can do your nails at the same time.'

She escaped into the freezing wind that whipped round the tall apartment buildings, fleeing to the warmth of the underground system. The route was familiar to her now and she reached Piccadilly with sufficient time to pick up a cappuccino on the way in.

Exhibitors greeted each other like old friends, wandering over to each other's displays to find out how sales were going.

'Hi. Did you survive last night?'

Mills looked up. It was a young man from one of the other stands.

'I mean, did you have a nice meal with the prof?' He was smiling conspiratorially.

'Yes, thank you. Do you know him?'

'He was my supervisor when I was doing my PhD. He has quite a reputation with the ladies.'

'I bet.'

'Doing anything exciting with your free afternoon?' he asked while he casually flicked the pages of the Yardley Forensics leaflet on the table in front of him.

'I have to see someone,' she said. There was no way she was going to admit she was having her hair done.

'Would you like to join us on our table this evening?' He looked up. 'I mean – do you have any plans about who…'

'No, that would be great. I mean, I hadn't thought about it really,' she replied, blushing.

'Great. It's just a bunch of us from work but… well…'

'Thank you…' She looked at his name badge. 'Alex.'

Her phone rang and he made his way back to his stand. The call was from Fiona, who sounded surprisingly annoyed.

'Mills, I need you to call your friend, Nina, – she has to talk to you urgently.'

'I can call her later – it's just that I'll be going in for the talks...'

Fiona cut her off. 'Ring her now, Mills, if you've got any sense. She said it was an urgent police matter. I hope everything is all right?'

Nina was apparently waiting for the call. She picked up immediately.

'It's me.'

Nina didn't give her a chance to continue. She demanded to know how Mills had access to the whereabouts of the missing vehicle. It was a very serious matter that she was going to get to the bottom of, right now. Did she not realise this could become a very serious investigation?

Mills had to think on her feet. She didn't want to drop Harry in it but she'd been increasingly concerned that he'd behaved in a very strange manner. It seemed that he'd not reported the missing Land Rover when they'd discovered it – certainly not immediately – and she was sure he'd taken an object from it and hidden it in his car.

She took a deep breath. 'I was with Harry when he found it in Mallerstang,' she explained. 'I had to leave soon afterwards but he assured me he was going to report it immediately. Nina... I only told you because you were off work. I didn't want it to go any further... I mean I didn't want you to get involved.'

There was a long pause.

'Send me an e-mail with what you've just told me.' Nina's

voice was cold. 'When are you back up in Yorkshire?'

'Friday night.'

'OK. Please don't contact Harry before then. You'll need to give a full statement to Hazel – preferably over the weekend.'

'I can't do that to Harry, Nina.'

'I thought you'd dumped him.'

'But…'

Nina stopped her. She gave her Hazel's number and e-mail address, ringing off abruptly.

Mills sat for a few minutes feeling slightly nauseated. The room had emptied for the first session of the day and she was missing a talk on footprint identification, but suddenly it all seemed rather trivial. She'd just betrayed Harry and she wasn't supposed to let him know. She turned her mobile on again and selected his number.

Margaret had woken Harry at nine with a cup of tea.

'I'll start cooking breakfast but there's no hurry; you take your time.'

Harry pulled himself up into a sitting position and took the mug, sipping the hot, strong brew. It had been a really late night searching the area round the arch in Mallerstang. There was no suspicion regarding the owner of the land, who'd been oblivious of the Land Rover being there. But Harry had already come to that conclusion; no-one in their right mind would leave it on their own doorstep if they were involved in a plot to hide it. A cursory search of the area had produced nothing but Harry knew that as well – he'd been searching on and off for three days with no result. He was sure if he'd had a little more time he might have found something that would lead to Jamie Reed's whereabouts. The vehicle itself would be taken apart now but his search had revealed nothing.

He was getting dressed when the call from Mills came through. Recognising the number he was tempted to ignore it but he was curious to know why she would ring. If she wanted to meet up again, he would explain as kindly as he could that he was seeing someone else. Shelley and he weren't exactly dating yet but he was sure she would agree if he asked her out, now that Valentine's Day was over.

'Hi,' he said, as cheerfully as he could.

'Harry, listen.' Her voice sounded shaky. 'They know that we found the Land Rover on Saturday. I had to tell them. I'm not supposed to speak to you so don't say I rang.'

'Mills! Mills!' he shouted but the call was over.

He sat on the bed for a minute or two, working out what to do. Eventually he finished dressing and went into the kitchen for breakfast.

'You were working late last night, love.' Margaret said as she served out the bacon and eggs. 'Was it something important?' She put the plate down in front of him. 'My Tom said it was probably about the missing lad.' She waited. 'Was it?'

'Yes it was. They've found his father's vehicle.'

She went across the kitchen to the door that led into the yard.

'It *was* the lad, Tom,' she called and stood looking out.

Harry ate as fast as he could but he was still finishing his toast when Mr Drysdale appeared.

'Where did they find it, lad?' he asked as he removed his boots and jacket.

'Mallerstang – near where the road crosses the railway line.'

'Is that right? Didn't get far then… and the lad?'

'No sign.'

'So what's to be done now?'

Harry was tired of his questioning. 'I really don't know. It's been handed over to CID in Carlisle.'

'Does that mean you'll be going back to Harrogate?' Margaret sounded disappointed.

'No – I'm helping with the sheep thefts. I'm here until that's sorted.' He got up from the table.

'That's nice then,' she said, taking his empty plate.

She was running the water to wash up as he set off for Kirkby Stephen.

He deliberately drove along the road to Mallerstang, interested to see if anything was happening at the scene of last night's discovery. The Land Rover had gone, everything was back to normal and he could begin to relax. The longer route gave him a chance to think and a plan was taking form. If he kept his cool he could probably carry it off. When he arrived at the station to find Sergeant Crossland waiting for him, he was prepared.

'I think you'll find it's a lot of nonsense,' Harry told him with a smile. 'It's my ex-girlfriend.' He emphasised the "ex". 'She's a bit down on me because I dumped her and she's trying to cause trouble.'

His sergeant looked perplexed. 'The message came from a colleague at Newby Wiske. They want to speak to you as soon as possible. I suggest you get over there now!'

'Now? But I'm supposed to be going down to Preston market with Graham.'

'If you've got any sense you'll do as I say, lad. When you

get back here you'll be needed for the search. They'll be covering every inch of Mallerstang, including Wild Boar Fell, looking for young Jamie and they'll need everyone they can get.'

'What do they think happened?'

'That the vehicle ran off the road and he set out looking for help, poor lad. Let's pray he made it to safety.'

The visit to the salon with Fiona was as embarrassing as Mills had anticipated. They manicured and painted her short nails and fiddled about with her hair while she fought to keep their styling under control. Eventually she compromised, accepting a small amount of conditioning and straightening of her unruly locks. When she admitted that she liked the effect, Fiona insisted on buying her the most expensive straighteners in the shop.

'I know you're feeling low at the moment. These will cheer you up – from your father and me.'

Mills accepted them graciously, giving Fiona a peck on the cheek.

It was unusual for her to feel satisfied with her reflection but that evening, before she left for the conference dinner, she gave herself a nod of approval. Fiona fussed over her and insisted that her father drive her to the venue.

'Don't be ridiculous,' retorted Hugh. 'It will take ten times as long by car at this time of night.'

'It's OK, it's easier to take the tube,' agreed Mills.

The dinner was being held in a smart hotel close to the conference venue. Mills pulled her coat round her as she emerged into the cold at Piccadilly Circus. The lights were bright and the streets busy, nothing could be further away than her life in the Dales. It was extraordinarily different and she tried to imagine what it would be like to live full time in such an exciting environment. Fiona and Dad enjoyed the buzz of the city but obviously they didn't miss the countryside. It was fun for a few days but she knew she would feel the usual swell of recognition as she arrived back in the Dales.

'Hi!'

Mills turned to see Alex on the pavement beside her.

'I thought I might see you coming from the tube. I wasn't sure if you knew where the hotel is.'

She smiled. Had he really made a special effort to come to meet her? She wished she hadn't worn her woolly hat with the dangly bits down the side. She felt oddly shy but he didn't seem to notice, chattering about the cheap accommodation they had booked him into.

The hotel was brightly illuminated and inside it was warm and noisy as they fought their way through the groups arriving for the evening. Alex took her coat and offending hat, and handed them into the cloakroom.

'I put them all on the same ticket,' he said as they made their way up to the ballroom.

His colleagues had taken a table near the bar and he took her over, introducing Mills as if he'd known her for years. She already knew that the firm they worked for specialised in forensic data recovery because she'd had a sneaky look at their stand in the exhibition room when it was quiet. But no-one was talking shop on their table. They were soon joined by more young people who had been at university with one or other of them and she was able to settle back, enjoying the conversation without the need to join in.

The food was surprisingly good and their glasses were topped up with red or white through all the courses. After they'd eaten and coffee was being served, the inevitable speeches began. They all turned towards the top table where the creepy professor was a member of the esteemed delegates.

'Are you all right?' Alex was asking in a whisper. 'Are you usually so quiet?'

She blushed. 'I'm fine. Just a bit tired.'

There was a round of applause as the conference organiser presented the administrator with a bouquet of flowers. The professor stood to give a short speech which was supposed to be amusing but was a self-promoting description of the development of computer forensics. It went on too long and her fellow diners were making faces at each other and looking at their watches. Finally the speeches ended, there was further applause and background music broke the expectant silence.

It was already after ten and Mills didn't relish the tube journey at that time, certainly not later, so she made to leave.

'I'll have to go,' she said to Alex as she stood up.

He immediately jumped up and followed her out to the lobby.

'I'll get the coats,' he said.

She tried to stop him but he insisted on walking with her to the tube. She was amazed how busy it was at that time, fighting against a stream of people on the pavement and down into the warmth of Piccadilly underground station.

Even there he wouldn't let her go alone. He produced a ticket and followed her through the barrier and down the escalator.

'I'll be fine from here, Alex. You must be in the other direction, surely?'

'I can't let you go on your own at this time of night,' he insisted.

So they travelled together to her station and he saw her to the door of the apartment block.

'Wow, is this where your dad lives?' he asked.

'Yes. They're up there somewhere. I'd invite you in but…'

'No, it's late. I must be off anyway.'

He took her hand and pressed a business card into it. 'Give us a ring if you need any digital forensics,' he said and turned away.

'Thanks,' she called and smiled as she put the card in her coat pocket.

The interview at Newby Wiske was worse than Harry had expected. At first it was just snooty Sergeant Hazel Fuller but then he was taken to see the DI. He'd insisted that it was all a mistake but they produced an e-mail from Mills which they accepted as the true record of events, despite his protestations that she was being vindictive. Hazel let slip that Mills was a friend of Nina Featherstone's and everyone knew that Hazel Fuller had worked with Nina for years. He insisted that his car had broken down and there was no signal on his phone to report finding the Land Rover, but he knew they didn't believe him. In the end he had to admit he'd been lying and then they went ballistic, threatening him with instant dismissal.

He wasn't sure whether to tell them that he'd spent every free moment searching for Jamie. When he did finally explain why he was working on his own they seemed shocked, incredulous even. He was told to wait in the interview room while they decided what to do next. An hour went by and he was allowed to fetch a sandwich from the canteen – not that he was hungry. He sat with a plastic cup of coffee going cold on the table in front of him while he waited to see what would happen next.

Eventually the Chief Superintendent came in and Harry jumped to his feet. 'Sir.'

The Chief Super "read him the Riot Act", as he referred to it. Harry called it a severe bollocking.

'Don't think this is the end of it, son. There will be a report and we'll be recommending a misconduct interview. Meanwhile you're very lucky not to be suspended. You're to go straight back to Kirkby Stephen. We need everyone we can spare to join the search for Jamie Reed. He *is* a PC worth his salt.'

Mills arrived at the exhibition room early but there was no sign of Alex all morning. The meeting finished at mid-day and as she packed up the posters she glanced across to where his colleagues were doing the same.

'I just came to say goodbye,' she said, wandering over.

She was too embarrassed to ask, but fortunately someone mentioned that Alex had been called to the office unexpectedly. They needed him for a mobile phone investigation, they explained. Disappointed, she made her way back to her father's apartment where Fiona was waiting to persuade her to stay the weekend.

Mills insisted she would be travelling back to Yorkshire on the following day, despite Fiona's protestations. It was a subdued evening meal with Mills excusing herself immediately afterwards to pack. She tried calling Nina but Nige answered, with an obviously fabricated excuse that Nina was in the bath and would be going straight to bed.

Early next morning, as her father went down to put her bag in the car, Mills thanked Fiona for their afternoon out together and promised to return soon. As she held Flora's little hands, she had a momentary desire to stay with her family for that extra day but it was too late now.

'You'd better hurry, Mills. Hugh won't be able to wait long in the street.'

The London traffic was crawling along roads lined with parked cars and Mills wondered why her father had even offered to take her to the station, she knew he hated driving in congested streets. Soon it was clear that Fiona had an ulterior motive in sending them off together.

'Fiona and I are worried about you, Mills,' he began.

You mean *Fiona* is worried, she thought.

'We think perhaps you're a bit down after breaking up with that boy.'

'Harry?'

'Yes, Harry.'

There was a long silence while they waited for the lights to change.

'Don't worry, Dad. It's not that.'

'What is it, then?' He looked round at her for a second.

'Just work.'

Another pause as he took a right turn into faster moving traffic.

'We were thinking it's probably time you were settling into a proper job.'

'I've got a proper job, Dad. In fact I shall have two soon.'

She described the arrangement at the university while Nige was on leave.

'Well, that's something I suppose, although we thought the forensic laboratory would give you a full-time job in due course.'

'I don't think Brenda can afford it… and anyway, I like the variety.'

'The spice of life, eh?'

Mills had hoped to be home before dark but, although the afternoon wasn't over, the taxi driver had his lights on during the last part of the journey. The snow was still forming a white layer on the fields and tops of the walls but the roads were relatively clear. It was a wonderful feeling to open the gate and walk up the path covered in pristine snow. But inside it was cold, very cold.

Mills lit the fire and turned on the immersion heater. It would be hours before the cottage was even slightly warm. She kept her coat on while she unpacked her bag and loaded the washing machine. Finally, she poured herself a cup of tea and rang Nina.

'Nige?' she said as soon as the phone stopped ringing, 'I don't care if Nina is fast asleep in bed, I have to speak to her!'

No-one answered for a few seconds.

'It's me.' Nina's voice was flat. 'What do you want?'

'I'm sorry, I'm so sorry, Nina,' Mills sobbed. 'I'm sorry.'

'Stop it… Mills, stop it. It won't solve anything doing that.' Her voice was cracking. Mills sensed a softening in her tone. 'We need to talk about this business with Harry. It's put me in a very difficult position.'

'But you're not working at the moment. What I told you was in confidence.'

'That's irrelevant, Mills, and you know it!' she replied sharply.

'I'm sorry…'

'Stop apologising. It's answers I want. I need you to give a statement. Hazel's waiting for it. Come over tomorrow and I'll go with you.'

Chapter 11

Harry threw himself into the search for Jamie Reed. This was proper policing and he would have happily carried on through the night if they hadn't been ordered to stand down as dusk fell. Back at the station there was almost a party atmosphere as they stood around with mugs of tea, discussing the chances of finding Jamie alive and well. There were suggestions that he might have broken his leg or got trapped in a snowdrift. No-one dared raise the possibility that he might not survive. Most of the constables were from Carlisle and had little local knowledge, less than Harry in fact. They huddled over the map, guessing where they would be working the next day. He was glad when the minibus took them away, leaving him alone in the outer office.

'No joy today then?' his sergeant called, without looking up from his desk. The atmosphere between them had changed since Harry's disgrace and now they only conversed about work.

'No, sir.'

'Well, perhaps tomorrow. Are you off back to my sister's?'

'Yes, sir.'

'Can you ring Graham Patterson? He's got something he wants you to help him with.'

'But I'm on the search operation...'

'You're on whatever we throw at you at the moment, lad. You're lucky you've got a job at all.'

Harry went to his desk and rang the number without comment. He was hoping that Graham wouldn't answer but, after a few rings, there was his cheery voice at the other end.

'Harry? Good. I've got the go-ahead to set up a honey trap!'

Harry waited for him to continue.

'Are you there, lad?'

'Yes.'

'Right. Well, we're going to lure that slime ball we met in Lancashire out of his hole. We're going to pose as buyers of his rotten meat. What d'you think of that?' He waited. 'Can you hear me?'

'Yes. How? I mean, what...'

'It'll take a bit of working out. We don't look very likely buyers, do we? I was thinking we need someone who looks like they might buy dodgy meat.'

'Such as?'

'Well, like owners of an Indian restaurant or a Chinese take-away.'

'Isn't that rather racist?'

'Why? It's common knowledge that unscrupulous Asian restaurant owners are buying dodgy meat because it's halal.'

'I suppose.'

'I've got a bit of a problem though. I need someone who looks the part.'

'What d'you mean?' Harry thought he knew exactly what Graham meant.

'Do you have any friends from Pakistan who could pretend to be a restaurant owner?'

'You *are* kidding?'

'No.'

'No… certainly not well enough to ask them that!'

'Have a think, Harry. We need to be authentic if this is going to work.'

When Harry put the phone down, he couldn't contain himself.

'I don't believe it!' he said to himself but loudly enough for his sergeant to hear.

'Sounded interesting,' he called. 'What's Graham up to now?'

When Harry explained, Crossland shrugged. 'What's wrong with that? If we needed an ethnic match for an identity parade we'd have to do it.'

Harry admitted that he didn't actually know anyone to approach with such a request.

'There must be suitable candidates in the force,' speculated Crossland as he struggled with his overcoat.

'Yes,' Harry replied, as he tried to think of any officers in his region. No-one came to mind. 'Anyway, don't you think an officer would be offended, being asked to do it?'

'No, lad. They'd be pleased to help.' He pulled on his gloves. 'Now, I'm off. Tell my sister we'll see her on Sunday – she's asked us over for our dinner.'

'Yes, sir.'

If that was the case, Harry decided, he would see Shelley that night then return to his flat in Harrogate at the weekend. As soon as his sergeant had left, he called a familiar number. It rang for so long that he was about to put the receiver down, convinced Mills was deliberately ignoring him.

'Hello.'

'Mills, it's me.'

'Harry? What do you want? I don't really want…'

'Listen. It's a quick question. You know Nina Featherstone, don't you?'

The voice at the other end was hesitant. 'Look, if it's about…'

'Listen, won't you? I know she's not back at work properly yet but I need to contact her urgently.'

'OK.'

'Do you have her number?'

'I don't know… I mean…'

'It's a police matter, Mills.' He was trying hard to remain patient.

There was a rustling at the other end. 'It's on my phone. Hold on…'

He waited until she returned then copied the number onto a sheet of scrap paper on his desk.

'Harry, I…'

'Sorry, got to go.' He put the phone down quickly before she could say any more. The last thing he wanted was to start another discussion about what had happened between them. Shelley was practically his girlfriend now, he'd call her… but first he would contact DS Featherstone and get *that* over with.

An icy wind was blowing when he finally left the station. The roads were empty and he passed no-one as he drove through Mallerstang. Although the lights of the farm were welcoming, he was beginning to tire of the Drysdale's hospitality. It was wearing having to be so polite all the time, to keep his room tidy and eat meals at set times. He yearned to lie in bed all morning at the weekend.

'Hello, Margaret.' He smiled as he entered the kitchen. 'Sarge says he's looking forward to Sunday.'

'Oh, yes. I nearly forgot to tell you that we'll be having company.'

'That's OK. I'm going back to Harrogate on Saturday night.'

'You don't have to.'

'No, I was going to anyway.'

He went to his room and lay on his bed until supper time. Shelley wasn't back from work until late on a Friday. He'd call her after he'd eaten and go round to hers. It would be the only chance to see her if he was out searching on Saturday before he drove home.

When Mills arrived on Saturday morning, Nige was keeping his head down, having given up trying to reason with Nina; but before he could warn their friend, she began on Mills.

'Do you know what that wretched guy asked me to do?'

Without waiting for Mills to respond, she repeated the conversation she'd had with Harry the night before.

'He said he needed someone who looked as if they needed halal meat, if you please! I asked him, "Do I look like I eat halal meat?" I'm from India, I'm Hindu, for goodness sake!'

Mills agreed with her friend that it was insulting, more out of a wish to keep her happy than any instinctive feeling that Harry was in the wrong.

'I don't see the problem, myself,' said Nige.

'What if you were specifically asked to pose as a Welsh…
I don't know… harp player?' Nina demanded.

Nige's expression of first puzzlement, then mirth broke
the tension.

Even Nina's expression softened. 'OK, I know… but…'

Nige put his arm round his wife. 'Look at it as using
bigotry to catch a criminal. Playing on his ignorance, same
as you would if you were tricking a burglar with an easy
break-in. You've got an unfair advantage over all your
white colleagues.'

She grinned. 'That's true. I suppose it might be
interesting.' Suddenly she looked serious. 'Anyway we've
got to go, Mills.'

She issued verbal instructions to Nige about when and
how the twins were to be fed and rested, then ushered Mills
out of the door. They drove most of the way in silence
except to agree that Harry really was the limit but by the
time they reached Newby Wiske, Nina had talked herself
into taking part in the sting to catch the sheep rustlers.

The police interview was difficult for Mills, even though
she'd met Hazel before. She asked her to go through
exactly what had happened when Harry found the Land
Rover in Mallerstang. That wasn't the problem. Mills
relayed a blow-by-blow account of her seeing the vehicle
and how Harry had told her to stay put while he went to
investigate. But as she described the events, she suddenly
realised that she'd overlooked something.

'Then he came back to the car and I said we should
report it at once.' She wasn't sure why she omitted the fact
that he put something in the boot of his car before getting
back in.

'But he didn't, did he?' Hazel asked. 'He didn't report it

immediately.'

'No. He said he would go back to Kirkby Stephen after he dropped me off.'

Nina was smiling encouragingly throughout the interview. Hazel was very business-like. She said she would get the statement typed up immediately so she could have a signature before Mills left. Once they were alone, Mills asked Nina what would happen to the statement.

'They'll add it to the file so they can decide on the next step. He'll probably be reprimanded for his lack of commitment.'

'Did he say why he didn't report it?' Mills asked.

'Car broke down… no phone signal…' Her face was non-committal but Mills guessed they would be considered lame excuses.

Nina went off to talk to a senior colleague while Mills promised to stay exactly where she was. Hazel returned in less than ten minutes with her statement ready for a signature.

'Did they find the man in the Land Rover?' Mills asked as she carefully signed the form.

'Not yet. They've got a full-scale search going on over there at the moment.'

Mills didn't know what to say.

'Look, it's none of my business,' said Hazel, taking the paper from her, 'but I would be careful of that young man.'

'Who? Harry?'

'Yes. There's something not right about him. Just a warning.'

Embarrassed, Mills explained that they were no longer an item, feeling herself reddening under the older woman's gaze.

'Well, you're well rid if you ask me.'

Mills was relieved to hear Nina coming back down the corridor. Her friend arrived looking pleased with herself.

'All systems go. Apparently they're keen for me to do it, so I suppose that's OK.'

Hazel listened as Nina explained what she had to do in the sheep-rustling investigation.

'So you've got to pass yourself off as a restaurant owner who doesn't care where her meat comes from,' she said in disbelief. 'Anyone looking at you wouldn't be taken in for a minute.'

Mills agreed that Nina's impeccably groomed hair and nails did not give the impression of someone without scruples.

'You forget,' Nina said with a laugh, 'I was the lead in my school production of "Romeo and Juliet" and my Cordelia is still talked about to this day!'

'But you'd better be careful, Nina. Harry doesn't seem to be a very reliable officer to work with,' warned Hazel.

'I agree but apparently Graham Patterson is leading the investigation and he has an amazing reputation. And it will allow me to keep an eye on young Harry.' Nina looked over at Mills before continuing. 'See what he's about.'

Hazel said nothing but Mills had the impression they were keeping something from her.

They barely spoke on the way back. Mills was worrying about whether she should have told Hazel about whatever Harry had taken from the Land Rover. Normally she would have asked Nina's advice but her friend was not likely to treat their conversation as confidential – as she had reminded Mills before, it *was* a police inquiry. When they reached the house, Nina wanted her to stay for tea but

Mills insisted she had to get back and drove straight home, determined to confront Harry as soon as she got the opportunity.

Mills put down the receiver when Harry's mobile went to voicemail. It wasn't something she could leave a message about. She wanted to find out what he'd taken from the Land Rover and for that she had to hear his unrehearsed response when she asked him. There was nothing much in the fridge so she opened a tin of beans and made toast but, just as she settled down to watch television with her meal on her lap, the doorbell rang. Thinking it was probably her neighbour, she left her plate on the sofa and opened the front door without bothering to switch on the porch light. There was a large figure on the front step.

'Hi. I thought I'd come round for my torch.' It was Daryl.

There was nothing to do but invite him in but Mills swept her plate off the sofa and into the kitchen before he came into the light of the sitting room.

'Something smells good,' he remarked, his eyes moving round her small room.

She pushed her hair back behind her ears.

'I hope I haven't disturbed your tea?' he asked with a smile.

'Oh no, would you like some tea – to drink I mean?'

'Yes, that would be good. I can't stay long though. Got to get back to my brother.'

'How is he?' Mills asked from the kitchen. He began to follow her. 'No stay there! I mean, sit down… please.'

'He's getting there,' Daryl called to her. 'He was at Gran's funeral yesterday but he'll not be working for a while.' He came to the kitchen door. 'Look, were you going out? You seem, well... dressed up. Are you going somewhere? I can leave if you want.'

Mills explained that she'd been out all day although she didn't say she was visiting the police headquarters. She pointed to her plate of beans on toast. 'As you can see I have no plans.'

He beamed. 'Well that's great because I've got a bottle of wine in the car and I love baked beans – if that's OK with you?'

'That's fine,' she said, hoping she sounded cool but when he'd left the room, she allowed herself to grin stupidly at her reflection in the window. When he returned, she asked about him having to get back to his brother.

'Ah. That was not factually correct,' he admitted. 'I just didn't want to outstay my welcome.'

Harry returned exhausted after another day searching for Jamie Reed in Mallerstang. It had been a bright morning and the snow-covered hills looked spectacular against the empty blue sky. But the wind was sharp and he'd got colder and colder during the day. Progress was slow, becoming slower as they climbed higher and they met snow drifts up to a metre deep. He had begun the day with enthusiasm but became more sluggish as time went on. By dusk he could barely lift his legs to climb into the van, his trousers were so sodden, his boots so saturated.

'All right if I have a bath?' he called as he took his boots off at the kitchen door and hung his coat on a spare peg.

Mrs Drysdale appeared from the hall. 'What's that dear?'

'Can I have a bath?'

'Of course, the water's hot.'

He made for the door before she engaged him in conversation.

'Hold on!' she called. 'There's a message. A Mr Patterson says he's been trying to get you on your mobile. Can you ring him urgently?'

Harry nodded and went through to the bathroom. As he waited for the water to reach a satisfactory level, he pulled off his wet clothes, leaving them in a damp pile on the floor. The temperature of the bath was hot but while he added some cold he stepped in, watching his feet and ankles turn red. Finally he was able to lower himself fully into the water and luxuriate in its warmth. However pleasant it felt, he couldn't stop picturing poor Jamie Reed. The thought had haunted him all day: how cold he must have been when he left the Land Rover that night. Harry's day on the fells had really brought it home to him and he couldn't shake it off.

'Any luck?' Mr Drysdale asked when they were having supper.

The old man had asked every night since he'd joined the search. Harry shook his head and carried on eating.

'I suppose they'll go on until he's found? Won't they?' Margaret asked.

Harry looked up. The couple were watching him, waiting for his response.

'I guess they'll have to stop sometime.'

Harry broke the respectful silence by helping himself to another roast potato.

His host pushed back his chair and stood up.

'You've not finished,' said his wife. 'Are you all right?'

'Got to get on,' he replied, pulling on his coat as he stepped outside, closing the door behind him.

They finished their meal in silence. Margaret began tidying up and Harry helped clear the dishes from the table. Normally she would be chattering away about something trivial – a television programme or something on the radio – but she was unusually quiet as she loaded the dishwasher.

She straightened up and turned to face Harry. 'Tom hasn't been himself this week. I think he might be coming down with a cold. I hope he'll be all right for tomorrow. I wouldn't want to cancel dinner with my brother and his wife,' she said, drying her hands and untying her apron. 'Well, that's that. I'm going to sit down for five minutes.'

Harry had decided to travel to Harrogate that night. He planned to lie in bed all morning and wander into town for brunch. As much as he liked the countryside, there were things he missed about his flat close to the town centre. He packed his bag before finding Margaret in her sitting room.

'I'm off now,' he announced.

'Oh. I thought you'd be going in the morning. It's dark now.'

'It'll be fine. I need to get back. I'll be there in an hour and a half.'

'Did you call Mr Patterson?' she reminded him.

'Yes,' he lied, as he left the room.

The farmer was in the yard, working on his quad bike.

'Got problems?' Harry asked, trying to be friendly.

'Aye, always problems.' The old man stretched back up to his full height and surveyed the vehicle. 'Time to get a replacement I reckon but…'

He stood in silence, watching Harry put his bag in the boot of his car.

'You off then?'

'Yep.'

'Coming back?'

'Yes, if they need me.'

'I hope they find out what happened to the lad. It's not right to think of him lying out in the snow.'

Harry knew Tom Drysdale well enough by now to know he was not one to indulge in speculation. Under the poor illumination in the yard he could see lines drawn across the man's brow; he was looking at Harry intently.

'Tom, have you heard anything. Have there been any more rumours?'

The man paused, his mouth moving silently as if deciding how to word his reply. 'There may have been... rumours, I mean.'

'Saying what?' Harry had moved closer to hear what the man had to say.

'That this policeman – Jamie Reed – he must've been onto summat. That's why he... disappeared.' He watched Harry, waiting for his response.

'Who's saying this?'

'They're just rumours.' He turned to fiddle with the engine again.

Harry addressed the back of his head. 'And would these rumours say how they made Jamie "disappear"?'

'No. They just think he was onto summat, so now he'll be lying out in the cold.'

'Right.' Harry wondered what to do about what the old man was saying. He needed time to think. 'Right then, I'll be off now,' he said, heading for his car.

'You will tell them, won't you? 'Bout the rumours like? Someone needs to know.'

'OK, I'll let them know,' Harry promised. He was sure

that the farmer knew more than he was letting on but he could wait. He'd wait until Monday anyway.

But before he left the yard, Harry lowered the car window and called across to where the dark figure was leaning over his quad bike.

'By the way, if you know anything else about Jamie Reed – anything however trivial – you must let me know. Otherwise you could be done for perverting the course of justice at the very least.' He didn't wait for a response but drove out of the yard, grinning to himself.

When he reached the road he stopped briefly, making up his mind about where to go. He had planned to drive straight to Harrogate but if he went via Hawes, it wouldn't be much further and he would pass close to where Mills lived. He wanted the opportunity to see her face to face, tell her to mind her own business and keep out of his affairs. He'd say what a troublemaker she was and convince her that he was delayed in reporting the Land Rover because of a series of unfortunate accidents. He'd wanted to do so for a while now.

Chapter 12

Mills was aware of the sound of a vehicle pulling up outside the cottage but she was too comfortable, snuggled up on the sofa, to take any notice. After they'd finished the wine with the beans on toast, she'd found another bottle and now it stood on the floor beside them, almost empty. As she looked round at Daryl, who was asleep beside her, the doorbell rang and he was jolted awake, looking at her questioningly. She shrugged, climbed off the couch and padded to the door.

'Harry?'

He stood on the garden path, staring at her. 'Can I come in?'

'What d'you want?'

'Have you got company?' He pointed at the truck.

'What d'you want?' she repeated.

He peered past her into the cottage and Mills guessed he would be able to see her visitor. Daryl, she noted, was keeping quiet.

Mills moved onto the step pulling the front door closed behind her. The stone felt cold under her bare feet.

'What do you want, Harry?' she asked in a whisper.

He seemed rattled. 'I wanted to tell you that you got me

into trouble over the Land Rover. I got in touch with Kirkby Stephen as soon as I could but the car broke down and there was no signal. I called in as soon as I could.'

'Really.'

'Don't you believe me?'

'It doesn't matter what I believe, Harry.' She turned to go inside then she remembered what she'd wanted to ask him. 'By the way,' she said, 'what *was* it you found in the Land Rover?'

'What d'you mean? I didn't find anything.'

'You did. You put it in the boot of your car. I saw you.'

He looked genuinely puzzled. 'There wasn't anything.'

'I don't believe you… and if *you* don't tell them, *I* will.' She pushed the door open, marched inside and slammed it behind her.

Daryl was standing by the window with the curtain pulled aside.

'Should I go?' He looked concerned.

'No, don't be silly. Anyway, you've had too much to drink. You shouldn't drive.'

He raised an eyebrow. 'I'd better have that coffee now then'.

He didn't ask about Harry and Mills didn't offer any explanation. It was two in the morning when Daryl finally left and Mills dragged herself to bed. She tossed and turned, thinking about Daryl and Harry, wishing she'd not consumed so much wine – or so much caffeine. Eventually she fell into a fitful sleep full of dreams she couldn't remember.

Harry lifted his head slowly and pulled himself to a sitting position on the edge of his bed. As his eyes focussed on the radio-alarm he could make out that it was already afternoon. He was grateful that he was in his own flat; it meant he could stagger to the kitchen in his pyjamas and carry a mug of coffee back to bed.

There was a message from Graham on his mobile, asking him to call.

'OK, old man, give me time,' he muttered at the phone as he threw it down on the duvet cover.

He struggled with the packet of headache tablets, removing two from their foil wrapping. He swallowed them quickly and sank back on the pillows.

Last night had been a disaster. He was an idiot to think that Mills would be alone on a Saturday night and she was obviously in no mood to discuss things rationally. He had no idea what she was on about towards the end of their exchange. She'd definitely accused him of taking something from the Land Rover – which he hadn't. Goodness knows what else she'd been making up. No wonder they were on his case.

He went over the conversation between them, trying to remember exactly what was said. His recollection was hazy but she'd referred to him putting something in his car. He pictured what had happened when he searched the Land Rover, checking the interior, carefully closing the doors, making his way up the slope – which was slippery with snow – and climbing back into the car. No, she was right... before that he threw the torch into the boot. Of course, she thought he'd taken something from the crime scene. But he hadn't – it was just his torch.

He smiled and finished his coffee. Feeling better already he climbed out of bed, ignoring another call from Graham. He would ring him later, but first he wanted to go into town and find himself a big, fat burger. He switched off his mobile and went into the shower.

At three o'clock Harry packed his bag with enough clean shirts, socks and underwear for the week and washed up. With a sigh he looked round the flat before stepping out into the hallway and locking the front door. It would be dark by the time he reached Old Hall Farm; Margaret would start fussing round him and Tom would be as enigmatic as usual.

The roads were quiet and he made good time but dusk was falling when he drove up the track to the house. He was irritated to see his sergeant's car still parked outside, expecting that they would have left by now. The house was unusually quiet considering they had guests and the kitchen was empty, so Harry went through to his room, past the Drysdales' sitting room where he could hear low voices. He took a deep breath, put on a smile and opened the door.

It took him a second to take in the scene. Margaret was lying on the sofa, a handkerchief clutched to her face. His sergeant was seated on a low chair beside her, holding her free hand. In the armchair sat an elderly woman who Harry assumed was Mrs Crossland.

When he saw Harry, Sergeant Crossland jumped up, indicating to his wife to take over responsibility for Margaret. Harry was quickly ushered out into the hallway.

'Didn't you get my call, lad?'

'No. What's going on?'

'There's been an accident.'

'Accident?'

'Well, not really an accident… I mean…'

The man looked grey, shaken. He rubbed his forehead as if to extract the right words.

'Has something happened to Tom?' It was obvious that it was the farmer who'd been hurt.

'Yes, lad. It has.'

'Is he in hospital?'

'No… it's too late for that… I'm afraid…'

'He's *dead*? How? What happened?'

His sergeant was moving back towards the sitting room. 'I'll explain later, I'd better…'

'Wait! What do *I* do? Should I go?'

'Stay put for now, Harry. We'll sort something out. I'll speak to you later.'

Without a signal, Harry couldn't check the message he'd been left. He wandered into the kitchen and filled the kettle, thinking that tea was always a good idea in these circumstances. While he waited for the water to boil, he wondered what sort of accident could have occurred to result in death. He wandered into the yard, thinking he might get an indication, but everything was in order. Back in the kitchen he used three spoons of tea in the old brown pot, unsure how much he should add but deciding to err on the side of too strong rather than too weak. It was only as he looked around trying to find cups and saucers that he noticed that the cupboard where Tom kept his guns was open. Inside there were a few cardboard boxes and a shotgun. One gun was missing but that didn't mean anything, did it? He shuddered involuntarily. He really didn't want it to be that.

The rest of the evening went quickly. When he took in the tea, they told him that Margaret would go home with them. Mrs Crossland took her off to the bedroom to pack a few things for her stay. Harry took the opportunity to ask his sergeant about "the accident".

'There's no point in beating about the bush,' he said, sighing loudly. 'My brother-in-law shot himself.'

'Today?'

'Aye, just before we arrived – in the barn. It was almost as if he planned it that way... so we'd be here for Margaret.'

Harry didn't know what to say but the silence was awkward. 'I'm very sorry.' It was all he could think of.

'I know, I know. Look, would you mind staying here overnight? It'll save me having to think about security and so on.'

'What about the farm?'

'I'll sort out the livestock in the morning. The neighbouring farmers are good friends, they'll help out.'

Harry couldn't stop himself from asking. 'Why did he do it?'

'We may never know that lad. Times are hard and he was feeling the pinch, I know that. He didn't have to do that though... he should've spoken to me. I could've helped.' He stared into the distance for a few seconds before pulling himself to his full height. 'You hold the fort, sonny. I'll see you in the morning.'

The house was strangely silent as Harry sat in the kitchen listening to the car disappearing down the track. Had his suspicions proved correct? Was Tom Drysdale involved in Jamie Reed's disappearance? He wished he'd pressed the man harder when they'd last spoken. On the other hand, had he pushed him too far? He washed the cups and saucers, drying them carefully and placing them on the dresser in neat rows. He sat in the cold guest lounge trying to concentrate on the television but it wasn't long before he began to wonder about the dogs. Tom always fed them after supper but he realised now that there had been no barking when he arrived at the farm. He went out and peered into the barn but their pen was empty so he assumed they'd gone with Margaret; at least that was something he wouldn't have to cope with.

He knew Tom always shut the gate at night using a padlock to stop thieves interfering with his machinery. There were a few stars visible between the clouds and the moon was casting a weak light across the yard. Harry made his way over but couldn't see well enough to fix the padlock to the chain. Cursing, he fetched his car keys to open the boot where he kept his torch. He found it easily enough but had difficulty turning it on. When he finally succeeded the beam was poor and hardly helped as he struggled with the padlock. In the end he abandoned the gate and returned indoors, relieved to lock the back door and retreat to his bedroom. He placed the torch on top of the chest of drawers to remind him to change the batteries.

He spent a restless night. He was hungry but didn't want to eat. The empty house seemed noisier than usual and he woke at every creak and bump. At one stage he thought he heard a vehicle but in the end he decided it was all in his imagination. By six o'clock he was wide awake, despite it being pitch black outside. He entered the kitchen, determined to cook breakfast, just as Margaret would have done for him.

He found bacon in the refrigerator but when he put it into the frying pan there was no sizzling: the hot plate was cold and a quick look inside the solid fuel stove confirmed that the fire had gone out. There was nothing to do but put two slices of bread in the toaster and wait. He covered the toast in thick layers of butter and marmalade, and sat with the plate in front of him, thinking how strange it was to be there alone. He left the table and wandered into the yard, and with no particular plan in mind, he crossed to the barn. He was curious about where Tom had chosen to take his life. He admitted to himself that it was morbid curiosity.

At first the barn looked as it always did, cluttered but in an organised way. The pen where the dogs slept had appeared empty last night but now he could see it was not. It looked like a heap of rags but as he moved closer he could see the outline of shapes that were the farm dogs, lying lifeless together where they had been left. Closer inspection confirmed they had been shot. Harry could understand that Tom wouldn't have wanted to leave them without a master but it seemed a cruel gesture. He went back to the kitchen, and threw the remains of his breakfast in the bin. He attempted to light the stove but gave up when he couldn't find any matches. He washed in cold water and dressed quickly. With nothing else to pass the time, he left for work an hour earlier than usual, locking up carefully behind him.

No-one had arrived yet so, alone in the office, Harry checked the messages on his mobile. The one from Sergeant Crossland simply said there'd been an accident and to come straight from Harrogate on Monday morning. The message from Graham was longer.

'Hello… right…yes… Harry, I just wanted to let you know that Sergeant Featherstone is on board… I mean it's on, lad. Oh, and so you're working with me from now on, until future orders. That's good, eh?'

Harry listened to it again and then called him back.

'Hi Graham. I got your message.'

'Right lad, I'll get down there as soon as I hear from Sergeant Featherstone. I've had an e-mail from him and he's up for it!'

'He?'

'What, lad?'

'You said *he*. She's not a *he*. Her name is Nina.'

There was silence at the other end. 'Graham?'

'No, it can't be... No, I can't... She can't...'

'Why not? What's wrong?'

'We can't put a woman in there. It might be dangerous. No, lad, definitely not.'

Harry considered for a minute. 'It might be less dangerous if a woman's involved,' he suggested.

But Graham was not to be convinced. After a few more protestations from Harry, he rang off, saying he would let Sergeant Featherstone know that he wouldn't be asking for her help. Harry was back on the search for Jamie Reed's body – no-one was pretending that they would find him alive now.

By ten o'clock the search team was assembled but there was no sign of Sergeant Crossland. Disappointed, Harry left in the bus with the other constables for another day out on the fells.

Nina was working her way through a pile of ironing, thinking that she would rather be back at work, even if it meant driving to Newby Wiske on a cold, dark Monday morning. Breakfast was over and the boys were asleep. She was pleased to be interrupted by a phone call and excited to hear that it was Graham Patterson calling her.

'I'm glad you rang,' she began, 'I wasn't sure when you

wanted me to start the operation?'

'Ah… well… the fact is…'

In the general scheme of things, Nina considered herself a patient person. She'd overcome any inhibitions she'd had about posing as an illegal meat trader – even a *Muslim* restaurant owner – but he was suggesting that as a *woman* she was not suitable for the job! That was intolerable. He stuttered and apologised; he gave all kinds of ridiculous reasons why it wouldn't be appropriate. She stopped him mid-sentence.

'Are you saying that you won't work with me under any circumstances?' she asked calmly.

'I don't believe it would be safe for a woman to take part,' the man replied apologetically.

'Your last word?'

There was a pause. His reply was barely audible, 'Yes.'

'This is not the end of it, *PC* Patterson.'

She slammed the phone down and paced the room. She was not proud of the way she'd emphasised the PC. She smiled as she realised that what was irritating her most was the fact he was far from "Politically Correct". Her immediate reaction was to call Hazel for advice.

'He said *what?*' her friend asked, after Nina had described the call. 'I don't believe it!'

'What should I do?'

'I'll talk to the Guv'nor. He'll soon put the dinosaur right. I'll call you straight back.'

Before Hazel rang, Nina had changed one of the boys, given the other a cuddle and gone back to the ironing while she chatted to her sons. But when the call came it was not what she was expecting.

'Not good news, I'm afraid. The boss agrees with

Patterson, it seems. He says it's a dangerous operation with potentially violent criminals. He emphasised your new responsibilities and wasn't comfortable...'

'You are kidding!'

'I know but...'

'Hazel, this is the first chance I've had to do something like this. I've got to do it!'

'Well girl, you'll have to convince the boss.'

'OK, I'm coming in.'

'What about the twins?'

'I'll bring them with me if necessary!'

There was a snort at the other end.

'Hazel – before you go – have you got Harry Clark's number?'

The snow had cleared from the roads and was beginning to disappear from the slopes, leaving the rough pasture in a bog. As the search party disembarked and set off down the road there was discussion about how much longer they would continue this fruitless exercise. Some of the lads were becoming disenchanted with the relentless operation which showed little hope of success. There was a cold easterly wind and Harry detected drizzle in the air. Before they had reached the gate onto open ground it had turned to heavy rain.

'With a bit of luck they'll stand us down,' called a lad from Carlisle, as they fanned out and began trudging up the hillside. 'It's a pigging waste of time if you ask me.'

'No-one's asking you, mate,' Harry muttered under his breath. But he tacitly agreed with his sentiments.

They continued with the rain beating on their faces. Harry could feel cold water running down his neck, a wet patch forming on his back. But he worked on determined that he would be as diligent as possible in the search for his colleague. That was how he thought of Jamie Reed now, a fellow officer and colleague. It was his duty to do everything possible to find him, alive or dead. It was just that he couldn't see why the body would be out on open moorland unless he'd wandered there by himself. Harry didn't believe it was that simple. The Land Rover had been deliberately hidden – it was obvious to him.

He was sure that Tom Drysdale had known something about Jamie's disappearance and it was why he'd killed himself. Was it possible he was responsible? What had Tom said to him on Saturday night? *He must've been onto summat. That's why he disappeared*

Harry had hoped that Tom Drysdale was going to give him some information when he got back to the farm. He wished he'd questioned him on the Saturday night but he'd tried to be clever, thinking that if he waited, Tom would be more forthcoming. How wrong he'd been. Whatever Sergeant Crossland implied about financial difficulties, Harry was convinced that money was not the cause of the farmer's suicide. The man had been fretting over the missing police officer all the time Harry had been at the farm and he'd been about to confess when he took his own life.

When the search party returned to the bus for lunch, they were told they would be returning to base immediately. The weather was closing in and they would not be required for the rest of the day. As soon as the team were aboard, they were on their way to Kirkby Stephen and Harry decided he would speak to his sergeant about Tom.

Crossland was in the office waiting for him. 'Sergeant

Featherstone wants a word,' he said sternly. 'His number's on your desk.' Without stopping to correct him, Harry dialled the number. The conversation began with Nina Featherstone explaining that she was helping with the sheep rustling case. Harry thought she was no longer involved but he assumed things had changed yet again. She asked him what had happened so far and even suggested "popping over to chat about it and update her with the details" – until he suggested she spoke to Graham.

'Look, Harry – may I call you Harry? – I just want to get up to speed on the case. Is that so difficult for you? I don't want to make life harder for you than it is right now, so…'

'OK.'

He gave her a quick description of what he'd done with Graham. 'And the last thing that happened was when we visited this farmer who threatened Graham. I wasn't there all the time but he seemed pretty upset.'

'So the idea was to see him about getting suspect meat by pretending to supply a restaurant?'

'Yes. I guess he needed someone who wasn't known to the guy. He's seen Graham and me.'

'That's where I come in. Can you find this farm again?'

Harry thought about it. 'Possibly. Why?'

'Well, if we're going to visit him, we'll need to know where to go.'

'Is that all right? I mean… Graham…'

'I'll speak to him; you don't need to bother Graham. D'you understand? I don't want *you* to do it – *I* will.'

'OK, Sergeant Featherstone. I understand.'

Harry put the phone down, puzzled by their conversation. But if it meant they were back on the case he wasn't going to argue.

Sergeant Crossland was hunched over his desk when Harry approached him.

'I just wanted to know whether I should pick up my things, you know... from the farm?'

He looked up at Harry. His demeanour was unnaturally dour. 'Nay lad, you stay put.'

'But...'

'No buts. It's an order. My sister will be with us for a while I reckon; she's in a right state. If you can keep the place going it'll give her peace of mind.'

'What about the farm?'

'That's all sorted. I've a cousin who'll take the livestock. There's nowt else to worry about.' He paused for a while. 'I've arranged for the dogs to be removed.'

'You know he...'

'Yes. I haven't told Margaret yet. It'll break her heart.'

'Why did he... you know... the dogs?'

'Who knows, lad.' He sighed and leaned back in his chair. 'Who knows what drove him to any of it.'

'I suppose *he* shot them, the dogs I mean?'

'Aye, it looks like it.' He looked up sharply. 'What d'you mean? What are you saying?'

'Nothing, Sarge. I was just thinking that... no, nothing.'

It occurred to him that he'd not seen the dogs when he left the farm on Saturday. It was around the time Tom usually fed them and yet they weren't about. He'd never been outside the house with Tom and not seen the dogs in the yard. Was it possible that the dogs were dead the day before Tom killed himself?

Chapter 13

The farmhouse was in darkness when Harry arrived back after work. He'd bought some groceries in town before setting off, including matches so he could get the Rayburn going again. The central heating ran off the stove so the sooner he got the fire lit the better. He locked the back door behind him and unpacked the shopping, reluctantly. The house was creepy as well as cold and he wished he'd arranged to move elsewhere. He could have found somewhere nearer Shelley for a start, he thought.

It took three attempts before the stove was burning sufficiently well that he dared leave it unattended for a while. He went into his bedroom, which was at the west end of the farmhouse and was always colder than the rest of the building. Tonight it was icy and he wondered if there was a heater he could use to warm it until the central heating kicked in. He changed into his jeans and opened the chest of drawers to find his thickest sweater. As he pulled it out a piece of paper fluttered to the floor. He finished dressing before picking it up to put it in the bin. Curious he unfolded it and read the scrawl. It was written in pencil, half the letters were joined-up, the rest in capitals and to his surprise it was addressed to him.

I don't want my Margaret to think of me as a bad person so I'm letting you know. When I saw that lad in the Land Rover I didn't think he would come to any harm. I hope they find him so he can have a proper burial. Keep it to yourself please.

It was signed Tom Drysdale, followed by a series of numbers. It seemed odd to put his mobile number but who knew what state of mind he was in when he wrote it. Reluctantly he went to the phone to contact Sergeant Crossland but stopped in the hall, reading and re-reading the note. Did he really expect Harry to keep it quiet from the investigation? Was it important? It told him nothing.

It made sense, thought Harry, as he made himself a cup of tea. The trailer parked down on the road that night must have belonged to Tom. Had he used it to steal Maynard's sheep? And had Jamie Reed found out? Harry took his mug to the kitchen table and sat down with the note in front of him. In his opinion, Tom was responsible directly or indirectly for Jamie's disappearance and, presumably, his demise. But why hadn't Tom realised until the weekend that his actions had caused the young man's death – if that *was* what had driven him to suicide? Harry decided it would make no difference if he waited until the next day before showing the note to his sergeant.

It was six thirty and he was supposed to call Shelley about going round that evening. Although he didn't feel very sociable, neither did he want to stay in the farmhouse alone. When she answered, he explained what had happened to Tom and she immediately invited him over for supper.

'Mum's made this enormous steak and kidney pie.'

An evening of normality among Shelley's large family

was exactly what he'd hoped for. He placed the note in his underwear drawer before making sure the stove was stocked up with fuel, leaving the kitchen light on when he locked up. Outside it was clear and cold, with a layer of frost forming on the car already. He scraped the windscreen and switched on the engine. But before he set off, he went round to the boot, grabbed the torch and went into the barn. He swung the beam into the corner where the dogs had been but it was empty now. Just a few cartridge cases glinted on the floor. He wanted to look at the trailer that had been at the centre of Tom's problems. It was kept inside "in case of thieves", although Harry now knew that he might have other reasons to keep it out of sight. It was too dark to examine it now but in the morning he'd get a proper look. He went back to the car, threw the torch on the passenger seat and set off towards Sedburgh, his mind now on the steak and kidney pie that was waiting for him over at Shelley's.

The situation had been worrying Nina all morning, although she didn't confide in her husband when he rang her at lunchtime. She knew it was unfair to be so moody but she'd been really upset by the rejection of her services because she was a woman. She knew Nige would just laugh it off. She knew exactly what he'd say. He'd point out that she'd been insulted they'd asked her to imitate a halal restaurateur anyway, so why was she upset that they no longer required her? Consequently she kept quiet while she decided what to do.

So, when she'd called Harry that afternoon, she simply wanted to tell him that although she wasn't going to be directly involved, she'd help out where she could. But because he wasn't there, and she'd had time to think about it, when he rang back she decided on the spur of the moment to pretend it was still on. To be honest she'd shocked herself – the way she'd spoken to him – but he was a rookie, a lying one at that, and she was going to show them at HQ that they couldn't mess her about.

Now she was getting cold feet. What if Graham Patterson found out? What if…? And then it suddenly dawned on her that she wasn't officially back at work and so they couldn't tell her what to do, could they? If she wanted to help Harry, it wasn't any of their business. One small problem – she hadn't explained that to Harry.

There was no way she was going to tell Nige that it was unofficial but he was going to have to take some time off to look after the kids while she worked with Harry, and that would mean asking Mills to cover for Nige. So when her husband was dozing in front of the television, and there wasn't a sound from upstairs, she crept into the kitchen to make the call. Mills answered almost immediately and expressed pleasure at hearing from her friend.

'You might not be so pleased when you find out why I'm ringing.'

'Go on then.'

'You know when you were here before, Nige asked if you would start covering for him on odd days before April?'

'Yes.'

'Well, I've got some work to do and I wondered if you could start sooner rather than later?'

'I don't see why not. Actually it would be a relief to cut down my days at the laboratory. Are you going back to work already?'

'No, well yes… not exactly.' Nina made sure the kitchen door was shut properly. 'Don't ask, you know I'm a terrible liar.'

'So what's up?'

'It's rather unofficial but don't say anything to Nige, he'll only worry.'

'Sounds intriguing.'

'I can't say any more. And not a word to Nige.'

'Really?'

'Yes. Promise.'

'I promise.'

'Oh – and can you give me Harry's mobile number?'

'Harry? Why d'you need his mobile? Is he still in trouble? *I* was going to ring *you* about him.'

'Oh?'

Nina moved back into the warmth of the sitting room to find her mobile.

'He came round late on Saturday night accusing me of getting him into trouble and it wasn't even as if I'd told Hazel every little detail.'

A low whimpering had begun upstairs but Nige continued to doze. Nina kicked his foot and pointed to the ceiling.

'One's awake – can you go?'

She waited until Nige had stumbled to the door.

'Righto, go ahead,' she told Mills, as soon as he'd gone.

'Oh, it's nothing.'

'No it wasn't. Tell me what you didn't tell Hazel.'

'I'm not sure. I thought I saw him… it looked like… I thought he'd taken something from the Land Rover when we found it.'

'What sort of thing?'

'I don't know. He put something in the boot of his car. It can't have been big because he was carrying it in one hand.'

'Are you sure?'

'That's the trouble; he seemed so surprised when I challenged him with it that I've begun to wonder myself. So please don't say anything.'

'I won't, Mills. Now please give me that number.'

Nina transferred it carefully to her phone, which she replaced quickly in her bag as she heard Nige coming down the stairs. In his arms was Tomos, red-faced and bleary-eyed.

'I'll have to go,' she told Mills. 'But thanks.'

'No problem,' her friend replied. 'Tell me when you want me – I'll just need a few days warning.'

Nina was surprised how accommodating her husband was about her "having a few days to carry out some important investigative work for Hazel". While she fed her son, Nige checked his commitments and gave her a series of dates when Mills could take over his lectures.

'So what's it all about?' he asked, sitting down beside her. 'It sounds rather exciting. What will you have to do?'

'It's not that interesting really.' She wiped her baby's mouth and handed him over to Nige. 'There you are, go to Daddy. Can you hold him for a bit before he goes down – I don't want him getting wind again.' She jumped up. 'Coffee?'

Having neatly changed the subject, she went to the kitchen and put the kettle on. There was little sound from the other room and when she returned with two mugs, Nige was fast asleep with Tomos lying across his chest.

*

Harry had set the alarm for six but must have dropped off again because it was twenty-past seven when he checked at the clock. He'd planned to look at the trailer in the morning but it was hardly daylight and he would have to leave if he was to catch the search team bus. Without time to eat, he drank from the milk carton and grabbed a half empty packet of biscuits that would have to be his breakfast.

On the journey to Kirkby Stephen he decided to come clean with Sergeant Crossland. He would tell him about the letter from Tom Drysdale. Honesty was the best approach, as his mother always said, and so far withholding the truth had been a disaster. No more lies. And he would tell him about high and mighty Nina Featherstone; she seemed to be side-lining Graham and that was out of order.

The search team bus was already outside the station but he went in to have a quick word with the boss. As he put his head round the office door, his mobile rang and the name Featherstone came up.

'Good morning,' he began, trying to sound cheerful as he moved into the hallway for better reception.

'Harry? I need to discuss our operation.' She sounded very business-like and although he was wary of her, he wondered now if it might be quite good for his career to work with her.

'OK. So has Graham, I mean PC Patterson…'

'Listen Harry, as your senior officer I am telling you that we are going ahead. You don't need to speak to Graham. I'm coming over on Friday morning. It will be best if we meet in Sedbergh – there's a car park by the Information Centre. There's no need to broadcast it, just tell Sergeant Crossland that you're on regional business.'

'I really don't think…'

'No, you're right, Harry, you really don't need to think – I can do that for both of us. Just be there, Friday at ten.'

'But…'

'Harry, listen. You are already in serious trouble over not reporting the missing vehicle and now I understand you've taken something away from the scene, yes?'

'Well…'

'So it's best if you just do as I ask and keep your head down, if you don't want it going any further.'

He was left holding the mobile to his ear but she'd gone. It was a shock to hear Sergeant Featherstone repeating the accusation that he'd interfered with evidence. Instead of going back to the office to speak with Sergeant Crossland, he went straight outside to board the bus. It was full of young constables dressed up against whatever the elements were going to throw at them that day. He leaned back in his seat by a window and listened to the banter, trying to forget the mess he was in because of his enthusiasm to investigate Jamie Reed's disappearance – even a busload of bobbies didn't seem capable of that.

It was another day of slow progress across boggy moorland and struggling against ferociously strong winds. There was some relief when Harry joined a group covering woodland where it was sheltered from the worst of the weather. But throughout the day as they worked across the fields and over streams, the atmosphere was one of dejected resignation. Few believed there was much hope of finding Jamie Reed's body.

Back in Kirkby Stephen at the end of the day, wet and cold, Harry stayed long enough to ask his sergeant how Margaret Drysdale was. The old man looked up from his desk with an exhausted expression.

'Not too bad, lad. Not too bad – considering.'

Harry repeated how sorry he was about it all but escaped as soon as he decently could and drove back to the farm, anxious to have a hot shower. The house looked almost welcoming with the lights still blazing where he'd left them on that morning. But he'd forgotten to top up the stove and without fuel the shower was tepid. Dressing quickly he put on his jacket and grabbed his torch off the chest as he passed, shoving it in his pocket as he made for the back door.

Outside, the kitchen lights provided enough illumination to get him across the yard. The bitter wind made it difficult to open the bulky barn door but eventually he was able to get inside out of the icy blast. It was as dark as it had been the previous night but he'd have no opportunity to return in daylight while he was on duty. The torch beam was pathetic and within a minute had gone completely and he was left in darkness. Cursing as he realised he'd forgotten to buy new batteries, he fumbled his way to the door and back to the kitchen, thinking he might be able to find a supply in one of the drawers. Frustration mounted as he exhausted all possible places they might be hidden.

Finally, abandoning his search, he made a mug of tea and sank into Tom's old chair at the head of the table. The torch had been fine last night, he was thinking, except... he hadn't used *that* torch, had he? It had been in the bedroom since Sunday when he'd used it to look in the barn and missed seeing the dead dogs. The picture made him grimace involuntarily. He thought back to last night, when he'd gone into the barn once more and the dogs had been removed. The torch had been fine then – it had picked up the cartridge cases – but he'd taken *that* torch from the boot of his car and left it back on the passenger seat. He fought his way across the yard against the strong wind and peered in. There was the torch, on the seat where he'd left it.

Back in the kitchen, he placed the two torches side by side on the table. He recognised the one his dad had given him for his birthday when he was a kid – he'd had it for years. That was the one with the dead batteries. The one beside it was a different make, although similar in appearance. He switched it on and off; it had a strong beam. He had no idea whose it was or how he came to have it but, as he thought back to when he last used a torch, he dropped it quickly onto the table. He had a sickening feeling that he now understood why Mills had accused him of taking something from Jamie Reed's Land Rover. The accusation was true – he'd accidentally taken a torch from the crime scene – and Sergeant Featherstone knew.

Chapter 14

Harry dreamt he was out on Wild Boar Fell in deep snow searching for Jamie Reed. He was with Graham Patterson and they were both in uniform. When they stumbled on the body it was fully clothed but showed signs of having been fed on by animals. That was bad enough but when the corpse began to move and cried out, Harry had turned to run but his legs were feeling heavy... He woke in the dark, sweating and disoriented, his head thumping.

Fumbling for the light, he struggled to sit up, licking his dry lips as he peered at the clock. It was four-thirty. He was anxious to get away from the claustrophobia of his bed with its memory of the figure calling out for help as it lay in the snow. He jumped up, grabbed his jacket and wandered down the passageway in his bare feet. But he didn't need a coat – the Rayburn was pumping out the heat. The kettle boiled quickly and Harry relaxed as he sipped tea, beside the warm stove.

He looked round the old-fashioned kitchen, thinking about the times he'd spent in there with the Drysdales. Tom's taciturn nature had obviously been due to his guilt over Jamie Reed. He'd been worried about what Harry might uncover. Several times he'd asked about the search for Jamie and now Harry knew the man's interest had been more than passing curiosity. He thought he understood why Tom was concerned and how it had led to his suicide, although it was a mystery why Tom would have shot his dogs. Margaret had loved them and they were devoted to him.

He thought of the times Tom would be out in the yard in all weathers feeding them at night and of the evening when he'd joined the farmer. It was when he'd become quite heated about the sheep rustlers from Lancashire. Harry had not seen him so animated before, or since. Presumably he'd been trying to divert police attention away from his trailer parked down on the road by suggesting the thieves came from outside the county. It was possible Tom was responsible for stealing sheep single-handed but unlikely because he'd need a contact to slaughter and butcher the livestock. Harry thought back to when he'd accompanied Graham to visit The Fox. The old man had mischievously pointed them in the direction of an old hall, which at the time had meant nothing. But now it began to make sense; Tom Drysdale – of Old Hall Farm – was the link.

If Tom was the thief, and he'd met Jamie Reed that night, the torch Harry had found in the Land Rover might prove it. He mulled over the possibilities as he drove to work. In the past he would have rung Mills to ask her to examine the torch for forensic evidence. She might not have helped but at least he would have been able to ask. Now he was unsure of her response and was concerned she would tell bossy Sergeant Featherstone and her stroppy mate Hazel Fuller. In the end he decided to keep quiet until he was better able to assess the situation. He really didn't know whether he was still in trouble with his old bosses at Newby Wiske or not.

His sergeant was waiting for him, looking more old and weary than before.

'Just wanted to let you know – Tom's funeral is on the first of March. It's a Thursday. I've cleared it so you can have the time off.'

Harry thanked him, wanting to sound suitably grateful. He had hoped he wouldn't be invited – it would be the first funeral he'd ever attended and he was unsure of what the procedure was.

'I've got to help Margaret with the solicitor and then I'm taking her to the bank,' his boss continued. 'I'll need you to hold the fort here today, in case there are any calls.'

It was an order and Harry sensed there could be no argument. Although he was keen to help find Jamie, the dream had left him with a dread of actually discovering the body himself. He'd dealt with many unpleasant corpses of animals but he'd never seen a dead or even a badly injured person.

Harry took a deep breath. 'Before you go, can I show you this note I got from your brother-in-law?'

His sergeant looked puzzled as he took the piece of paper in his chubby hand. Opening it clumsily, he read and re-read it.

'Where did you get this?' he asked sharply.

'I found it in my chest of drawers at the farm.'

'Do you know what it means?'

'I thought it might suggest... I mean, it could imply...'

Crossland held up a hand while he read the note again.

'It's difficult to know what he meant. He was very depressed. Money matters, you know. He met Jamie when he went to ask them about the road accident. I expect he felt sorry for him when he heard that he'd gone missing.'

He folded the note carefully and put it in his pocket. 'As he says, let's not worry Margaret with this.'

'But I thought… that it might be…'

'Important? No, lad. The man's dead – he can't help us now, can he? She's suffering enough. Let it be, for her sake.'

Sergeant Crossland had left him with nothing to do, so he went on the internet and tried to work out where Graham had taken him to see the meat vendor. It was south of Sedbergh; they'd driven for about half an hour. Say that was fifteen to twenty miles, they hadn't turned off to Ingleton and they hadn't reached the motorway, which meant the farm must have been off the A683. He sat with his head in his hands trying to visualise the route. Nothing. If only he could remember the name of the farm. He was a hopeless police officer unfit to wear the uniform, just as they'd said.

There were just a few routine calls that morning so Harry had plenty of time to explore the area south of Kirkby Lonsdale using the satellite map. As he zoomed in, he could make out the smaller "B" roads and lanes leading off to farmland scattered to right and left. He remembered going over a river, which meant that they must have turned west. The road crossed open farmland and then there was another bridge; it could have been the railway line – he could just make it out. After that, he was unsure, but at least he would know roughly the area to make for with Sergeant Featherstone.

When he'd arranged to meet her on Friday, he'd not thought about whether it would be all right with his boss.

He'd not mentioned anything to Sergeant Crossland yet because he wasn't sure what to say. There was something a little clandestine about the way the arrangement had been made. Clearly Graham wasn't involved; possibly he knew nothing of it and certainly he wouldn't approve. Harry had his suspicions that she wasn't being honest with him and planned to ask her straight out on Friday whether she had authorisation from the top for what they were doing. He didn't want to get into any more trouble.

Mills wanted to arrive at the laboratory early. Work had been going very slowly and she was determined to catch up with staff, to ensure they understood the urgency of their tasks. Brenda seemed distracted these days and refused to hear any suggestions that they were having problems carrying out their routine assignments. Mills assumed she was busy going ahead with plans to increase their capabilities into other areas of forensics.

The set of samples they'd received from three similar crimes carried out thirty years ago had been the most challenging and they'd been getting nowhere with them. Mills was determined to get to the bottom of the problem and headed straight for Glyn's office.

'Before you ask – no I haven't got any further with the batteries. I've tried the superglue on one but it didn't show anything.'

'Oh, you've done it.'

'Don't sound so disappointed!'

'Sorry, I wanted to see how it's done.'

'I know, but you were enjoying yourself down in London.'

She ignored him; she knew his views on her representing

the laboratory at the conference.

'So no results from the screwdriver at all?'

'None .' He took off his glasses and leaned back in his chair. 'Donna's finished the hair sample and I've told her to get on with the handkerchief. I've passed the screwdriver over to her as well.'

'Did you use superglue on both batteries?'

'If I do that, Donna won't get any DNA.' Perching the spectacles back on the end of his nose, he sat upright again and turned to look at the computer screen. 'Was that all Dr Sanderson?'

It was spoken with a degree of humour but Mills knew he was irritated by her presence. 'Fine. I'll go and see Donna.'

'She's off sick.' He didn't look up but tapped on the keyboard as he spoke.

'Are there any results yet?'

'Don't know – they'll be on the server if there are.'

Mills went back to her office, depressed that her working relationship with Glyn was getting worse. It took her some time to find the relevant folder but, when she opened the files, she could see that Donna's work was far from complete and nothing would happen now until she was back at work.

She deliberately timed her coffee break so she could catch up with Brenda, knowing that her boss would walk out of her office at exactly eleven o'clock. So with time to spare, Mills went down to the kitchen and put the kettle on. A few minutes later the door burst open.

'Mills! Lovely to see you. How did the conference go? Did you find lots of new customers for us?' Brenda's ample figure filled the tiny kitchen.

'I got rid of a few brochures.' There had been little interest in their stand but Mills wanted to sound upbeat.

'Let's hope they don't all rush at once then.' She laughed. 'We seem to be a bit short on the ground at the moment. Donna's got 'flu.'

'I wanted to ask you about that. I've been waiting ages for the DNA on the cold case samples.'

'Oh I told her to leave it for now,' said Brenda airily as she unscrewed the lid of the coffee jar and dropped two heaped spoons of granules into her mug.

Mills couldn't believe what she was hearing. 'Leave it? Why.'

'She wasn't feeling well and it's more important to get on with the current cases.'

'But they still want the handkerchief tested?'

'Oh yes. Sometime.' She put the lid back on the jar and replaced it in the cupboard slowly. When she turned back she had that smile on, the one she wore when she'd had one of her "clever ideas".

'I've been thinking,' she said, 'about what we should be concentrating on. That's partly why I sent you down to London – to get up to speed on the current state of play. Bring your mug, we'll go and talk about it now, while it's fresh in your mind.'

Mills knew she would have to report back on the conference and had made notes but they were on her tablet PC and she had expected some notice to gather her thoughts. Despite protests she found herself in Brenda's office at an impromptu debriefing.

'So what should we be doing to keep ahead of the competition, Mills?'

'There was an interesting talk on using isotopes to

identify what part of the world a body originated from.'

Brenda viewed her over her reading glasses. 'That sounds like forensic archaeology.'

'And some clever devices for buried bodies.'

'Forget the bodies.'

'Speech patterns?'

Brenda shook her head.

'Blood spatter patterns?'

'These are not things we can offer here, Mills. We need to move the lab into the twenty-first century, we need something modern, up-to-date, like smart phones and tweeting.'

'Digital forensics?'

'Which is... ?'

'Mobile phones, computers, that sort of thing,' Mills offered.

'Now that's more like it! That sounds cutting edge. Who do you know that does that, eh?' Brenda sounded triumphant.

'Well, actually there was someone at the conference, who knew all about it.' She felt herself redden and saw Brenda smirking.

'Oh yes? Good looking, was he?'

'No, it's just that we were chatting. I've got his card somewhere.'

'Well find it, girl! We'll see if he'll help us get going with it.'

'I think it's quite sophisticated. I'm not sure we could set it up ourselves.'

'Of course not, silly girl. We'll get him to come and work for us – where is he based?'

Mills wasn't sure. The business card Alex had given her

would have the address on and she knew exactly where to find that – carefully placed in her handbag, which was hanging on her chair.

Brenda picked up her mug and was on her way to the door before she could reply.

'Find him and tell him to come for a chat. Next week would be good.'

The door slammed and Mills sighed. It was good to work for someone who was go-ahead but Brenda had a way of delegating – no, dumping – the effort onto someone else, leaving her free to move on to her next bright idea.

She carried her coffee back to the office and found Alex's card. His full name was printed in bright blue across the middle: Dr Alex White. His company address was in tiny print below. She punched the number into her phone without considering what she would say and was about to put down the receiver again, to gather her thoughts when he answered.

'Alex White.'

'Alex… it's me… Mills, Mills Sanderson. We met at…'

'Mills! How nice to hear from you. I was thinking… that is, I was going to…' he sounded uncomfortable.

She interrupted quickly. 'I'm ringing you about work. Dr Yardley asked me to contact you.'

'Oh, right.' There was definitely disappointment in his voice. 'How can I help?'

She kept it simple. Her boss was interested in digital forensics and wanted advice on how to get it set up. There was no way she was going to tell him that Brenda wanted to give him a job. It was far too embarrassing.

'I could come Wednesday,' he offered when she suggested coming over the following week. 'I can be there by ten o'clock – it can't take long from Manchester.'

'That should be fine but I'll confirm it when I've spoken to Brenda.'

'Great. It will be good to catch up – I really have been meaning to call you but it's been mad here... and I wasn't sure... you know...'

'It will be great to see you again.' Mills chose her words carefully. 'Not just because of work.'

'Sure. I guess I should go now but look forward to Wednesday. Maybe we could have a drink or something to eat?'

'That would be nice.'

When Mills put the phone down she couldn't stop herself smiling. Well it was more of a grin really.

'Yes!' she said aloud, but softly in case anyone was within earshot.

As soon as his sergeant said he could leave, Harry raced back to the farm, determined to make a thorough search of the trailer. He'd been thinking about it all afternoon and was sure there must be electrics in the barn. It was already dark as he turned through the gate and parked in the pool of light shed by the kitchen window. The key refused to turn in the back door and he struggled for a while until he realised it was unlocked. Cursing himself for failing to secure the farmhouse, he went inside and put the kettle on. When he went through to the hall he was aware that something was wrong but couldn't make it out at first. The door to Tom and Margaret's bedroom was open – perhaps she'd come for some of her things. He peered in and was surprised to see it was not the neat and tidy place he expected it to be. Cupboards and drawers were open, clothes strewn on the bed and on the floor. If her brother had been sent down to collect Margaret's things, Harry thought, he could have been a little more careful.

When he approached his own bedroom, he was surprised to see that door wide open as well. A look inside confirmed his fears; someone had ransacked the room and left it in the same state. His clothes had been pulled out of the chest of drawers and left in a pile on the floor. Books were lying open and damaged where they'd been thrown. This was no professional break-in, someone had created the mess by throwing things across the room.

He began folding his shirts and jeans, placing them back in the drawers. The spine on the hardback copy of "Moby Dick" he'd found in the sitting room cracked as he folded it and his own paperbacks were worse for wear. He picked up three separate pieces of the vase that had perched on the table by the window and put them in the wastepaper basket.

He supposed he should report the break-in and, after he'd tidied his room as best he could, he went to use the phone in the hall. Harry tried repeatedly to get a dialling tone but the phone was dead. Initially he was fooled by the red flashing light on the answer machine until he realised that the landline had been cleanly severed close to the phone. Frustrated and disturbed he examined the rest of the farmhouse. The sitting room was untouched but the room where Tom and Margaret spent their evenings was in a similar state of disarray with papers scattered over the desk and floor. The room was icy cold and Harry went across to close the window. There were gouges in the frame where it had been forced open. He went to the kitchen, looking for the spare back door key that hung with the other keys. It was missing. That was how the intruder or intruders had left. Harry wondered whether they still had the key, and if so, whether they'd be back.

Suddenly he was anxious to get to the barn. Grabbing a flashlight from the shelf above the sink he ran across the yard, pushing the big doors open. A quick sweep with the beam of intense light showed everything as it has been before. In the centre of the barn was the trailer and Harry wasted no time in pulling open the door at the back. There was a strong smell of sheep dung but nothing to see apart from a layer of straw and faeces. He climbed inside to make a meticulous search, starting at the front and working back until he stepped down into the barn again.

He stood, shining the light into the trailer, unsure what to do next. He knew that his superficial inspection was not adequate – if there was even a speck of blood in there from Jamie Reed, forensics could find it. But how could he persuade them that there was any link between Tom Drysdale and the stolen sheep, let alone a connection with Jamie's disappearance. As he turned to push the door back into position, he noticed something at eye level: tufts of thread wafting as he moved the door. He shone the full beam on the piece of wool that was caught on the rough metal cross bar. He carefully removed it, tying it round his finger to ensure he didn't lose it. Perhaps this was what he was looking for, a small thread to link Jamie Reed to Tom Drysdale.

Chapter 15

The CSI woman arrived mid-morning and he gave her coffee. Until then, Harry had struggled to decide how much of his suspicions he should divulge. It was difficult to tell your boss that his brother-in-law was mixed up in a sheep rustling operation before he died and even worse that it may have led to the disappearance of one of his own young officers. So he sat impassively as they dusted around the lock of the back door.

'They touched the telephone in the hall,' he called as she went off to the sitting room to examine the damaged window frame. In an hour she was finished.

'Probably a couple of amateurs looking for loose change,' the young woman suggested.

'Really?'

'No professional burglar would leave such a mess.'

'Did you find any prints?'

'Nothing round the window or the door. Must've been wearing gloves.'

'Not so amateurish then?'

'They watch criminals on the telly.' She packed her bag and picked it up from the table. 'Thanks for the coffee. I'll be off,' she said indicating the back door.

Once she'd gone, Harry set about tidying the clothes, doing his best to fold and put garments into the chest of drawers. There was one suit, still on its hanger, probably kept for special occasions. He'd only ever seen Tom in his cords, an old sweater over a checked shirt. He sighed and dusted down the trousers and jacket, hanging them in the old wardrobe carefully. He put pairs of shoes together on the bottom shelf and did his best to find hanging places for Margaret's dresses. The wardrobe smelled of mothballs and reminded him of his grandmother's house.

Sergeant Crossland said he wasn't going to tell his sister about the break-in. He didn't want to worry her unnecessarily – she was stressed enough over Tom. So Harry said he'd tidy the place up. He surveyed the bedroom when he'd finished and nodded. It looked all right although Margaret would find nothing in the right place when she came home.

He moved to the sitting room to see if he could shut the window properly. Its closure was adequate but he would lock the door to the hall to stop anyone getting into the rest of the place. It looked as though the contents of the desk had been emptied and hurled round the room, so he supposed he would have to tidy up in there as well and began collecting sheets of paper off the floor, piling them on the sofa. Some were bills and he couldn't help but notice there were red demands. Others were receipts for fuel orders and straw. He put them all in a heap. There were envelopes that had been carefully opened with a paper knife and the contents replaced inside; they formed another pile. He collected a number of old catalogues for animal feed and brochures for farm vehicles.

Everything was put on the desk and adjacent table to be sorted by the family. All that remained were little scraps of paper dotted around. One was a shopping list, another was a memo for tasks to be done, including topping up the diesel, filling in his tax form and getting the MOT booked. The last item was to call JE. Harry wouldn't have taken any interest but for the number scribbled beside it. He was sure it was the mobile phone number on the message Tom had left for him when he killed himself. Even more interesting was the date scribbled alongside: 4th February. That was the night Jamie Reed went missing.

Harry ran back to his own room, to look for the torch he'd taken from the Land Rover. He hadn't seen it when he was tidying up and searched anxiously through the drawers. Eventually he discovered it almost hidden under the bed, where it had rolled. The wool thread from the trailer was still safe in his jacket. He quickly pocketed Tom's memo as well. At least he had the phone number and when he had a signal, he would ring it.

It was still dark when Mills left Swaledale to travel to the University of North Yorkshire. She knew that some, including her father, considered her lifestyle unsettled with her temporary posts and part-time commitments but it suited her. She enjoyed the variety and was looking forward to spending the day teaching archaeology students, after her week in the forensic laboratory. The roads were empty and she arrived in plenty of time to grab a coffee and catch up with old friends. Nige, of course, was at home with his children while Nina went off to work but Jake was in the office. It had been a few years since they were together but it still felt awkward when they met.

She put her head round the door. 'Hello!'

He was not alone. A skinny blonde woman in a smart wool dress and really high heels was standing close to his desk.

'Hi Mills! This is Claire.'

'Hi!' She had a strong American accent.

'Hello.'

'Claire's over here for a holiday,' explained Jake, taking the girl's hand. 'We met when I was in the States.'

'That's nice.' Stupid thing to say, thought Mills. She looked at her watch. 'I'd better be going, I'm teaching at nine.'

'Plenty of time,' Jake said, looking at the clock above his desk.

'Um, I've got to find the room and...' She excused herself clumsily and hurried out before they could see her blushing.

To her relief, a good number of students were already seated when she arrived. She was unsure how well they would accept a new lecturer halfway through the course but Nige had obviously given her a good build-up because there was quite a buzz in the room. She couldn't help noticing an older man seated at the back, looking incongruous behind the rows of fresh young faces. Usually mature students asked more questions but he sat placidly throughout her lecture. Nige had suggested she talk about modern forensic techniques for studying disinterred bodies, so she presented much of what she'd learnt at Yardley Forensics. The students seemed to enjoy it and were happy to accept an assignment from her, to be handed in later that term.

Everyone piled out through the door in one large crowd at the end, except for the older man who stayed behind and introduced himself as Dr Green, the course organiser for the forensic science option that the department had introduced last year.

'I remember the Head telling me about it,' remarked Mills.

'Yes,' said Dr Green archly. 'He said you would be getting back with some ideas of how you will be contributing.'

'Did he?' Mills had a vague recollection of the conversation but she'd forgotten all about it.

'I thought I'd sit in. See how the lecture went.'

Mills waited.

'Some of it was quite interesting.' He stood up and edged along the back row until he was able to come down to her level. 'Send me an outline for a series of six lectures as soon as possible.' He walked out before she could respond.

What an unpleasant individual, she thought, but made her way to the departmental office to obtain more information about the option and to see the administrator about how it might work financially.

Nina had also left home in the dark that morning. Although Rosie was awake, the boys were thankfully still asleep, and so was Nige. It was easier to give her daughter a kiss, leaving her playing with her doll, and tiptoe out quietly pulling the door behind her. It was the first time she'd been out on her own since the twins were born and, although she enjoyed the prospect, it was with some apprehension that she left them, telling herself it would only be for a few hours. She planned to reach Sedbergh early so she could sit and enjoy a cup of coffee alone, something that hadn't happened for months.

It was a beautiful morning when the sun finally appeared. She parked at the edge of town and found a cosy café where the atmosphere was warm and the coffee was good. She was feeling charged by the caffeine, determined to make the day a productive one. She had decided to be honest with Harry once she was sure she had his trust. He had secrets and she would play on that but she wasn't unscrupulous and she was sure they could come to an understanding.

Harry was a few minutes late. He'd slept badly, imagining noises in the night, scared that the intruders had returned. When he'd tried the mobile number on Tom's memo, there had been no response and he'd spent the night trying to imagine who was at the other end. Finally he'd fallen asleep in the early hours of the morning and not heard the alarm. He hadn't wanted to keep Sergeant Featherstone waiting but there she was, sitting in her BMW looking supercilious – not a good start to the day.

'Good morning, Harry.' She was straight over before he could get out. He lowered his window.

'Shall we use your car?' she asked, walking round before he could respond and opening the passenger door.

Although she had a thick jacket on, Harry could see she was wearing a long tunic over trousers and a voluminous scarf round her shoulders. Her clothes were brightly coloured and foreign looking. She had a pleasant smell that reminded him of spices. Her hair was long, sleek and shiny. Maybe the scent was in her shampoo.

'Perhaps you could get me up to speed with progress so far?' She was giving him a friendly smile which confused him.

'I went with PC Patterson to see an old boy he reckoned was supplying Preston Market with illegal meat.'

'And?'

'Then we drove to this other farm where Graham, I mean PC Patterson, went on his own.'

'Why?'

'I think he wanted to... he wanted... he had a chat with him. I went up to see what was going on.'

'And?'

'He didn't let on to the farmer that he was in the force but he didn't get anywhere.'

'He was pretending to be a buyer?'

'I think so.'

'So that's where we start, I suppose. Are you ready for this?'

Harry nodded but his passenger did not seem convinced.

'Are you sure?'

'Yes, Sarge. It's just – I'm not absolutely certain about the location.'

She sighed. 'Well, we'll have to see what we can do, won't we? Off we go.'

Harry had memorised the route to where he thought the farm might be and had also put the nearest village into his sat nav, in case he got lost. It was daunting to have a senior rank sitting beside him, ready to criticise if he failed. He set off towards the motorway and hoped he wouldn't make a fool of himself.

As the stone walls flashed by, Nina asked herself what they should do if and when they reached the farm. She'd dressed as best she could to look like a Muslim woman and assumed she wouldn't need to speak Punjabi but she was nervous.

'Has the man we're going to see met you before?' she asked.

'Sort of. I was outside when Graham came out of the farm but he wouldn't have more than glanced at me before

I turned my back.'

Nina considered for a moment. 'Best to keep in the background again,' she suggested.

'But…'

'No buts.'

They passed the road to Ingleton and eventually Harry found the turning into the lane that wound round fields, over the river and eventually over the railway line. The countryside looked familiar and he was confident they were on the right road when they passed a field with two black sheep in.

'I'm sure it's not much further now,' he informed Nina, who was leaning forward, peering into the distance.

The road forked and neither of the two narrow lanes in front of them seemed familiar. He risked it and kept right. The walls closed in on either side and, after about a mile, the lane became a track with a farm in the distance.

'Is this it?' His companion sounded excited.

'No, it's not,' he replied. 'I'll have to find somewhere to turn round.' He tried to hide his irritation. He'd not wanted to appear incapable.

'At least there's only one other option,' she said.

He found a field entrance, turned in three attempts and drove back to the fork as fast as he could, making the sharp turn with little room to spare. This road also looked unfamiliar but fortunately there were no more decisions to be made. The track petered out at the gate where he'd waited for Graham to return.

'This is it,' he said, delighted that he'd found the place at last.

Nina was pulling the scarf over her head, hiding her face from him as she sat in silhouette. When she turned, her face was tense.

'We'd better leave the car here, out of the way. Take it a bit further down this track and I'll walk back.'

'Don't you want me to come with you?'

'No.'

He was left by the car, watching her make her way slowly across the field towards the farmhouse until she disappeared from view behind the stone wall that surrounded the field. The name on the gate was partially hidden by snow; he brushed it away to reveal the weathered sign: "Mildroke Farm".

Nina was thinking fast as she picked her way along the track. The chippings on the snow-covered path were large, making it difficult to walk. She'd borrowed the leggings and kurti top from her friend, and it had been hard to find suitable shoes to wear with the outfit. Normally she would have chosen sandals but it was February and boots were more appropriate. In the end she had selected a pair with a small heel; even so, her progress was slow.

It gave her time to address what she would do when she met the owner of this farm, if he was there. She'd not formed a plan and was ill-prepared for the meeting. Originally she was going to act the quiet Pakistani woman but realised that she would not be approaching a remote farmhouse on her own if she really was so timid. By the time she reached the farm she was an independent woman, owner of a chain of restaurants in West Yorkshire, who had little regard where the meat came from as long as it was cheap.

The gate was padlocked, a sign there was no-one home, she assumed. After searching for an alternative means of entry and finding none, she prepared to climb the gate. Looking round, she pulled up the kurti to her waist and placed one foot on the bottom rung of the gate.

A door flew open and a large man dressed in camouflage jacket and trousers appeared wielding a shotgun. His shaven head added to the impression that he was ex-army. By his side were two collies, baring their teeth and barking aggressively.

'Oiy!' he shouted in a deep voice that filled the yard. 'You! What are you up to?'

He stopped, lowered his weapon and peered at her.

Nina climbed back down onto the ground, pleased to be on the other side of the gate.

'Hello. I wonder if you can help me?'

He didn't move and made no attempt to answer.

Good, she thought, he was clearly nonplussed by her appearance. 'I don't know whether I'm in the right place.'

No response.

'I was told you might be able to help me?'

'I don't think so, lass.'

Nina detected a Merseyside accent.

'I run my own restaurants.'

'Do you now and what's that to me?'

'They said you supplied meat... Halal meat.'

He straightened up and started to raise his gun. The dogs began barking again and he shouted at them to be quiet. 'And who told you that?'

'Harry.' It came out without thinking. She was in the part now and it was a battle of wills. If he thought he had the upper hand she would lose and be sent away with her tail between her legs.

'Harry? Harry who?' he shouted at her.

Nina thought quickly. 'We don't use surnames, it's too risky.'

'So what's your name then?'

'You can call me Huma. I don't use my birth name with business associates. What's yours?'

There was a long pause but, while he cogitated, the dogs wandered off to sniff at corners of the yard and Nina knew he'd relaxed.

'You can call me Reg.'

The tide had turned in her favour and she took the lead.

'It's very cold out here, Reg. May I come in?'

He felt in his jacket pocket, pulled out a bunch of keys and came over to the gate. When he opened it the dogs ran forward but with a word from him, they retreated to the corner of the yard. She followed him into the house.

The room was a kitchen – of sorts. A table and two chairs took up most of the space but Nina could see a free-standing cooker and a cupboard in the corner. There was an electric heater on the floor but it was so cold Nina doubted it was on.

'Sit down, girl,' the man ordered, laying the gun on the table before making himself comfortable on the chair opposite.

'I was told…' Nina began.

'Hold on… hold on… I've got some questions, like,' he interrupted.

'I want to know if you can supply me with halal meat. It's simple.'

'Not that simple. I need to know you're kosher – if you'll pardon the expression.' He was laughing at the pun but watching her closely.

'Kosher or halal it makes no difference to me – so long

as it's prepared the same way.'

'Oh aye, we know the right way to do it and we'll give you good stuff.'

'Do you do it here, then?'

'You don't need to know the ins and outs.'

'I need to know I'm getting the right material. I don't want any rubbish and I don't want to be robbed.'

He rubbed his bristly chin, staring at her until she felt uncomfortable. 'I need to see the colour of your money before I sell you anything.'

'That's as expected. I thought a small consignment to begin with. What would be a sensible amount?'

'Depends what you're after. Half a cow, a goat, a sheep?'

'Let's say a sheep.'

'Right. Will your husband bring the money? Or a brother?'

Nina stood up to emphasise her point. 'Reg, I own five restaurants… successful restaurants. I have built my business up without the help of a useless husband or lazy brothers. You don't need to worry that you will be bothered by any of my family. I'll return next week. Do you have a phone here?'

The man rose, ignoring her question.

Nina tried again. 'How can I contact you?'

'Do you have a mobile?' he asked. 'Give it here.'

He typed a number into her phone and returned it.

When Nina checked, he'd put a mobile number in under 'Reg'.

'Do you have a signal?' she asked. 'I don't have one here.'

'Just leave a message with the day and time. We'll be ready for you.'

He opened the door, waiting for her to leave. The dogs were there but this time they came up and gently sniffed her. She deliberately made a fuss of them, delaying her exit for a few moments while she sniffed the air. She was sensitive to the smell of blood, having been brought up in a strict vegetarian household. It seemed to her that there was a strong odour coming from the outbuilding across the yard.

She heard the door slam behind her and saw Reg watching her as she made for the gate. She shut it carefully behind her, allowing time to look round one last time. She memorised the number plate of the vehicle, hoping that it was registered to the man who was still looking out of the window.

Chapter 16

'So you think he was really convinced?' Harry asked as they drove back to the main road.

'Completely!' Nina was feeling elated.

'So tell me what happened.'

'Not yet. Let's go back to Sedbergh for something to eat.' The combination of adrenalin and relief made her light-headed.

'Kirkby Lonsdale is nearer.'

Once they were seated in the bakery and had ordered coffee and cakes, Nina described almost word for word her conversation with Reg.

'Is that his real name?' Harry asked.

'No, no more than Huma is mine.' Nina laughed. 'But I do have the registration number of his vehicle.' She pulled out her diary and put in the details as she had memorised them. 'And he gave me a mobile number.'

'What is it?' Harry asked.

His interest surprised her but she recited it. He sank back in his chair looking disappointed.

'Did you expect to recognise it?' she asked.

Reluctantly, he admitted that he also had a mobile number that he suspected was associated with the illegal meat traders.

'So where did that number come from?'

He tried to avoid the question but when Nina insisted, Harry told her about the note that Tom had left him.

'So he committed suicide? Do you have the note?'

Harry explained that he'd given it to Sergeant Crossland, who'd dismissed it as unimportant. Then he also told her about the break-in at the farm. 'I think it was related to Tom's death in some way. I believe he was using his trailer to steal sheep and he knew something about Jamie Reed going missing.'

'So who was searching the farm – and what for?'

'I don't know but I think they wanted to ensure there was nothing incriminating in the house. He was trying to tell me something before his death.' He hesitated before continuing but decided to tell her his theory. 'I think they shot Tom's dogs as a warning to him and that sent him over the edge.'

'It all sounds rather dramatic, Harry. I assume you've reported it to your senior officers.'

'Yes it does sound far-fetched and that's why I've not made a report because I don't even have that note now.'

'But you do have that mobile number?'

'Yes.'

'Have you tried ringing it?'

'Yes but no answer.'

'But they'll have your number now.'

'What?'

'A missed call. It'll be recorded.' She shook her head and smiled at him. 'You'll not make a good detective will you, Harry?'

'I discovered a thread of wool in Tom's trailer,' Harry

said, searching his pockets and producing a plastic bag. He handed it to her, reaching into his pocket again. 'And I found this torch as well.'

'Does anyone else know about these?' Nina asked, turning them over in her hands.

'No, not yet. But at least it's something.'

'Yes it is, Harry.' She put them in her handbag. 'And I have a vehicle registration. And there are fingerprints on my mobile phone belonging to this Reg character. The question is: what are we going to do with them all?'

Harry was fiddling with the crumbs on his plate. Nina sipped her coffee and waited.

'I was thinking...' he began. 'I was thinking perhaps we should talk to Graham – PC Patterson.'

'Let's call him Graham, shall we? And you should call me Nina, OK? So how will Graham help?'

He didn't look up; a pile of crumbs was forming in the centre of his plate. 'Well, it seems to me that he doesn't know about today... and I think he should.'

Nina considered her options. If Harry realised she wasn't working on anyone's authority but her own, he could get her into trouble. He obviously got on well with Patterson and he was the wildlife officer who was leading the meat investigation.

'Do you think Graham would be pleased to know the progress we've made today?' she tried.

Harry looked across with a serious expression. 'I think he would be. If we can get him on our side it would make life a lot easier.'

'Good. Would you like another coffee?' She left the table, relieved that at last they understood one another.

Reg had offered her a sheep, presumably butchered and

ready to use in her fictitious restaurants. It had occurred to her that she could not arrive home with a car full of lamb and she had no idea how much it would cost. Probably more than she could afford in cash. There were arrangements to make that could be difficult without official help.

When they finally left the warmth of the café, they had agreed that Harry would speak to Graham, leaving Nina to ponder over how she might get some of these pieces of evidence examined.

As soon as Nina had climbed back into her own car at Sedbergh, Harry called Graham. He was going to have to explain their actions quite carefully and he thought he knew the best approach.

'Graham? It's Harry. I wondered if you fancied a pint... Where are you...? How about I see you in Kirkby Stephen then?'

An hour later they were seated beside a roaring fire with a pint in front of them, waiting for their pies to arrive.

'Well, this is very nice, lad. Are you not out with the search party today?'

'No. Actually I had something else to do. It involved Sergeant Featherstone. She asked me to help her.'

'Well that's good, lad. It's always good to be asked by a senior officer.'

It was harder than he'd imagined, broaching the subject, and he was pleased when he saw the barman bringing their food over. Graham attacked his pie and chips with vigour and they ate in silence for a while. Then the older man put down his cutlery and took a long swig of his beer.

'So, lad. What was this work you were doing with

Sergeant Featherstone?'

There was no point in messing about. He might as well get it over with. 'We were investigating the meat traders down on the Lancashire border.'

Graham was wide-eyed and silent for a second or two as if incapable of taking it in.

'You what?' he asked under his breath.

'We went down to Mildroke Farm.'

'And did what?'

'She had a chat with the man there. He called himself Reg.'

'Reg?'

'She's arranged to buy some meat off him next week.'

Graham was grinning, a strange humourless grin of disbelief. 'So all the work I've been putting in has been a waste of time, has it?'

He turned back to his pie, finishing his beer once he'd put his knife and fork down for the last time.

'Shall I get another,' Harry asked tentatively,

'I think you better had, lad. I think you better had.'

At the bar, Harry ordered another pint for Graham and a half for himself – he needed to keep a clear head if he was going to put a positive spin on what had happened. Graham needed to feel that he was back in charge.

'There you are,' he said cheerfully as he placed the full glass carefully down in front of his mentor.

'So, he was willing to talk to her, this chap at the farm?' Graham was looking straight ahead.

'Yes, she managed to convince him all right.' There was silence while he took the top few centimetres off his pint. 'And he's going to sell her some meat, is he?' he went on.

'Yes, next week. A whole lamb.' Harry didn't know why

he laughed but it helped.

'A lamb or a sheep?' Graham asked with a flicker of a smile. 'You know what they say…'

'Might as well be hung for a sheep as a lamb!' Harry exploded with laughter, relieved that the tension between them had eased.

'When is she going back?' Graham's expression was serious again.

'We don't know yet… we wanted to talk to you first. We need you to co-ordinate things.'

'You mean you need to get everything above board again. Make it official.'

'Yes.'

'Sorry lad but I'm not sure I can do that…'

'But…' Harry interrupted.

'It's nothing personal. I don't have the authority to rush in and raid a farm just because he offers to sell a young lady a sheep. Plenty do that. We'll need evidence that it's an illegal business.' He picked up the pint glass and sipped his beer slowly. 'We need proof Harry.'

'So what should I do?'

'Get some background checks done on the farmer – your Sergeant Featherstone's a detective, she can do that.'

'She got his prints on her phone,' Harry offered.

'Clever girl.'

'So we won't go back until we've done the checks?'

'No. But I'll square it with them in the office. I'll tell them you're investigating the farm with Sergeant Featherstone.'

'Thanks, Graham.'

'That's OK. But next time I want to know what's going on *before* the event.' He lifted his glass and drained it in one slug. Harry wondered if it was wise to offer him another.

Once her lecturing duties were finished, Mills headed for the car park. It was mid-afternoon and there was nothing to keep her; she didn't particularly want to bump into Jake and his American girlfriend again. Nina had suggested she drop in for tea and she was looking forward it. She enjoyed the atmosphere of their tiny, terraced house, full of the chaos of a family with three small children.

Nige opened the door looking as unkempt as usual, wearing his signature eclectic mixture of clothing that combined cord trousers with a flowery shirt and striped tank top. Nina called it his charity shop look, not that all his clothes were acquired that way. Rosie had followed him and was peering out at Mills with a shy smile.

'Hello sweetheart!' Mills called.

'And hello to you!' replied Nige with a grin.

Mills was laughing as she went into the sitting room, where Nina was seated by the fire.

'Wow!' exclaimed Mills.

Nina stood and gave a twirl. 'Do you like it? It's not mine.'

Mills had only ever seen her friend in western attire, except of course at the wedding. She looked wonderfully exotic in the brightly coloured tunic and trousers. Her long dark hair swung round as she turned and her daughter ran to join in the fun.

'It's her working clothes,' explained Nige.

'Really?'

'Undercover work. Hush, hush.' He was tapping the side of his nose with his forefinger.

'And how are the boys?' Mills asked, squatting down by

the play mat where the babies were lying contentedly.

'Nige is going to the supermarket, aren't you dear?' Nina gave her husband a piece of paper. 'Here's the list.'

He grabbed a jacket, disappeared into the kitchen, returning with a bundle of plastic bags and left with a wave. Nina made a pot of tea, returning with scones which she announced had been made by Rosie, with her father's help.

'You love baking, don't you?'

Her daughter gave a shy smile then sat down beside her baby brothers.

Nina asked about her day at the university but Mills was much more interested in what Nina had been up to.

'So you've started your undercover work then?' she asked.

'Is it obvious?' Nina laughed. 'We were over in Lancashire today. It was fun.'

'Who's we?'

'Just me and Harry.'

'Harry Clark?'

'Yes. You know, I've changed my opinion of him. I think he's all right, just a bit inexperienced. You have to remember, he is a wildlife officer not CID.'

'So what did you have to do in Lancashire?'

'We visited a farm trading in illegal meat. I've arranged to go back next week to buy a lamb.'

'A whole lamb?'

'I suppose so. It'll be dead but I didn't like to ask whether it will be in pieces or not.' She giggled and began pouring the tea.

'Where do they get the meat from?'

Nina passed Mills a scone. 'Stolen from farms.'

'So where is it slaughtered?'

'I think it's done on the farm. It had this smell, like a butcher's shop. Horrible.'

'That's awful. So how are you going to collect this sheep – in the back of your car?'

'I've been thinking about that. We need someone with a truck or a Land Rover.'

'Can't help you there, I'm afraid my Mini won't be big enough. Surely the police have a van you can use.'

'No – I'm supposed to be a restaurant owner, not a police officer. I hope Harry's fellow wildlife officer will sort something out.'

'Daryl's got a truck,' Mills said, without thinking.

'Daryl?' Nina asked with a mischievous look.

'He's just a guy I met. He mends walls and stuff.'

'Really? He must be fit!'

'I suppose.' Mills felt herself redden.

'Can I have another one, Mummy?' Rosie asked, gently shaking Nina's knee.

Pleased by the distraction, Mills asked Rosie to show her the toy dog she'd been playing with and then had a cuddle with Owen and Tomos. By the time the babies had been changed and fed, Nige had returned, making two journeys to the car to fetch all the shopping.

Mills stayed until it was Rosie's bedtime. While Nina bathed the children and changed into more conventional attire, she fetched fish and chips from the shop round the corner. Nige opened the beers and they sat round the fire, eating from the paper to save washing-up.

'I spoke to the guy who runs the forensics course today,' Mills told Nige. 'He wants me to design an option on modern forensic techniques – six lectures.'

'Sounds cool,' Nige said with his mouth full.

'D'you think so? I wasn't sure. But the money's good.'

'That course could be filled ten times over,' Nige explained. 'There are members of the department who would kill to be able to have an option on it. It'll raise your profile in the department, that's for sure.'

Nina took her friend's hand. 'You should go for it Mills. It would be so nice if you were back at the university. We'd see more of you and you could live here or...'

'Steady on, love,' Nige interrupted. 'We can hardly move in here as it is.' He turned to Mills, 'Not that we don't...'

'I know what you mean, Nige. And don't worry. I wouldn't want to leave the cottage, even if I did spend more time over here.'

There was a faint cry from above and Nige jumped up. 'I'll go!'

As soon as he'd left the room, Nina turned to Mills with an earnest expression. 'I know it's not official but if I gave you a couple of items for forensic analysis, can you have a look at them?'

Mills hesitated. 'Sorry but I'm not supposed...'

'Just a couple of things, Mills.'

'What are they?'

'I've got fingerprints on my phone from someone at the farm. I've got a registration number that Hazel's checking for me.'

'Can't you do the prints through official channels?'

'I suppose I could ask Hazel but it can't be used in evidence not with me working undercover and no proper chain of custody.'

'If you give me the phone it won't be back with you until at least Tuesday.'

'That's not a problem, I can't use it until it's done

anyway.'

'Give it to me,' Mills offered. 'I can get it processed while we wait for Hazel to authorise a request.'

'There's a torch for fingerprints and a piece of wool as well.' Nina produced the items from her bag.

'Are they connected?'

'I don't know – Harry gave me these.'

Mills was a little uncomfortable with the unofficial arrangement she was going to have to present to the laboratory but her friend had put her neck on the line to help her before.

'And when are you and Harry going back to the farm?'

'I haven't rung him yet because of the transport issue. If I need a truck…'

Mills made an audible sigh. 'I can ask Daryl.'

Harry struggled to light the Rayburn. It had gone out yet again, leaving the house cold and uninviting. He watched the firelighter burn under the sticks of wood until the flame flickered and died for the third time. It was no good; he couldn't keep the place going when he was out all day. He called Shelley, who was delighted to hear that he was taking up her parents' offer to stay with them.

'I'll just pack my things and be on my way.'

'Cool.'

He wasn't sure if it was a wise move. Shelley was sweet but she was quite young and seemed overly attached to him. On the other hand, he would get his meals cooked and the place would be warm. Shelley's house was a modern semi with gas central heating and double glazing; there was a shower room where the water came out at more than a drip.

He made sure the sitting room door was locked – the window had not been repaired – and carried his bags to the car before returning to turn out the lights and lock the kitchen door. Suddenly he was in total darkness. The sky had cleared in parts and he could make out bits of familiar constellations. No sound, no sight, just the familiar smell of the farmyard. As he stood adapting to the dark, he could hear the drone of a vehicle in the distance, getting nearer. Soon it was too close to be on the road and Harry saw headlights coming up the track.

Instinctively he moved behind the car, waiting to see who appeared. It seemed an age before the headlights were switched off and a bright beam of light swung round the yard. The smell of cigarette smoke wafted across as a man's figure followed the light to the kitchen door and Harry could hear him struggling to fit a key in the lock. Eventually the door opened and the figure went inside. The kitchen light snapped on and he became a dark silhouette: tall and bulky.

Harry considered whether he should confront the man but whatever he was doing in the kitchen took very little time. Soon he was out and moving quickly across to the barn. Harry ducked down as the torch beam swung towards the car but he stretched up gingerly to watch the intruder drag the barn door open and disappear inside, stopping only to wave towards the gate with his torch. Suddenly there was a revving of engine and a Land Rover appeared, manoeuvring until it was reversing into the barn. A minute or two later, it reappeared pulling Tom's trailer. The other man ran out and jumped in before they sped away down the track.

When he was sure they'd gone, Harry went into the

house. On the kitchen table was a note. Just six words in capital letters: KEEP YOUR MOUTH SHUT OR ELSE.

Chapter 17

Mills spent much longer than usual preparing for her date. Daryl had invited her for a meal in his "local" but early on Saturday morning he'd sent a text asking if she minded if his brother came too. He was staying with Daryl so she supposed he felt awkward about leaving him at home. It would be strange meeting a member of Daryl's family when she hardly knew anything about the man himself. Her hair was all right and she wasn't getting dressed up, but now she checked in the mirror she felt that she'd overdone her makeup. As she began hurriedly removing the eyeliner, she heard a car outside.

From her bedroom window she watched Daryl jump down from the truck. She quickly wiped a tissue over both eyes and grabbed her coat before running downstairs to open the door.

'Ready?'

'I'll just get my bag.'

Daryl introduced Len as she squeezed in beside him.

The heater blasted hot air and the bass on the heavy metal music pounded. It was impossible to talk so she sat clinging onto the edge of the seat as they swung round bends in the narrow road at speed. After a while Mills felt quite sick – she'd never been a good passenger – and shut her eyes, hoping they would soon reach their destination.

The cold wind was a relief when she climbed out in the car park. She took deep breaths of fresh air before following the brothers as they strode quickly to the back entrance of the pub.

She chose a soft drink and made her way to an empty table. The fruit machine was flashing; the speaker above her head issued music louder than necessary. Daryl was waiting at the bar as his brother came over to sit beside her. There was a family resemblance, although Len was shorter and had a gaunt appearance.

After an awkward silence Mills asked him how he was feeling.

'I'm fine really. Just getting used to being out in the world again.'

'It must have been horrible,' she said, meaning the period in hospital.

'I've never been in a crash before,' he replied. 'It was like they say: everything goes into slow motion but I couldn't do a thing.'

'What happened?'

'There was this vehicle in the road as I went round the corner. I swerved and I hit the wall…'

Daryl arrived with the drinks – two pints and a glass of coke. 'Is he boring you with his war wounds?' he asked.

'No, he was telling me about the accident…'

'The mystery trailer?' Daryl laughed as he picked up his glass. 'All in his imagination I reckon,' he teased.

'Well that's where you're wrong,' Len responded indignantly. 'I had a call from the police about it and they said they believed there *was* a vehicle parked on the road that night. That's why they rang – to tell me they believed me and to see if I'd remembered anything more about it.'

'And did you?' asked Mills.

'Not really. They asked if it could have been a trailer but I'd already said that's what it looked like. I was just pleased they know I wasn't lying.'

'Does that mean you're off the hook?' Daryl asked.

'I think so. Yes I'm sure that's what they said.'

'That must be a relief,' Mills offered.

'It is. I don't like coppers.'

'Careful,' warned Daryl. 'Mills has friends in the force, don't you?' He was smiling but Mills sensed he was worried how she would react to his brother's remark. 'That guy that came round the other night, he's a copper isn't he?'

At mention of Harry, Mills felt unnecessarily defensive. 'Yes… so?'

'I thought it was him! He stopped and questioned me when I was repairing the wall you demolished,' he said, nodding at Len.

'What did he want?' Len asked.

'Don't know but he didn't let on he was police. There was just something about him.'

'Might've been the same one that came to see me in hospital.'

'Doubt it. He went missing. They're still looking for him.'

'No. There was another one… later on. Wanted to go over it again. It was him that rang me about the trailer.'

'His name is Harry Clark and he's a wildlife officer,' Mills announced. Her tone was deliberately cold and they got the message.

'I'll get some menus,' offered Daryl, getting up.

'They had to pin my arm,' said Len after a moment. 'It hurts like hell sometimes.'

'I reported it straight away,' confirmed Harry.

'Have you written a statement?' His sergeant was rubbing the back of his balding head.

'Yes, sir.'

'And they only took the trailer?' Crossland looked puzzled. 'Well, that's what they were after then.'

'There was the note as well.'

'I heard. Well, they wouldn't know about Tom, would they?' He sank back in his chair. 'You did the right thing, lad. It was best to lie low and take the registration. Sometimes these lads from outside are armed.'

'Yes, sir.'

'Harry, for that reason I need to ask a real favour and you can say no if you want to. Can you keep an eye on the place? I've arranged for the window to be replaced today and it sounds like a new lock is needed on the back door. I've not told Margaret about these break-ins but I'm sure she'd appreciate it if...'

'That's OK, Sarge. I just need to get the hang of the Rayburn.' He grinned to reassure his boss.

'Good lad.' He straightened up and looked hard at Harry. 'Graham Patterson has sent an e-mail. He wants you to concentrate on the sheep rustling investigation. He says Sergeant Featherstone is leading it – is that right?'

'Yes, sir.'

'Well keep me informed of what you're up to. And be careful; I'm still responsible for you while you're over here.'

Harry went back to his desk to ring Nina with the good

news and was disappointed that she wasn't picking up. He left a message then contacted CID in Carlisle to see if there had been an identification of the vehicle that had visited the farm on Friday. The phone rang and rang with no option to leave a voicemail. Frustrated he dashed off an e-mail then tried Graham Patterson's number.

'Hello lad, how's tricks? Anything back from Newby Wiske yet? Have they traced the vehicle at Mildroke Farm?'

'No, I can't get hold of Nina this morning.'

'It all takes time, their priorities are sometimes not ours, lad.'

'Well, we need to know before we go back this week.'

'Don't go running before you can walk, lad. Get the intel first, then we'll move in. I'm out most of the week on a course but keep in touch with any progress.'

On screen, an e-mail had arrived from Carlisle. 'Righto, Graham, I'll keep in touch, bye!'

The message was brief. The registration had been traced to a Nissan 4x4 in Scotland but since it had been in the dealer's for major repairs for the last ten days, they were either false plates or he'd got the number wrong.

Irritated by the lack of progress on any front, he went back to his boss.

'I'm going to join the search again – if that's all right with you.'

'Yes, you carry on.' His sergeant didn't even look up. 'They're somewhere near Outhgill today. You'll see the bus.'

He hurried to his car, pleased to be outside. It was a frosty morning but the sun was shining and there was always the possibility of spotting a red squirrel in the area of the search.

*

Mills decided to take the bull by the horns and approach her boss directly about the items Nina had given her.

'They're not official police evidence,' she began, placing the bags on Brenda's desk. 'Because of the way they were obtained they won't be admissible in court.'

'I see.' Brenda scrutinised the contents of the bags, one by one. 'The phone?'

'For fingerprints, same as the torch. DNA if possible.'

'And what do you plan to do with the prints and DNA if there is any?'

'Look for a match?' Mills knew she was on thin ground.

'Without police authority? I don't think so. We can't access the database without authority.'

She placed the bag on the desk in front of Mills and squinted at the third bag. 'This thread?'

'Yes.'

'I can have a look at it and tell you what it is.'

'Thanks, if you have the time?'

Brenda smiled. 'I like to keep my hand in.'

'Well you are *the* international expert in textiles.' Mills smiled and left with the other two bags before Brenda could respond.

After checking that Glyn was busy at his desk, Mills located Donna in the sample preparation laboratory. She knocked on the window, indicating she wanted to speak to her. Donna waved and made as if she was drinking.

Five minutes later Mills was waiting for her in the tearoom. Donna was a bright girl, fresh from her forensic science degree and keen to progress. Mills knew she would help analyse the items she was holding, enthusiastically.

'Good morning, Dr Sanderson.'

Despite being asked to call her Mills, Donna had continued to address her formally and she suspected that Glyn was behind it.

Mills made coffee and asked Donna if she had fully recovered from the 'flu. Once the girl had assured her she was well enough to return to work, Mills raised the subject of testing the phone and torch, without going into details.

'Will you give me the submission forms?' the girl asked, as she washed her mug.

'Ah. It's not actually a police investigation at this stage, Donna. So I'd be grateful if you could treat this as a public enquiry for now.'

She looked confused. 'You just want me to test for prints and DNA. Do I put them on the database?'

'No, don't do that. Just keep the results until we decide what to do.'

'What name should I use?'

'Put them in my name – treat them like a request from me.'

'OK.'

'And you don't need to mention this to Glyn – he'll only get confused.'

Alone, Mills wondered whether she'd done the right thing. It would be impossible to ignore Glyn. As manager he would need to view anything that went through the laboratory. She would have to discuss the rogue samples with him at some stage, preferably before he found out by accident.

She spent the rest of the morning struggling with the paperwork that Brenda either couldn't or wouldn't manage herself. There were orders for laboratory supplies that had to be paid for, and invoices to be sent out to clients. As she pored over a particularly confusing message scribbled by her boss on the back of an envelope and stapled to a report for a customer, the phone rang. Mills was relieved to have a diversion and answered with a cheery hello.

'Mills, it's Nina.'

'Hi. I've got the lab working on the samples but they won't have anything for a day or two,' Mills hoped she sounded apologetic.

'Thanks, but that's not why I'm ringing. I wanted to take you up on your offer of a truck.'

'What?'

'The truck... you said that your Daryl would let us use his truck.'

'He's not *my* Daryl.' Playing for time while she thought of an excuse, she asked, 'When do you need it for?'

'Thursday.'

'To collect your sheep?'

'It's OK, it will be dead.'

Mills digested the information.

'And where does he have to go for this sheep?'

'We, Mills, not "he". Harry and I will be going over to Lancashire on Thursday morning – twelve o' clock.'

'Nina, I can't *borrow* Daryl's truck. I can ask if he'll drive us somewhere but I can't ask to take it without him.' It would be difficult enough for that favour; they hadn't parted on particularly good terms after Saturday night as it was.

'Could you just ask him, Mills? It's important police business.'

That's just the problem, Mills thought as she put the phone down.

Things got worse when Glyn marched into the office

later that afternoon.

'I'd appreciate an explanation of what exactly this request for unauthorised analyses means, Dr Sanderson.'

He placed a request form down on the desk in front of her. She didn't need to read it – she recognised her own writing. She took a deep breath.

'It refers to an important undercover investigation, Glyn. I am waiting for details from Newby Wiske now. Please get them done as soon as possible. I will give you the authorisation papers the moment they arrive.'

'But…' He was turning red.

'No buts.' She deliberately handed him back the request form without meeting his gaze.

He snatched the paper from her and left, slamming the door behind him. Mills sighed. Her head was beginning to ache as she stretched across for the phone again and rang Nina's home number. It went to voicemail.

'Hi, it's me. Please can you send me something that looks official to keep the lab happy? I really need to have an authorisation from Hazel… now. You owe me Nina Featherstone.'

As far as the request to Daryl was concerned, she couldn't face a direct conversation. Instead she sent a text asking if he was doing anything on Thursday morning and then buried herself in paperwork again.

Much later, Brenda bounced in looking pleased with herself.

'Busy?' she asked as she passed on the way into her office.

Mills muttered under her breath. Almost immediately Brenda reappeared with a plastic bag in her hand.

'That thread you gave me… most interesting. Had me

puzzled for a bit but not much gets past Brenda Yardley.'

'So they say.' Mills looked up.

'Tweed. Good quality tweed. Judging by the colours, I'd say camouflage cloth.'

'Like the army use?'

'No, not the army – the shooting fraternity. I'm sure it comes from a good quality tweed shooting jacket. Do you know the provenance?'

'No idea but I'll ask. Can I tell Nina that's what you think?'

'Yes, by all means. I don't change my mind once I've made my decision. Tell her it comes from a jacket belonging to someone who shoots or maybe a beater.'

Pleased to have a distraction, Mills called Nina again and this time she answered.

'I got your message and I've spoken to Hazel. She's sending you a formal request by fax as soon as she can get it signed. Happy?'

'Happier. I've got some news about the thread sample. Brenda says it's from a tweed shooting jacket. She wondered what you know about where it came from.'

'Not sure. Harry gave it to me. I'll ask him. I've got to call him about Thursday.'

Mills was not going to be drawn into a discussion about the truck again. 'Good. And any additional information about the torch would be useful.'

'About the truck, Mills. I have tried to get an alternative. I suppose I could hire something.'

Mills was tempted to tell her friend to do so but was becoming intrigued by whatever Nina was up to.

'No, it's OK. I'll speak to Daryl this evening.'

There was a pause at the other end. Mills imagined her

friend weighing up the options.

'Really?'

'I don't see why not. I'll tell him it's vital police business.' She laughed.

'Mills, this isn't a game. It's an important investigation.'

'If it's *that* important they'd provide transport.' She'd called her friend's bluff.

'OK. But please don't tell him why I need it.'

'No problem. Do you need a driver?' She giggled.

'No!' Nina put the phone down on her.

Mills sank back in her chair and swung round from side to side. At last there was a way she could find out more about her friend's undercover work.

Nina made herself a coffee. She was calling in too many favours and making plans with no backing at all. She'd bamboozled Hazel into covering for her on the forensics request and cajoled Harry into smoothing things over with Graham. There was now a sort of legitimacy for the investigation but no resources and she'd left everyone a little hazy over the details of the case. Worse still, she was organising the collection of a dead sheep on Thursday and had no clear idea what to do with it when she'd got it.

Fortunately Harry was back in the office when she rang and told him it was on for Thursday. She asked if he had access to transport but he said no, only his own vehicle and he didn't fancy trying to fit a dead sheep in his boot. So Nina offered to arrange it, without mentioning that they might be driving a truck belonging to his ex-girlfriend's new man – it could prove a bit sensitive, she felt.

Before finishing their conversation, Nina asked Harry to send her the particulars of exactly where and how he'd found the items of evidence he'd given her. When the details came through, she added her own information and faxed it to Mills with a note saying they really did need the use of the truck.

Mills called Daryl that evening. She had concocted a story about needing to visit an archaeological site with a large selection of tools. Initially he said no because he had a job on that day but when Mills pointed out she could drive it herself if necessary, he reluctantly agreed he could get his mate to take him to work.

'He's helping me fix a new gate on Thursday so he can pick me up on the way. You'll have to get over early though – before I leave.'

He offered to cook a meal for them in the evening.

'You can tell me all about your exciting day's digging,' he teased.

'Yes.' Mills had never been good at bending the truth and did not relish lying about how she had actually spent her time.

Replacing the receiver, she picked up the page Nina had sent over to the lab, studying it as she ate her microwaveable dinner for one. To an outside observer the items for forensic examination seemed diverse but Mills was looking for connections. Grabbing a sheet of scrap paper and a pen, she began to make notes.

The thread came from Tom Drysdale's trailer, and Mills wondered if it could be the same trailer Len had swerved to avoid when he had his accident. Nina's mobile phone carrying the prints of the man selling dodgy meat was presumably unrelated to the above. But there was something missing. Nina had also given her a bag containing a torch for forensics. Somehow it had been left off the list.

Mills pondered over her notes, wondering if the hypothesis was that Tom Drysdale was responsible for stealing sheep and selling them on for meat. Presumably the torch belonged to him or to the meat man, so it would be logical to compare prints on both. It might even be possible to get some DNA from the prints on the torch and the phone. If not, they might have to find a way of getting DNA from the meat man when they visited him on Thursday.

Mills rang Nina later, when she was certain that bath and story-time would be over.

'Good news, Nina! I can get the truck for Thursday.'

'You are a star, Mills. Did he mind? You didn't tell him why I needed it, did you?'

'No, it's fine. I told him I wanted it for work. Of course that means I'll have to drive.'

There was silence at the other end.

'Mills, I can't involve you. It's a police investigation.'

'Take it or leave it, Nina. It's up to you.'

Chapter 18

'Dr White rang, he's been held up on the motorway,' Brenda shouted from her office.

Mills was half an hour late, delayed by the thin covering of snow that had fallen in the night.

'Who's Dr White?' she called back as she hung her coat over the radiator and removed her boots.

'The digital guru you found in London.'

'Oh… Alex!'

She'd completely forgotten he was coming or she wouldn't have dressed in a ridiculous Scandinavian sweater that made her look fat. In a panic, she ran to the "Ladies" to use a bit of eye make-up. She even considered washing her hair in a basin and drying it under the air dryer. Instead she ran a comb through it and applied lipstick. She wasn't impressed with the result.

'Damn.' The face in the mirror frowned back at her.

It was another hour before Alex appeared, by which time the anticipation had made Mills nervous and excitable. The coffee she'd made in expectation of his arrival had gone cold, so she was in the middle of making a fresh pot when Brenda announced that their guest was finally here. Mills carried the tray with three cups and saucers carefully into the office, where Alex was already seated opposite Brenda. He leapt up to shake her hand and tell her how pleased he was to meet her again. Mills hoped her blush was not as noticeable as it felt.

'Alex has been telling me about the work he's been doing on the hum from the electricity mains to pinpoint the date and time of recordings. Fascinating.'

'That's rather more novel than most of the work we do,' he said, taking a couple of sips of coffee before replacing his cup on the tray.

Mills hoped she hadn't made it too strong.

'I thought digital forensics was looking at people's computers to see what they've been up to,' Brenda went on. 'But Alex tells me they can tell where people are from their mobile phones too.'

'Yes, forensics has had to run fast to keep up with the digital age,' he agreed.

'Well Alex, when we've finished our coffee, Mills can show you what we do here. We're not up to speed with these digital applications and I want you to help us with that.'

Alex smiled at Mills. 'Of course.' He picked up the cup and drained the contents before standing up. 'I'm looking forward to seeing your facilities.'

Mills smiled and led the way down the corridor.

'She seems a nice old dear,' Alex said quietly when they were out of earshot.

'She is. And very clever in her own field.'

'I read that she's an expert in textiles.'

'She is. Come and meet our laboratory manager.'

Mills introduced her visitor to Glyn and he accompanied them round the laboratory, describing the different techniques. He expressed no interest in why her visitor was there, so Mills explained that Alex was an expert in his own field of digital forensics.

'Oh that. We don't have anything like that here. There's no call for it.'

Mills smiled across at Alex, who winked at her.

At the end of the tour she escorted him back to Brenda, who wanted to talk to him alone. Mills sat reading through a report without concentrating on its content. She'd got on really well with him when they were in London but now, back in Harrogate, Alex seemed so much more professional than her. It wasn't just her stupid sweater; it was his manner, the suit and tie, the briefcase. He seemed so... so grown-up. She laughed at herself and tried to do some work.

Eventually, after about half an hour, they reappeared. Whatever they'd been discussing, they both looked pleased by the outcome.

'Mills, I've booked a table at "Sasso's" but I've got to go to a meeting. Would you take Dr White for lunch?'

They always booked the same venue for visitors. Mills didn't know why but she assumed Brenda wanted to impress their guests with the smart atmosphere of an Italian restaurant. Left on her own, Brenda was more likely to be seen in the local pub eating fish and chips accompanied by a pint of best bitter. Mills suspected that Brenda would be there while they were lunching in style.

The snow had stopped when they left the laboratory so Mills suggested they walk into town.

'It'll only take ten minutes,' she assured Alex, who was looking up at the grey sky.

'I'll get an umbrella,' he said. 'I've got one in the car.'

Wet snowflakes began beating on their faces almost as soon as they set off and Mills was so engrossed in keeping her hair dry that she missed the kerb and went over, landing on her bottom. She had tried to save herself by grabbing at Alex's arm. He supported her under her armpits, pulling her back into an upright position.

'Are you OK?' he asked.

'Yes, I'm fine. Honestly.' She could feel the damp patch through her jeans as they walked the rest of the way.

She was so embarrassed she couldn't speak until they reached their destination. She sat down gratefully and ordered a glass of wine to calm her nerves, even though Alex insisted on a soft drink because he was driving. He was talking rapidly about his work as he studied the menu but she wasn't listening. She was getting cold as she sat in her damp clothes.

Once they'd ordered a starter and main course, Alex told her what Brenda had discussed at their private meeting.

'She said to tell you about the offer.' He began toying with his glass. Bread arrived and he pulled small pieces off as he spoke. 'She's very keen to expand the business, isn't she?' he asked.

'I suppose so. She likes new projects.' Mills was waiting to hear what Brenda had been saying.

'She wants me to be a sort of consultant. Advise on digital stuff.'

'Wow.' If Brenda had offered him a job, Mills hoped her boss had looked at the finances to check they could afford it. 'Does that mean she's going to offer digital forensics as a service?'

'Not immediately. She wants me to do a feasibility study; what sort of things would be possible... you know.'

'Sounds good.' She had mixed feelings. It would be fun to have Alex around but she wondered how it would affect her own position in the company.

'Sorry,' he said. 'Are you OK? That fall must have shaken you up. Should we get you another glass of wine?' Without waiting for an answer he called the waiter over.

Once their food arrived the conversation flowed more easily. Mills realised afterwards that it was probably the wine that helped her get over her feeling of discomfort, literally. By the time they were served their main courses, Mills felt the same spark of excitement that she'd experienced when she first met Alex. Not only was he charming and funny but he was also very like her in many respects. She felt they were on the same wavelength in a way that she'd never been with Harry or Daryl.

It had been snowing hard outside throughout their meal. As they waited for coffee, Mills saw Alex glance out anxiously and check his watch.

'I think I'd better leave when we get back to the laboratory,' he said. 'I would have liked to have stayed but it's looking pretty bad out there – as much as I would like to spend more time with you.'

Mills shook her head. 'Don't apologise, please. It's been really nice and if you're coming back as a consultant…'

He grinned. 'That's right. I'll start my secondment in two weeks; as soon as Brenda has sent me a letter of appointment.'

On the way back, Alex insisted that Mills hung on to his arm and sheltered her with his umbrella. He saw her to the front entrance of the building and went to shake her hand but then changed his mind and kissed her on both cheeks. The unexpected embrace took Mills by surprise and he'd turned to leave before she had time to gather her thoughts.

She looked up as she opened the door and saw Glyn staring down at them. Inside there was no sign of Brenda so Mills went along the corridor to find Donna. She'd promised the results of the fingerprint analyses on the mobile and torch. It would be good to return the phone to Nina, but her main concern was to see if the lab had a match for the prints.

She found the analyst in the office busy on her computer keyboard. She looked up when Mills went in and reached for a folder.

'All done, just as you asked.'

'And?'

'The mobile was a right jumble. I've got a few bits and pieces – here.' She offered Mills a printed sheet covered in partial prints. 'There are definitely two sets, at least. One's bigger than the other. I put them on the system.'

'Ah.' Mills wasn't sure they had authority to do that.

'There's not a bad match for the smaller prints – like it said on the paperwork – belonging to a police officer. Let me find…'

'Yes I know. Sergeant Featherstone.'

'There's no match for the other one.'

'Not even with the torch?'

'The torch?' She picked another sheet from the folder. 'Nope. Nothing on there of any use.'

Mills thanked her and left, disappointed. Halfway down the corridor she turned and retraced her steps.

'What about the batteries, Donna?'

The girl looked confused. 'I didn't have any batteries.'

'In the torch?'

Donna looked blank for a second. 'Magic! The batteries

in the torch – I'll do them straight away!' She was out of her seat and struggling into her lab coat. 'I won't be long!'

Mills went back to her desk knowing it would be more than a few minutes before she would get the results. It was already dark and although it had stopped snowing, she was anxious to get home. At four-thirty she returned to the laboratory and spotted Glyn and Donna hunched over the bench where the laboratory manager had shown Mills how superglue could be used to find fingerprints on difficult surfaces.

It had taken Mills longer than she'd anticipated collecting Daryl's truck and driving to Sedbergh. She was ten minutes late and Nina was already waiting for her. She was wearing the same colourful outfit under her winter coat that Mills had seen before and the clothes looked incongruous as she stepped gingerly across the snow-covered car park.

'Hi, we'd better get going or we'll be late,' she said as she climbed up beside Mills.

'Where's Harry?'

'Let's get going, I'll tell you on the way.'

She drove carefully onto the main road, aware that the conditions were not ideal and the vehicle was not hers. Once they were out of town, Mills asked her friend why she was alone.

'It's Mr Drysdale's funeral this morning and his wife particularly wanted Harry to go. He asked me to change the day but there was no way I could do that at the last minute.'

'Did he have to be there?'

'Apparently Mrs Drysdale asked him to do a reading. He couldn't refuse.'

They sat without conversation – Mills needed to concentrate on the road, which was not completely clear of snow in places. Nina seemed preoccupied, speaking only to tell her which direction to take. The route became less well defined once they branched off the main road, leaving Mills wondering if they would even reach the farm. There was a layer of icy snow on the narrow lanes and she was grateful for four-wheel drive – the stone walls were getting nearer the closer they got to their destination.

'This is ridiculous.' Nina looked agitated. 'If we get stuck there's no-one to help.'

'Check your phone,' suggested Mills. 'See if there's a signal. It's in my handbag.'

Nina didn't answer but pulled out the mobile and busied herself. 'I don't believe it,' she said. 'Three bars!'

'You townies! We do have means of communication out here in the Pennines.' But privately Mills was relieved to know they were within contact of assistance.

'So did you get the prints off it?' Nina asked, waving her mobile.

'Yes and no. They were a real muddle but we got yours and a second set.'

'And?'

'No match. And…'

'Left, now!' Nina shouted suddenly as they almost passed an inconspicuous turning. Mills swerved violently and nearly hit the wall to her right. She reversed with a grating of gears and revving of the engine before making a second attempt to steer down the even narrower lane.

'And, what?' asked Nina.

'And no prints on the torch – but they're checking the batteries. What I didn't know was where the torch came from.'

'Didn't Harry put it on the list I sent you?'

'No.'

'Odd.' Nina sounded puzzled. 'I'll have to ask him. I assume it belonged to Mr Drysdale.' She leaned forward in her seat. 'Nearly there now. We may not be able to get down the farm track, unless it's been cleared.'

Mills was struggling to keep the truck on the road and was glad to stop at the farm gate. They both peered across the fields towards the roof of the farmhouse showing white above the walls.

'No smoke from the chimneys,' Nina pointed out. 'D'you think anyone is there? I can't see any car tracks going through the gate.'

'You're right. Perhaps they're not in. What shall we do?'

'Let's try to get to the house,' Nina suggested.

Mills was not used to driving in such conditions. She hesitated for a moment. To hell with it, she thought, let's do it!

'OK. Open the gate!' she ordered.

Nina clambered out, picking her way across the drifted snow to struggle with the iron gate. At first it wouldn't budge but eventually she'd pushed it back far enough for Mills to move into first gear and nudge the vehicle forward.

'I left it open,' Nina explained as she slammed the passenger door and shook snow off her boots. 'There aren't any livestock in the fields.'

There was silence as Mills concentrated on finding the route to the farm across the fields. Occasionally she would veer off onto softer ground and have to find the track again. After making very slow progress they were within sight of the house and Nina pointed out the gate she'd used on the previous visit.

'Park here,' she ordered. 'I'll go and knock.'

Mills watched her friend pick her way across the pristine snow and pause. Then she took the chain that was securing the gate and shook it to show that it was padlocked. Her friend shrugged in an exaggerated manner to indicate that she couldn't get in. Mills knew exactly how to attract their attention – she pressed hard on the horn several times until Nina waved vigorously for her to stop. There was no movement, nothing to suggest there was anyone around. Mills turned off the engine and climbed down.

'Stay there,' Nina ordered.

'I thought we could have a look around,' said Mills, making her way over to her friend.

'No. Don't you see? It will be obvious that we've been in by our footprints. I'm not venturing over the gate. I want them to trust me.' She turned and went back to the truck.

It was not for Mills to disagree. She reluctantly joined her friend and started the engine. Turning the vehicle was not easy – several times she thought they were stuck – but finally she was retracing the twisting route back to the lane. She kept the engine running while Nina closed the gate and as soon as she was in the passenger seat, Mills set off back along the lane.

'Well, that was disappointing,' remarked Mills once they were out of sight of the farm.

'Yes.' Nina sounded pre-occupied.

'What happens now?'

'We go home.'

'With the investigation, I meant. Do you think they forgot?'

'I don't know. Maybe they got jumpy – don't trust me.'

They were approaching the main road. A Land Rover was parked on the opposite corner of the cross-roads and Mills could make out two indistinct figures seated beyond the misted windscreen. She deliberately slowed down as she pulled out.

'Can you see them, Nina?' she asked.

'Not clearly.'

'D'you think they're watching for us?'

'I don't know; it's an odd place to stop. They may just be farmers.'

'What should I do?'

'Drive on. We can't do anything now.'

She was taking a notebook from her bag and Mills assumed she was checking the registration number. She drove off, watching in her rear-view mirror. As soon as they were past, the Land Rover turned down the lane. There could be no other place they could go but the farm.

'Should we go back? Perhaps they're just arriving late…'

'No. It was them.' Nina was insistent. 'It's after twelve o'clock. If they were running late they could have called me – I've got a signal again here.'

'So we just leave it?' Disappointed, Mills suggested she should have made a call when they were at the farm but Nina insisted there had been no signal. 'But you could call them now.'

Mills drove while Nina sat staring at her phone. Finally her fingers moved and she held it to her ear. It seemed a long time until she suddenly straightened up, indicating for Mills to keep quiet.

'Hello, it's Huma. I was at the farm but no-one was there. Where are you?' She sat for a moment then looked at her mobile before lowering it onto her lap.

'Did they answer?'

'Yes,' she said slowly, 'but when I said who I was they just hung up on me.' She sighed. 'I guess they've got cold feet. It's disappointing.'

'So that's that? We just leave it?' Mills knew she wouldn't change her friend's mind so she was already thinking ahead. 'Do you think Harry will be around this afternoon? We could go and ask him about the torch.' Then she remembered the twins. 'I suppose you've got to get back now?'

'I should but...' She consulted her watch for a moment. 'No, I'll just let Nige know I'll be late.'

'He seems to cope really well – considering how tiny they are,' commented Mills.

'That's the easy bit – they just feed and sleep when they're this small.'

By the time they were back in Sedbergh, Nina had spoken to Harry and arranged for them to meet him early that afternoon. She gave Mills the postcode for Old Hall Farm before she went off to get in her own car.

Mills let Nina lead the way. She didn't want to arrive first, fearing that the meeting with Harry would be awkward. As it was, she needn't have worried because he wasn't alone.

'This is my friend, Shelley,' he said as he introduced the young blonde in a very short black dress.

Mills hadn't seen him in full uniform before – it made him look taller and more grown-up. He might have added "my girlfriend" but it wasn't necessary. The girl hung on to his arm in a proprietorial manner. Mills gave her a smile of reassurance.

Harry had looked uncomfortable when Mills followed her friend into the kitchen 'What's *she* doing here?' he'd asked Nina.

'I'll explain if we can talk alone for a few minutes. Is there somewhere… ?'

He indicated the door that led from the kitchen into the rest of the house and she followed him, leaving Mills alone with his "friend".

'D'you think I should make us some tea?' asked the girl. 'I don't know where anything is.'

'I don't suppose it matters,' Mills answered. 'We won't be staying long.'

They stood facing each other as the sound of raised voices drifted from the other side of the door.

Shelley looked embarrassed and pulled at the strands of hair falling round her face.

Mills wandered to the back door and stared out to avoid having to look at her.

'Hope he's not in trouble,' Shelley said. 'It's been horrible today at the funeral, everyone crying and that. He's been really unhappy about Tom, really sad.'

Mills hadn't heard Nina's voice raised in anger before but it was clear she was giving Harry a hard time. It was difficult not to eavesdrop and neither Mills nor the girl made any attempt to converse while they listened. It was impossible to make out what was being said until the door was opened partially then closed again but not fully. They were right outside.

Mills could hear Nina clearly now. 'I want you to write a report to that effect. Explain exactly what happened and send it to me by e-mail.'

She came into the kitchen followed by Harry, who

looked upset. Then, unexpectedly, she put her arm round his shoulder. 'Don't you worry. We know the truth now – that's the most important thing.'

As soon as they were alone in the yard, Mills asked Nina what had happened.

'I quizzed him about the torch – he said he found it in a Land Rover that was abandoned up Mallerstang.'

'What? You mean the one that Jamie Reed went missing in?' exclaimed Mills.

'Yes.' Nina's voice was level, emotionless. 'He took the torch from the Land Rover when he... you found it. He didn't realise... He used it to look inside and just carried it back to the car. He didn't know what it was until he found his own torch much later.'

'Are you going to report him?'

'No need,' responded Nina. 'Once his report goes in, everyone will know. He's not bent; he's just a useless copper. He might make a decent wildlife officer yet if someone like Graham looks after him.'

'Do you want me to carry on looking for prints and DNA on the torch?'

'You might as well finish the examination but I expect it will just show that the torch belongs to Jamie Reed or his father.'

Nina unlocked her car and opened the driver's door. 'The most important thing now, Mills, is to find out what's going on at Mildroke Farm and I'll need Graham Patterson's help. Please look for a match again, Mills, I've got to identify this man Reg somehow.'

Chapter 19

The reprimand from Nina had stung Harry. Whatever he did seemed to go wrong. Shelley wanted to go out but he didn't feel like socialising with her juvenile friends.

'So what are we going to do, sit here like dummies all evening?' she asked.

'There might be something on the telly,' he offered.

'Have you seen their telly?' she asked contemptuously. 'I doubt they've even got "Freeview".'

They bickered until, irritated, he suggested she went back home where it was warm and they had all the channels. 'I wouldn't want you to miss any of your favourite reality programmes.'

It wasn't what was said so much as the way he'd said it, he knew that. She picked up her coat and bag.

'Call me when you're in a better mood,' she snapped, making for the door.

He watched the headlights disappear down the track before opening his last bottle of beer, making a mental note to stock up at the weekend. He'd need it if he was going to be stuck in this dump on his own.

He went through to the freezing cold sitting room, switched on the television and slumped down in the least uncomfortable armchair. He must have dozed because he woke to hear a vehicle on the track. Thinking it was Shelley, he smiled and rushed to the back door only to be confronted by a burly man dressed in camouflage gear, shouting at him.

His voice was muffled by the scarf covering half his face.

'I don't understand you,' Harry explained, wondering whether the man was lost.

Pulling the scarf off in frustration, he revealed a chubby face. 'I said: who owns the Mitsubishi Warrior that was here today?' he asked angrily in a strong Liverpool accent.

'I don't know,' Harry replied, trying to think what he meant.

'It was down the road the other week. A guy mending the wall.' The man moved forward in a threatening manner.

Harry took a step back. 'I don't know who you mean,' he said.

'Don't mess me about, pal. Wi' a paki woman. Just give me the name and address.'

Harry considered his options and made a decision. 'I'm a police officer. I suggest you clear off before I arrest you for intimidation.'

The man guffawed. 'Oh, now I am frightened. Please don't arrest me, officer.' He turned and called out. 'Hey, Tyler, he's only a effing copper!'

Harry went to tackle him but he was off down the track. He watched him jump into the same Land Rover that had visited the farm on the previous occasion.

Mills was in work early the next morning, wanting to finalise the forensics for Nina. But her boss had other ideas.

'Come in and sit down, girl,' she called from her office door. 'I want to have a chat.'

Mills was curious. Brenda rarely offered more than a few well-chosen remarks at her before she was off. She went in, closing the door behind her.

Her boss looked agitated and fiddled with an empty vase on her desk. She gave a sigh. 'There's no point beating about the bush,' she said at last, 'I'm just going to come out and say it…' Then she fell silent.

'Is something wrong?' Mills asked. 'Is it about those samples Nina gave me?'

Brenda shook her head. She took out a large cotton handkerchief and blew her nose loudly. 'No, pet, it's not that.' She leaned back in her chair and Mills noticed how drawn she appeared. 'I've been told by my GP to cut down on my drinking and smoking – *and* to lose weight. Would you believe it?' She laughed.

Before Mills could concoct a suitable response, her boss banged her fists on the desk, straightening up indignantly. 'I've got a bloody lump – here!' She pointed at her ample bosom. 'And it's bloody malignant. How about that?'

'I'm sorry,' stuttered Mills. The words affected her physically. Whenever breast cancer was mentioned, she was a young girl again, standing beside a hospital bed, watching her mother gradually fading away.

'… so it will be several weeks and then there'll be chemo and all that rotten stuff they want to do to you.'

'When will you…' Mills tried to keep her voice from wavering.

'Next week, they said. I'll need you to take over while I'm out of action. I'll tell Glyn you have full control.'

'But…'

'No, pet. The way you can help me best is to keep this place on an even keel. And on a happier note, young Alex says he's willing to help us get into the digital age – how about that?'

'Very good.'

'Well, you could sound more enthusiastic – I thought you were a bit soft on him. I assumed you'd be delighted.'

Mills shook her head slowly and smiled at Brenda. She really was the limit.

'Right then, pet, off you go. Lots to do before next week. I want to leave everything ship-shape.'

During the course of the morning, Mills watched Brenda making a point of seeing each of the staff in her office and then she went off. Their faces confirmed that they'd been given the same news and it was the talk of the tearoom at lunch-time. Mills decided not to bother Donna until the afternoon, knowing there would have been little work done that morning.

'Donna, I need to know if you've got any prints from the torch batteries.'

'Yes. Glyn's working on it.'

'Any DNA on the torch case?'

'Yes, but it's too much of a jumble. But Glyn did try to get DNA from the batteries – he says he could have done the mobile if you hadn't taken it away.'

Mills reddened but wasn't drawn. 'Thanks. Can you give me the report as soon as you can?'

She returned to her desk to give Nina an update but before she could text, she noticed a missed call from Daryl on her mobile. It rang while she was sending Nina's message and without thinking she answered it.

'Mills? It's me.' The voice was low and husky.

'You sound like you've got a cold,' she remarked. 'Did you get the keys – I left them in the glove box like you said. Sorry I couldn't wait for you last night...'

'No. Not a cold. A broken nose.'

'What?' She assumed that he'd been in a fight. 'What happened?'

'Two blokes jumped me outside my house last night. I'd just gone to put the bin out.'

'Have you been to hospital?'

'Yes. I've only just got back.'

'Have you told the police?'

'Oh yes, but I couldn't give them a description so there's nothing they can do.'

'Did they take anything?'

'Oh no, they weren't muggers. They said they were teaching me a lesson. I have no idea what they meant.'

'They didn't tell you why?'

'Their exact words were "If you come over the border again, we'll finish you off." I have no idea what they meant, unless they've started a turf war in the Dales.'

'How odd,' said Mills. It was the reference to the border that struck a chord. Nina had made a joke about going over the border to Lancashire. Had the men attacked Daryl because she'd used his vehicle?

'Anyway, it's not your problem and it's not the first time my nose has been damaged. I'm going to have black eyes tomorrow, that's for sure.'

'Poor you.'

'Just thought I'd let you know I'm going to be lying low for a few days until I look prettier.'

'All right for some!' Mills hoped she sounded normal.

'I'd better get back to work now.'

As soon as she was off the phone, she rang Nina and told her what had happened. Her friend asked if Daryl would be able to identify his attackers.

'I don't think so. He said he couldn't see them – it was dark.'

'If they wanted to warn us off, something must have spooked them,' Nina suggested. 'Did you say anything to Daryl?'

'No – I felt really bad about it but there didn't seem any point, if he didn't see them.'

'I think you should give him an explanation.'

'You mean tell him about the meat man?'

'No, of course not.'

So later in the afternoon, after wondering how to approach it, Mills rang Daryl back to admit that the attack might have been caused by her using the truck.

'… you see I was going to this dig in Lancashire and I cut up a car with two men in it and they got angry… really angry. I thought they were going to ram me, they were so close behind. I had to shake them off and so I suppose…'

'Are you telling me that the reason my face is swelled up like a balloon is because of your stupid driving?'

'I…'

'No, don't answer. I can't believe it. I don't want to know. Just leave it there, OK? Unbelievable.'

Silence. Mills checked her phone – he'd gone.

Despite calling and leaving messages, Daryl ignored her for the rest of the afternoon. Of course she felt bad but what if it *had* been a case of road rage? she'd asked Nina. Would he really have taken it that badly?

'I don't see why not,' her friend had replied. 'The poor

guy's got a broken nose because of you.'

'I'd like to remind you that it's because of *you*, actually. He won't be lending me his truck again in a hurry. In fact, I doubt he'll ever talk to me again.'

'That's not the only problem; they've obviously suspected that I'm not what I seemed.'

'So that's it?'

'I'll have to tell Graham that I failed. It's really embarrassing.'

'You just need to find out who owns the farm.'

'I know but it's not that simple.' She couldn't admit to Mills that her visit hadn't been entirely official.

Nina went back to the sofa and picked up baby Owen to feed him. She sat looking down at him as he sucked contentedly, his eyes slowly closing, while she decided what to do. When he'd finished feeding, she held him against her shoulder, pacing the room until she felt he was ready to join his brother for an afternoon nap. It was a quiet time of the day with Rosie in day nursery and the boys in their cots.

Graham would need to know that she failed to keep her cover. He would tell her to keep well out of his investigation in future. Her thoughts turned to Harry and the severe reprimand she'd given him for removing the torch from the crime scene – which she'd promised would be between him and her. The damage had been done; the evidence would be inadmissible without chain of custody, so what was the point of airing the issue?

She put off her call to Graham, which was not going to be easy, and instead rang Harry to tell him what she planned to do. First she asked how the search for Jamie

Reed was going.

'They're still out there.'

'What do they think happened to him, Harry?'

'That he got lost in the blizzard after he abandoned the Land Rover.'

There was a short silence at the other end, followed by a sigh.

'About the sheep rustling investigation, Harry...'

'I think Tom Drysdale was behind it.'

'Why d'you say that?'

'Because I had a visitor last night asking about the vehicle you were in yesterday. I guess they must have come from Mildroke Farm. It was the same Land Rover that took Tom's trailer and left a note for him.'

'What did they want?'

'Just to find out whose truck you came in – I didn't know. But you see there *is* a connection.'

'I think you're right, Harry. It belonged to a friend of Mills – he had a visit from them last night.'

'What happened?'

'You'd better ask Mills. Right now I need to speak to my Chief Inspector.'

'What do I do?'

'*You* are going to do nothing, Harry.'

It was Friday afternoon, there was no guarantee one of the boys wouldn't wake up in the middle of a call now. She would have to wait until after the weekend to visit Newby Wiske, if Nige could look after the babies for a few hours. Perhaps it was for the best – she would consider carefully what she was going to say to her superior. After all, she had her own back to cover as well as Harry's.

*

Mills stayed late at the laboratory finishing off overdue reports. It had been a rotten day and she had no desire to go back to the empty cottage for another night in front of the telly. Just yesterday it was going so well but Brenda's devastating news had left her feeling lower than she had been for a long time. Normally she would have rung Daryl to cheer herself up but he wasn't answering her calls. Finally, at seven o'clock, she left the building, carefully setting the alarm before stepping into the biting east wind. She selected a CD and turned it up loud. As she manoeuvred the Mini out of the car park, her vision was clouded by the tears that were slowly forming.

Her mood was not improved as she arrived at Mossy Bank. The windows of the other cottages glowed brightly and porch lights shone in doorways. Her cottage was the only one in darkness. Inside it was cold and uninviting. In no mood for cooking, Mills found some old crackers; the cheese was covered in green mould so she used marmite instead. Despite knowing that a cup of tea or coffee would be sensible, she went to the cupboard to fetch the bottle of red wine her father had given her at Christmas. "It's a good one," he'd said, "so keep it for a special occasion." She supposed he'd meant a celebration, such as a birthday, but today seemed an appropriate occasion… after all, it's not every day you are told by your boss that she might die and your new man dumps you. Grabbing a glass she took the bottle to the sofa, where she shivered with cold as she took the first sip. Dad was right, it is good, she thought, pouring a second glass.

She was having a strange dream about her mother when she was woken by the phone. It was after ten and she struggled to focus on the name of the caller –it was Harry.

She'd forgotten to remove his name from its memory.

'Mills, are you there?'

'What d'you want?' She attempted to sound cross but it came out like a single word.

'Sorry, did I disturb you?'

'No. What… do… you… want…?' It took considerable effort to separate out the words.

'I spoke to Nina today. She told me about your friend who owns the Mitsubishi Warrior.'

'He's… not… a friend.'

There was a pause at the other end. 'Anyway, she said he'd had a visit from these people that…'

'I'd prefer not to talk about it.' Mills was sitting up properly now, her mouth felt dry.

'Listen, Mills, it's important. I think these people are the ones that Tom Drysdale supplied with stolen sheep. Nina thinks so too. That's why I'm ringing. I thought you'd be interested – clearly you're not!'

'No I'm not.'

'OK that's fine. I was going to take a look at Mildroke Farm again over the weekend, that's all.'

Mills put the phone down, returned to the sofa to collect the empty bottle and tossed it into the recycling box with a satisfying crash before going to bed.

Chapter 20

Harry usually spent Saturday morning in bed when he wasn't on duty but today he was up before it was light, deliberately choosing to have a big breakfast. He'd already demolished a three-egg omelette and was finishing off with two pieces of toast and marmalade. While his tea cooled, he prepared some sandwiches – "doorsteps" his grandmother would have called them but he was never any good at cutting bread. He put them in his backpack with extra warm clothing, a torch, a penknife and a screwdriver he found in a drawer… just in case.

His plan was to get to Mildroke Farm early, preferably before they were up. He could watch until, hopefully, they went out, allowing him plenty of time to have a look round. If he had to wait all day… no, all weekend… so be it. He opened the rucksack and added a packet of biscuits and two cans of lager, just in case. Once he'd donned his padded jacket, hat and gloves, he finished the mug of tea and went out, locking the door behind him. Now he was on the move he felt the exhilaration of what he was about to do.

It was still dark and he met no cars until it began to get light and then it was only the occasional white van or delivery lorry. He'd checked the map to locate the farm but wasn't entirely certain of its position until he turned off the main road. Finally, he was confident that he was heading in the right direction and he just needed to keep a watch for the final left turn.

He slowed down just past the entrance to the farm then carefully turned the car round, parking close to the wall. The plan was to make his way across the fields, away from the track, to peer over the wall that hid the building from view. Just one thing he wanted to check – his phone. Just as he thought, no signal – not even for emergency use. He shoved it back in his pocket and climbed out into the freezing morning air. There was a strong wind blowing across the fields and he quickly pulled on his woolly hat before locking the car and pocketing the keys.

The drystone wall was not too difficult to climb and he was soon running across the open field as fast as he could through the snow. He threw himself onto the wet ground, keeping cover until he recovered his breath. Gingerly, he straightened up to peer over the top. In front of him was a field of sheep. They stared at him. A few started bleating and began moving towards him. He quickly ducked, aware that beyond the sheep was the farmhouse. I know you're hungry, he muttered under his breath, but please keep quiet while I have another look. He popped up quickly, this time focussing on the house. There were lights in the windows on the ground floor. Clearly someone was at home and he was pretty sure he recognised the Land Rover parked outside.

He stooped low as he ran back to the lane, pulling himself over wall, landing awkwardly as he misjudged the drop. His plan was to watch and wait until "they", whoever "they" were, left the house. He'd parked the car so it would be out of the line of sight of anyone driving onto the lane from the farm. It had seemed a good idea but it meant he wouldn't be able to see them leave. He'd assumed he would rely on hearing the diesel engine but when he opened the passenger window, a freezing wind blew in from the fields.

He sat for a while, pulling his scarf tighter round his ears. He thought of putting the radio on or perhaps playing a CD, but it might be heard when "they" came down the track. In the end he folded his arms tightly, sank down in his seat and waited. After an hour he needed to pee and crept into the undergrowth on the other side of the road. It was quite sheltered in the dense woodland and, better still, he could just see the entrance to the farm. Once he had relieved himself, he chose a fallen tree propped against a large oak and sat down. His phone was in his jacket pocket – no signal but hours of music. He inserted the earphones and leaned back, watching and waiting.

After an hour, now feeling chilled to the bone, Harry wondered if it was too soon to have a snack. He would have liked a hot drink but at least there were biscuits. When he stood up he was hardly able to feel his feet, walking awkwardly back to the car, stumbling over a fallen branch on the way. He pulled the packet of chocolate digestives from the rucksack, tearing at the wrapper with numb fingers, biscuits flying. Cursing, he retrieved them from the floor, eating greedily. It was only three minutes past ten. He took the rest of the packet with him back to his hide-away in the woods and resumed his vigil.

Mills clutched her head as she made her way carefully

down the stone stairs. It had been a tormented night with dreams she would rather forget. The one she always had when she'd been thinking of Mum; the one where she was lost and was running down corridors, looking for her mother – calling, screaming until she woke herself up. Her head was pounding as she searched in vain for some painkillers. The tea didn't help, nor did the shower, however long she stood under it. In the end she put on her towelling robe and climbed back into bed. There was no point in getting up anyway – if Daryl wasn't speaking to her, she had a pretty dull weekend to look forward to. She could call Nina but it was her fault she'd borrowed the truck in the first place; never again would she do her a favour. Even Harry had been involved with it all, yes – what business was it of his that she'd borrowed Daryl's truck?

When she woke again it was half past twelve. She still had a bad head but it had stopped throbbing. Downstairs she made tea, managing a piece of toast. She dressed, made more tea, followed by a large piece of the ginger cake that Muriel had made. She was beginning to feel almost human again. There were loads of things she should be doing: washing, ironing, cleaning, shopping... the list was actually endless. Guiltily she thought of Dad – she should ring him before Fiona, rang accusing her of neglecting her poor father. She flopped onto the sofa, staring at the phone. Someone had rung last night, she recalled, but she had been *very* drunk.

At one o'clock Harry felt justified in starting on his lunch. Pretty damn good, he thought, as he finished off the other half of his cheese and pickle sandwich. It was freezing in the car now, even with the windows closed, but using the heater meant running the engine, which was out of the question. So he marched up and down the lane, stamping his feet. It helped, so he ran the short distance to the end of the lane, then back to the car. After a few laps he felt considerably warmer. As he was jogging back for the tenth time, he thought he heard a car. In the distance, he could just make out the roof of the Land Rover moving slowly down towards the road. He pressed himself against the wall, although he was sure there was no chance they would see him when they turned out onto the lane. The sound of the engine gradually subsided as the vehicle disappeared from view.

Now he needed to find out if the place was empty. He locked the car, climbed the wall, and scooted across the field, as he'd done before. This time the sheep were far too interested in a pile of hay to take notice of him. No lights, no vehicles. He moved along the field until he met the wall that followed the track up to the house. He shinned over swiftly and walked up to the house as if he had every right to be there, no point in skulking about if he was being watched. When he opened the gate he could hear dogs barking but no-one came. He walked slowly toward the window, peering inside. The kitchen was small and dark, not neat and tidy like Margaret Drysdale's. Then he saw the dogs staring up at him from the corner of the room. Clearly he was not going to gain access to the house without difficulty.

He turned round to scrutinize the outhouses that formed the rest of the farm buildings. The stone barn looked as old as the house but the large wooden structure next to it was new. It was the one Nina had mentioned after her visit – complaining it smelt like a butcher's shop – but he couldn't detect anything, even when standing right outside the entrance.

The big double doors appeared locked but on closer inspection the padlock was not closed. Harry moved it so he could undo the fastening and hung it back on the open latch. Pushing at one of the doors just enough to squeeze in, he dragged it closed behind him.

Harry was expecting it to be like Tom Drysdale's barn: full of farm machinery and animal feed. But it was a very different place. In the few seconds before his eyes became accustomed to the semi-darkness, he was overpowered by a smell that caused his stomach to heave. Although there were no windows, there were places where daylight streamed in between the wooden planks. It was like a factory or a big kitchen with a long steel table down the middle of the room covered in large knives, axes, hacksaws, even a circular saw. He stopped as he felt something sticky on the floor and stepped back from what he could imagine was blood, as he caught sight of a large box in the corner, a large rack of bones protruding from it. There were a number of similar boxes along the wall, each containing parts of animal carcasses. Harry held his hand over his mouth and nose as he peered into them one by one. His inclination was to run out into the fresh air and drive away but this was what he'd been wanting, it was the illegal slaughterhouse they'd been looking for. Here was the evidence that Graham needed. All he had to do was to make the call.

There was no mobile signal, not even outside in the yard. Unwilling to leave without something, he went back to collect photographs on his useless phone. He took a general view, one of the boxes of bones, and the instruments on the table, presumably for butchering the carcasses. He found a bin full of foul-smelling entrails, blood-stained aprons hanging on a rusty nail and chain mail gloves. A soft humming noise was becoming more noticeable as he approached the big metal door at the back of the building. He tried the heavy handle but it was locked. He assumed there was a generator in the next room.

Using the torch on his phone, he explored the rest of the building until he was certain he had pictures of as many items of evidence as possible. Anxious to get away from the smell of rotting carcasses, he made for the gap in the doors, only to freeze at the sound of a diesel engine. Peering through the crack he could see a Land Rover coming towards him across the yard, stopping directly in front of the barn. Stepping back, he pressed himself flat against the wooden wall, hardly daring to breathe.

'You left the barn unlocked, idiot!' The Liverpool accent was thick and harsh.

A car door slammed, then a second. Footsteps coming towards him, the doors being flung open. Harry flattened himself harder against the wall and held his breath.

There was a click and suddenly the room was flickering then filling with bright fluorescent light. There was nowhere to hide. Harry stared at the man's back, waiting for the moment when his gaze would fall on him. It took about five seconds and when he turned, Harry recognised the man who had come knocking at Old Hall Farm on Thursday night dressed in camouflage gear.

'Well, well, well, it's the effing copper!' he said, swaggering towards Harry. 'Did you want something, pal?'

Now the man was standing right in front of him, Harry could smell his breath, too close for comfort.

'Come and see what's here, Tyler!' he called.

Soon they were joined by his mate, a lanky, youth who looked no more than sixteen.

'What d'you think we should do with this copper, eh?'

The lad shrugged, looking sideways nervously as the older man wandered away towards the table, picking up a knife.

'Fancy a few copper chops?'

As the knife was held under his chin, Harry gulped and the man guffawed. His young companion grinned but appeared anxious.

'I tell you what, son. You get some string from over there and tie this gentleman so he can't get away, while I think what to do with him.'

The lad fetched a large ball of string and allowed the man to cut a length with the knife he was still holding in a threatening way. Harry could feel the boy's hands trembling as he bound his wrists together in front of him and then onto a wooden stay in the barn wall.

'Is it secure?' the older man asked, as he threw the knife back at the table. It missed, clattering to the floor. 'Don't matter. We'll lock the barn this time. Keep nosey parkers out.'

He flicked the switch and indicated for the lad to follow. Harry watched the light fade as the doors closed together and heard the padlock click shut. He'd been tied where he stood, so however he turned there was no way he could rest down on the floor. I can't remain in this position, he thought, wondering how long they intended to leave him strung up. The barn was gloomy and soon it would be dark.

Presumably, unless they planned to let him out quite soon, he'd be there for the night. The thought frightened him and he yanked at the string tying him to the wall but it was secured firmly. The only way to get out was to cut himself free. He held his hands apart until the string was taut then made a sawing motion against the wooden plank. The surface was rough and he was sure that in time he'd be able to fray the string sufficiently.

At first there seemed to be little progress. He stopped to rest his arms but soon resumed his effort, determined to get free. He had to stop at intervals and it had become so dark he could no longer judge how he was doing. So when the moment arrived for the string to break it came as a surprise – suddenly his hands were free and he was able to rub his sore wrists to relieve the pain. Now he was able to move, he was unsure what to do next. He could only summon help by reaching a phone and that would mean getting back to his car and to the nearest phone box. Any attempt to get through the double doors could be seen from the house so he would have to attempt his escape from the side or the back of the building.

Using the light from his phone, he selected a hacksaw from a selection of tools on the big metal table and went over to the side wall, well away from the doors, and started to saw at the wooden planks. It was difficult to gain purchase on the wood – his hands were aching from the exertion of freeing himself and the saw kept slipping. He persisted for what seemed like hours but made little progress and eventually fell back exhausted, tossing the hacksaw onto the floor. He sat down beside it, defeated.

According to his phone it was seventeen thirty-two and he was still trapped. He stared at the screen as it died; the battery had finally given up and he was in darkness. He sat for a while considering his options. Surely they would come back tonight, if only to give him something to eat and drink, he thought. Wouldn't they? Then, determined not to be beaten, he devised another plan. Feeling his way along the rough wooden wall of the barn, he edged towards the door at the back. If he could get through it into the back room, he might find a light that wouldn't be seen from the house and possibly a way out.

Progress was slow in the unfamiliar environment – at times he wondered if he'd lost his bearings – but finally he reached a corner and began feeling his way along the back wall. He knew as soon as he felt the cold metal that he was at the door, his hands following the frame until he was at the top. Suddenly his fingers sent something flying, followed by a metal jingle on the concrete floor. He stopped, alert, thinking fast. The noise wouldn't be heard from the house but what was it? A nail or a loose piece of metal? He fumbled across the door, trying the handle. It was locked but was that the key? His grandfather used to do that, hide the key above the door.

He knelt down and stretched his hands out as far as they could reach, sweeping them in a circular motion across the floor, hoping to gather whatever had fallen towards him. Nothing. He edged forward and tried again. This time his fingers touched an object that was metallic, a ring? It was a large metal ring with a key attached. He stopped himself from calling out in excitement. At last there was a chance to escape. He straightened up and felt across the door for the keyhole. Holding his breath, he inserted the key and turned it.

The door was extremely heavy. Harry had to use both

hands to open it. Holding it back as he went inside, it slammed shut with a loud bang. He stood for a moment in the pitch black, feeling the sudden drop in temperature before fumbling to either side for a light switch. The fluorescent light flickered on and off several times before it came on properly and he was able to confirm that he was in a cold store. There was no way out except the way he'd come in.

There were carcasses hanging on large metal hooks and closer examination convinced him they were sheep. As he wandered amongst the dangling lumps of meat, he spotted one covered in a cloth. He stepped over a pile of ropes and chains on the floor to reach it and pulled the dirty rag back. At first he couldn't comprehend what he was seeing but stood staring until it became a coherent sight. In front of him... suspended from a meat hook... was the inert body of a young man, dressed in jeans and a tweed shooting jacket.

Chapter 21

Mills had spent much of her weekend in pyjamas, watching television. Her headache lasted until Saturday evening so she went to bed early, hoping she would feel better in the morning. On Sunday she ventured into the garden to sprinkle breadcrumbs for the birds. A biting wind was blowing fine rain from the fell and she pulled her dressing gown round her, escaping back inside to spend the morning on the sofa. Finally, in the afternoon, she showered and washed her hair. She even got dressed, in case anyone came round. Tempted to ring Daryl but afraid of his reaction, she sat in front of the television all evening, hoping for a call, and went to bed disappointed.

Monday mornings were usually bad but Mills was feeling so much better than she had over the weekend that she jumped out of bed and was setting off well before her normal time. The traffic was heavy but she sat patiently in the queue crawling slowly into Harrogate.

For once she was early and Glyn was the only one in before her. He was at his desk but quickly folded the newspaper as Mills approached.

'Good morning.' He sounded uncharacteristically

cheery.

'Hi, Glyn.'

'Got some good news.'

'Don't tell me… you've won the lottery.'

He frowned. 'No. I've got DNA from the torch batteries you submitted under your own name.'

Mills stood absorbing the information – he meant the torch Harry had admitted came from Jamie Reed's Land Rover.

'Do we have authorisation to check the database?' he asked.

'I don't see why not.' Mills turned to leave but Glyn called her back.

'Has Brenda spoken to you yet?'

'About… ?'

'Yes, about… her…'

'Illness?'

'Yes.'

'Yes, she told me on Friday.'

'She explained about the "arrangements" and asked if I would agree to them.'

Mills went to speak but he held up a hand.

'Let me finish, please. I just wanted to say that I told her my role in the lab was too critical to be covering her paperwork as well, so I thought *you* should be given the task. I promised I would keep an eye.'

Mills paused to regain her composure. 'Thank you, Glyn,' she said, making for the door before she said anything she might regret.

'No problem, Dr Sanderson.'

Mills kept herself busy all morning and only caught up with Donna at lunchtime. A swift interrogation revealed that the DNA from the cold case hair sample matched a known criminal who was already in prison for a more serious attack, which had left someone dead.

'It's a good match,' said Donna. 'It's got to be him.'

'Thank you, Donna.'

'No, wait. That's not all. Did Glyn tell you that he's got a match on the DNA from that torch you brought in?'

'Are you sure?'

'Positive.'

She almost ran down the corridor to find Glyn.

'Yes, it's good news and bad news. The good news is that we have a match but it's not a perfect match.'

'How come?'

'It's close to a man with previous called Atkins, although he has quite a few aliases. He comes from Merseyside and has been in prison for theft and assault.'

'But it's not him?'

'No, the DNA belongs to someone very closely related – probably a sibling but could be a cousin.'

'OK.' Mills was thinking hard. 'And the prints on the second torch battery?'

'Couldn't get any.'

'Oh no…'

'Let me finish! Couldn't get any – at first – but then we used the more sophisticated method with superglue.' Glyn was obviously enjoying keeping her waiting.

'And?'

'And we found a good thumb print.'

'On the database?'

'No,' replied Glyn, 'but a good match to the one on the phone.'

'What did you say?' Mills was confused.

'The prints on the phone and torch match – isn't that what you wanted?'

'But the cases aren't related!'

'Aren't they? You'll have to ask Donna, I haven't seen the final report yet.'

Donna was still in the tearoom. Mills was so worried she was hardly coherent when she asked Donna about the prints.

'Can we check them again?' Mills asked, aware that Donna was only halfway through her lunch break.

Thirty minutes later, Mills was on the phone to her friend.

Nina was in the middle of getting the twins dressed when Mills rang.

'Slow down, Mills. You forget I'm a mother of three with no brain left,' she said.

'Don't be silly – you're a detective!'

'I don't feel like one at the moment, covered in baby sick!'

'Well, I've got some interesting news.'

Mills explained that the prints on her phone and on the torch batteries were a good match. More importantly, they had picked up someone on the database who was a close relative, living in Merseyside.

Rosie was occupying the boys on their play mat and Nina took the opportunity to give Harry a call. There was no answer on his mobile so she rang the office, hoping to catch him there. Sergeant Crossland answered, informing her irritably that he hadn't turned up for work and there'd been no word from him. He'd tried the mobile and the farm landline but there was no response.

'It's not like him,' he complained. 'To be honest I was getting worried. You know it's not the first time one of my lads has gone off the radar.'

'I'm sure there's no problem. He's probably forgotten he's supposed to be on duty, that's all.'

'Let's hope so. I'm going to call Graham to see if he's seen him over the weekend.'

'That's why I was calling, to update him on the illegal meat investigation. You can tell Graham that we've had a breakthrough – we have DNA that links the suspect to a relative in Liverpool.'

'Right I'll let him know, Sergeant Featherstone.'

'Please call me, Nina. Do let me know when you catch up with Harry… and tell him I'm trying to contact him.'

Immediately she rang Mills and came straight to the point.

'Have you spoken to Harry recently?' she asked. 'No-one can get hold of him.'

'Have you tried his mobile?'

'Yes, it's not switched on.'

'No way; he's always on it. Must be out of range.'

'When did you last speak to him, Mills?'

She considered. 'Not for ages… no, hang on.' She thought back to Friday night; a phone call from someone and it wasn't Daryl. 'He might have rung on Friday.'

'You're not sure?'

'I was… tired… and it was late. I don't know if it was him.'

'It doesn't matter; I just thought it might help us find out where he is.'

As soon as she put the phone down her daughter ran to her, begging her to play. Babies were fun for a while but

Rosie quickly lost interest when they went to sleep. Nina took the boys upstairs for their nap and suggested that Rosie did some colouring. Soon the little girl was sitting up at the table absorbed in her colouring book, carefully selecting her pencils from the large tin containing a choice of seventy-two colours.

When Nina called Hazel at Newby Wiske to update her, it took some time to explain the details of the case involving the meat trader and she wanted to make it clear that she'd already informed the Merseyside force of the connection with their man Atkins.

'So the guy from Liverpool is the one who carried out the robbery?'

'No, but there is some similarity with him – a close relative perhaps.' Nina didn't confuse her colleague by mentioning the fingerprints which connected the meat trader with Jamie Reed's disappearance.

'OK, I'll do a report if you e-mail through the details from forensics. By the way, I thought you weren't coming back yet?'

'Well, I wasn't... I'm not... I'm just doing a few bits for the wildlife investigation... you know.'

'I don't and I won't ask. Just get back soon, we need you!'

'I will. As soon as Nige gets a break.'

'Looking forward to it, girlfriend!'

Nina smiled as she put down the receiver. She'd missed Hazel and it would be fun to be back at work.

She lay back on the sofa and was soon joined by Rosie, who snuggled down beside her. Nina closed her eyes and felt herself drifting off...

'Mummy! Mummy!'

Her daughter was shaking her awake. She could hear one of the boys wailing. She ran upstairs as, below her, the phone started ringing. Her daughter looked at her and Nina shrugged. 'We'd better sort Tomos and Owen out hadn't we? It's time we went to your dance lesson. Whoever it is can wait.'

Mills sat in the office while the phone rang and rang. Eventually it went to voicemail.

'It's me, Nina. It's just about Harry. He *did* call on Friday night but I can't remember why. To be honest I wasn't really concentrating at the time. I was... well, anyway, he definitely rang.'

She put the receiver down gently then picked it up again, trying Harry's number for the third time. It was unlike him to ignore messages but perhaps she'd been rude to him when he called – she really couldn't remember.

Harry had been dozing on and off throughout Sunday morning, following the rough treatment he'd received from Scouse, as he had named him. He'd shouted foul names, kicking out at Harry's legs as he sat on the floor of the stinking barn. He seemed frustrated that Harry had found his way into his territory and was uncertain what to do about it. It was the first time he'd been in to see him since he'd discovered him loose in the barn on Saturday night, preferring to leave it to the young man to deliver the odd sandwich and can of drink.

Harry knew from that first evening what Scouse was capable of. He'd said he was teaching him a lesson, that it would stop him from trying that again.

'Did you get a good look at your copper friend in there?' he'd asked nastily. 'Would you like to join him?' He'd guffawed. 'Pigs on hooks!'

Harry could still picture every detail of the scene he'd been confronted with in the cold room. He'd been unable to move, even when he heard the doors being unlocked. They'd been alerted by the light and come to investigate. The older man had literally dragged Harry back to the barn entrance after knocking him to the ground. His face felt tender and one of his eyes was only half open. Since then he'd been chained to a metal strut supporting the roof so now there was no way to escape. He'd begged them to release him to have a pee but they refused. You can shit where you sit, Scouse had said, with a great belly laugh.

'You can rot in here until the rozzers find your body, rotting away, being eaten by the rats!' Scouse aimed a kick at his groin before walking out, leaving the young man standing awkwardly alone.

'Nice guy,' commented Harry. No response. 'Is he your boss?'

'He's my uncle,' he replied as he left. There was no emotion in his voice.

The worst part was waiting to see what was to become of him now that he knew Jamie Reed had been killed by his captors. They wouldn't release him to tell anyone about that, so it was only time before they would have to kill him too. He'd been there for two nights; someone would notice he was missing now but no-one knew where to find him. Without any possible means of escape he could do nothing but wait for the arrival of something to eat and drink. They'd given him a plastic bottle of water which the young man refilled when it was empty. Daylight wasn't so bad but at night he was sure he could hear rats moving about the barn floor.

Last night he'd managed to doze and was dreaming that he'd been saved by his sergeant but woke with a start to find he was still in chains. It was the sound of a car engine and the blast of cold air through the barn door that had woken him. Terrified, he thought the two strange men had come to take him away but they walked straight past him to the back of the building. Straining to hear, he recognised the sound of the heavy door of the cold store being dragged open.

Then Scouse arrived. 'Turn round,' he ordered.

Harry expected his chain to be removed, certain they'd decided to finish him off.

'Keep facing that way 'til I tell you.'

Were they going to shoot him? He tried in vain to hear the instructions Scouse was shouting to his mates. The cold store door slammed, everything went quiet except for the engine waiting in the yard. The sound of feet shuffling through the barn was followed by the door shutting and the padlock clicking. More doors slammed, the engine revved and the beam of the headlights disappeared. In the silence that followed, Harry wondered if it had been one of his bizarre dreams.

It was another series of nightmares that left him disoriented, with a heavy head and a dry mouth. Harry was wide awake before it was light and it felt like several hours before the young man arrived with a bowl of cereal and a mug of tea – the first hot drink they'd given him.

'Thank you, mate,' he said, deliberately trying to sound friendly as he struggled to a sitting position.

'It's cold this morning. I thought…'

'You on your own?'

'Uncle Jack's busy.'

'What was all that commotion last night?' Harry asked, hoping the lad might open up while Scouse wasn't around.

He didn't answer but Harry could tell he was nervous. He stuck his hands in his pockets and shrugged. 'Don't know what you mean, mate,' he said as he left.

Sergeant Crossland was alone in the office waiting for the search party to return before he went home. His wife was anxious for him to be on time because she was finding his newly widowed sister hard going. He was working on the duty roster when the phone rang.

'Hi Mike, Graham here. I just wanted to have a quick word with Harry.'

'I'm sorry, he's not here. Can I help?'

'No, it was him I wanted. He's not answering his mobile. Is he with the search team?'

Crossland sighed. 'No he isn't. No-one has seen him. That Nina Featherstone has been chasing him.'

'Oh aye?'

'Yes. She says she's made some progress on the illegal meat investigation.' He referred to his scribbled note. 'There's been a breakthrough. DNA from someone in Liverpool, apparently.'

'I'd better call her.'

'Right you are. And if you speak to her, let me know if she's heard from young Harry. I've got a bone to pick with him, he's supposed to be looking after my brother-in-law's farmhouse and he's not been there this weekend according to the neighbours.'

Crossland returned to the roster, wondering how to manage if Harry was off sick. Only a few minutes later the phone rang. It was Graham again.

'I've just got hold of Nina Featherstone. They've got a connection with a family in Bootle – right load of villains by the sound of it. Anyway, this illegal trader is related to them in some way. Merseyside have spoken to an old boy who's got three sons. Two live in the Liverpool area but one left for Preston years ago. They've lost touch – or so they say.'

'Have they got a name?'

'Yes, Earnshaw, it's being traced now.'

'That's good news.'

'Yes but she doesn't know where Harry is. She's been speaking to a girl who knows him – an old girlfriend I think – who spoke to Harry on Friday night. She's going to ask her again if he told her what he was doing at the weekend. She'll be in touch if she hears anything.'

Mike Crossland replaced the receiver, stared at the blank wall opposite and sighed. Young people these days didn't take their work seriously enough. He shut off the computer and was preparing to leave for the evening as he heard the bus arrive back with the search team. Wondering why they were so late, he went to the front door. He could see something was wrong by the way the team members disembarked from the bus with grave expressions.

'How did it go?' he asked the team leader.

'At the bottom of Wild Boar Fell – not far from the road. If the teams had been doing their job properly, they would've found him weeks ago.'

It took a few seconds for Mike to absorb the news.

'You've found Jamie?'

Chapter 22

Mills hadn't noticed the answering machine flashing until she was about to settle down in front of the television with her supper. She stretched over to press the button and waited. She didn't recognise the voice at first and couldn't comprehend what the woman was saying, until Harry's name was mentioned. She replayed the message and noted down the number. Apparently the police had found Jamie's body and she wanted to talk to Harry. Mills guessed it was the blonde girl that she'd met at the farmhouse.

'I had a message from a girl...' Mills explained when a man answered the number.

'That must've been our Shelley,' he said and shouted out for "Shell" loudly, several times.

'Hello?' The high-pitched voice wavered.

'Shelley?'

'Yes.'

'I'm Mills Sanderson. You rang me today?'

'Oh yes... I'm sorry... it's just ... I've got to talk to Harry. He's the only one that understands. I suppose you know where he is?'

'No, I'm sorry but I don't.'

'But he was with you this weekend?'

'No, Shelley, he wasn't. Why do you think that?'

'Because when he dumped me, I thought… well, I assumed… because you were… you know, before…'

'Look, I don't know what he's been telling you but I haven't been seeing him for some time and have no intention of doing so again.'

There was a wail followed by the sound of the receiver being dropped, then a man's voice. 'Sorry but my daughter is very upset. Her boyfriend's body has just been found.'

'Harry?' Mills gasped.

'No, Jamie Reed. They've been searching for weeks and now they've found his body. Shell is in a right state. She wants to talk to Harry; he's a nice lad and being in the force…'

'I understand and I'm sorry I can't help but I haven't seen him. He rang me Friday evening that's all.'

'Thanks anyway, love. I expect he'll be in touch when he gets the news.'

Mills picked at her meal and scraped half of it in the bin. As the evening went on, she tried to remember why Harry had rung so late on Friday. She'd been drunk and he just wanted to tell her something that didn't seem important at the time. He'd mentioned Daryl, which had been like a red rag to a bull, something about his truck and the people who'd beaten Daryl up. He'd seemed excited by the news and was going to do something about it. She even tried to recreate their conversation. Late that night it dawned on her what he'd planned to do – he was going to visit Mildroke Farm, he'd said – the farm where the meat man lived.

She realised that she should have done it earlier but it was past midnight before she decided she should have called someone. Unable to sleep at first, she lay in bed worrying about what might have happened to Harry. What if they found another body? What if he had met the same fate as Jamie? Gradually she began to doze but woke several times from dreams where she was looking for him.

Eventually, at five in the morning, dressed, full of coffee and feeling more anxious by the minute, she decided there was only one thing to do. She put on her warmest jacket and lined gloves before leaving the cottage as quietly as she could. She fought the freezing wind as she opened the door of the Mini and struggled inside, throwing her bag on the back seat. As she drove, she felt less confident with her plan. It was easy to go to the farm but she had no idea what she would do when she arrived. Hopefully she would find out if Harry had been there. There was no reason why the owners would be suspicious of her. She had a rucksack in the boot and could pretend she was a lost hiker – or had a puncture. Yes, she would say her car had broken down.

She chose the quickest route that took her up the dale and over to Hawes, before turning onto the road to Ingleton. Her headlights cut through the dark, casting eerie shadows as she wound round the lanes. Very occasionally a car went by in the opposite direction but it was a lonely journey. Once she'd turned off the main road, she had to drive slowly to find her way. Things looked very different from when she'd done the route with Nina. She could detect the beginning of daylight on the horizon but it would be another hour or so before dawn. When she reached the final fork in the road she decided to park the car and wait until it was light.

It had seemed like a good idea but the car soon became very cold without the heater running and once her eyes became accustomed to the darkness, she felt confident she would be able to manage to walk the last part of the journey without a torch. So she waited just half an hour then set off down the lane.

The walls on either side were dark; the trees were tall shadows swaying above her. The ground was uneven under her feet and she moved very slowly, feeling her way cautiously. A few times she tripped over ruts and nearly fell but at least she forgot any fears she had, concentrating hard on keeping upright. She identified the gate to the farm by the gap in the outline of the wall and edged forward slowly to peer up the track. She could see nothing. Further along the lane was a dark shape that took the form of a vehicle as she moved closer. It was covered in frost, the windows white with ice. Closer examination confirmed it belonged to Harry.

Edging back along the wall until she reached the opening, she made her way steadily up the track. Seeing a light in the farmhouse, she slowed down, considering her next move. It would be wise to approach the place with caution, she told herself. She knew now that Harry had been there for some time – at least overnight, which was worrying. She had to explore the farm and hoped the rucksack would convince anyone who confronted her that she was a rambler who had got lost in the dark.

As she approached the gate to the farmyard, she could see light in the big barn. The doors were shut but there was yellow glow emanating from the cracks. She tried the gate but it was heavy and creaked when she moved it slightly. Climbing over was more difficult than she'd imagined; her hands were numb with cold inside her gloves and the metal rails were slippery with frost. Picking herself up and adjusting the rucksack on her shoulders, she walked quietly towards the barn, and stopped to one side of the doorway, where a shotgun had been left casually leaning against the door jamb.

It was the voices she noticed first. A quiet conversation was taking place just inside the doors. They were speaking too softly to hear what was being said but it sounded like two men have a friendly discussion. Mills was shaking, whether with cold or fear she wasn't certain. She found a gap in one of the wooden boards forming the barn wall and put her eye to it. The slit was just big enough to see a young man standing with his back to her. He was looking down. She bent down until she found another split board and this time she could see Harry, sitting sprawled on the floor. He had a chain round his waist and his face was bruised and bloody.

She crept back to the front of the barn and was about to pick up the shotgun when the door swung open, knocking her over. A tall figure emerged, swung the door closed and disappeared towards the house carrying a bucket. Her heart was pounding as she lay on the ground clutching the shotgun that had fallen on top of her. Struggling to her feet she dragged the door open far enough to get inside before the man saw her.

'Harry!'

Mills was horrified at the state of him, covered in bruises and filth. He looked dazed and Mills wondered if he'd been drugged.

'What are you doing here?' he asked, clearly confused.

'Quickly,' Mills whispered. 'We need to get you out.' The building stank of blood and excrement; she didn't know how long she could bear it before she threw up. She grabbed at the chain holding him.

'It's padlocked,' Harry said.

'Has he got the key?'

'Who? Tyler? I don't know. Not sure he'd be trusted with it.'

'Was that Tyler?'

'Yeah, he's all right really. It's his uncle that's the problem apparently.'

'Where is he – the uncle?'

'Dunno. Tyler says he's on the booze, might be gone for days.'

Mills bent down to examine the chains wound round Harry's body. The padlock seemed to pass through several links, making it impossible to loosen the chain sufficiently to release him. She straightened up, taking hold of the shotgun.

'You be careful with that, Mills.' Harry warned. 'Have you ever used one of those?'

'No, of course not.'

'Well put it down then.'

'No.'

'Someone will get hurt if you're not careful!' Harry shouted.

As they were bickering, the door opened and a young man came in. He put the bucket he'd been carrying down and stood looking from one to the other.

Mills lifted the gun and pointed it at him. 'Stay where you are!' she shouted, despite the fact he seemed incapable of moving.

'Who are you?' he asked. 'Is that my gun?' he added, as if simply curious.

'Never you mind,' Mills shouted angrily, hoping it was

having the desired effect. 'Go over there.' She pointed the gun towards the side of the doorway and then straight back at him. He sauntered over slowly.

Harry was trying to attract her attention. 'Mills…'

'What?'

'This is Tyler. Tyler this is Mills. She's a friend of mine.'

'Hi.' The young man lifted his hand slightly to give a nervous wave.

'Tyler helps his dad on the farm, don't you Tyler?'

'Yep – and I do stuff for Uncle Jack.'

'Although you'd rather have your own farm, wouldn't you?'

He nodded.

The gun was getting heavy but Mills carried on pointing it at the young man while Harry continued talking gently to him.

'I was telling Tyler about the work I do as a wildlife officer and he was quite interested. He likes animals.'

'Does he?' Mills had seen the tools of the butchery trade on the table beside her and guessed what went on inside the stinking barn.

'Tyler…' she began, following Harry's example and speaking to him as if he were a child, 'do you know where the key is, the one to open this padlock?' She waved in Harry's direction.

'My uncle's got it.'

'And he is… where?'

'I don't know.'

'He's gone drinking, hasn't he?' Harry suggested.

'Yes. He took the carcasses off on Sunday. He always gets pissed when he's sold them.'

'When will he be back, Tyler?' Mills asked. 'Today?

Tomorrow?'

He just shrugged.

'What about your dad? Where's he?'

'He's gone to find my mum. She left when he set this up for my uncle.' He pointed at the metal table that dominated the barn.

'Is there a phone in the house?' Mills was becoming impatient and the lad seemed harmless. 'Here.' She handed Harry the gun. 'Keep an eye on your friend, while I go and call the police.'

She could hear Harry calling her back but she took no notice. The farmhouse door was unlocked and she stepped into the chaos of the kitchen. As soon as she was inside, she could hear a low whining, followed by barking and heavy thumping against a door leading from the room. Clearly there was a dog or dogs on the other side.

A grimy telephone hung on the wall near the sink. She felt the stickiness as she held it gingerly to her ear and pressed nine – once, twice, three times. Before she'd finished a man's voice asked her "Which service?"

'Police, I need the police... now!'

Graham Patterson was disappointed with Harry at first. He'd left several messages over the weekend with no response and assumed he wasn't interested in helping his investigation anymore. By Monday he'd admitted he was annoyed, ringing Mike Crossland again to ask what the lad was playing at.

'So what's being done to find the lad?' he demanded.

'Graham, when we've established he's missing, and not skiving, I'll let you know.' Sergeant Crossland's voice was strained. 'Sorry,' he went on, 'they've just found young

Jamie. He's been lying out there in the snow all this time.' He sounded close to tears.

He went on to give Graham the news that the body of his young mentee, Jamie Reed, had been at the foot of Wild Boar Fell for weeks right under their noses. He told Graham he was up to his eyes in paperwork and would give Harry "what for" when he did turn up.

Graham absorbed the news. Jamie Reed was a good officer by all accounts – a bit green, but with a future in the force. It was unsettling when Harry had disappeared to think that his body could also be out on the fells.

'What was he doing last week?' Graham asked.

'You know that better than me. He was with that Sergeant Featherstone at the farm you're investigating. That's all I know and I don't have time for it now!' He was beginning to sound stressed.

'OK mate, not to worry. I'll deal with it.'

He put the phone down, considering what to do next. It wasn't long before he grabbed his coat to walk to his local pub.

Usually he enjoyed such an outing but today he was bothered. The pie was nearly cold, the beer cloudy. He finished his lunch quickly and set off for Mildroke Farm – it would be easy to find out if Harry had been poking around down there.

The man who took her call told Mills to stay on the line and when the gun was mentioned, he said it might be a while before the police arrived and on no account should she leave the house.

'I have to make sure Harry's all right!' she said but the man insisted.

The dogs continued to bark and scratch at the door. After a few more exchanges with the emergency services, she simply said, 'Sorry, I have to go!' and hung up.

She ran back into the barn, expecting Harry to still have the gun aimed at Tyler.

'Stay there, Mills!' Harry shouted when he saw her, indicating that the gun was now back in the other man's possession. He was leaning against the wall, white as sheet, pointing the gun at Mills now.

'What happened?'

The chains rattled as Harry shrugged. 'Sorry. I put the gun down, it was heavy and Tyler's a friend, aren't you?'

Mills looked at the lad, who nodded but continued to aim at her. She edged forward slowly until she stood next to Harry. Smiling she asked if she could loosen Harry's chains, thinking that between them they might be able to overcome him.

'Leave 'im!' he demanded, the gun oscillating between the two of them.

Mills tried to move back but he ordered her to stay still.

'You wouldn't shoot us, would you Tyler?' Harry's voice was measured. 'We're mates now, aren't we? And Mills is my friend so she's yours too.'

'Yes, Tyler. I want to be friends.'

Unexpectedly he started moving backwards, still training the gun in their direction.

'You shouldn't have gone for the police. I won't shoot you but you mustn't move. Stand exactly where you are and it'll be all right.'

He edged towards the back of the barn, disappearing into the gloom. Mills heard a metallic sound, like a key in a lock, followed by creaking.

'They won't get me now!' he shouted and a door slammed.

Harry looked shocked. 'He's gone into the cold store!'

'What for?'

'I don't know but there's a body in there. I'm pretty sure it's the missing officer.' He was shaking.

'Let's get you out before he comes back!'

Mills grabbed a hacksaw and began working on the chain where it was linked to a padlock behind Harry's back. It was thick metal and she made little impression. All the time she was listening for the door of the store to open again. After considerable effort she stopped to rest her hands, she was only about a quarter of the way through the metal link.

'What's he doing in there, Harry?'

'I wonder… you don't think he's shut himself in deliberately?'

Mills straightened up and walked slowly towards the cold store door. It was firmly shut. She turned the handle and pulled but it was either extremely stiff or locked.

'There's a key on the ledge above the door,' Harry shouted.

Mills felt along. 'No there isn't.'

'He must've used it to get inside. Perhaps he's locked himself in.'

'That's pretty daft.'

'Well, he's not the brightest kid on the block. We have to do something. Go and ring for help again.'

Mills went slowly to the farmhouse, worried that the dogs might have got into the kitchen by now. It was quiet until she opened the back door, then the barking and scratching resumed. Once more she rang the emergency services and told the police operator how the situation had changed.

'But there is still a weapon on the premises?' she was asked.

'Yes but...'

'In that case you should stay in the house – the police are on their way.'

She returned to the barn and picked up the hacksaw. There was nothing to be done except work to free Harry and wait.

Graham was a careful driver but his original training had been as a traffic cop and now he was using all his skills to manoeuvre the old Ford Mondeo round tight bends at speed. Even so, his progress was frustratingly slow and it took him half an hour to reach the farm. Ignoring the cars parked along the lane, he turned into the farm track and put his foot down, only to slam on the brakes as he turned the bend. In front of him was a line of blue flashing lights and he was confronted by a burly uniformed officer.

'What are you doing here?' he demanded as he approached the car. Then he stopped. 'Graham Patterson?'

'That's right. What's going on?'

'Hostage situation; you'll have to stay here.'

Graham switched off the engine and climbed out, pocketing the keys. He deliberately walked past his colleague, making for the front of the queue of cars where he'd spotted the Chief Inspector. Before his superior could say a word he held up a hand.

'Sir, if it's Harry Clark, I'll go in.'

'What do you mean, Graham? We're waiting for experienced negotiators.'

'It's my case, sir. I put him in there – I'll get him out.'

'Don't be ridiculous. We need specialists. It's very delicate. There's a gun.'

'Can I speak to him?'

'Who? No. There's no phone contact. We have to wait. And what do you mean: it's your case?'

Graham outlined the details of his investigation. '…so you see, I've met the guy from the farm before. I know him. He'll talk to me.'

'You reckon?' He seemed to consider the situation, sizing Graham up. 'Time is of the essence with someone trapped in the cold room but unfortunately we can't use you – procedures, you know. There's a shotgun involved but it'll be a while before the armed response vehicle arrives, they're coming from Central Division.'

Graham wandered off as if returning to his car until no-one was taking any notice, all too immersed in their duties. He skirted the edge of the field until he reached the drystone wall. Waiting for the moment when everyone was looking away, he struggled over, landing in an undignified heap in the slush on the other side. Peering over the wall to his left, he had an excellent view of the farmyard and the officers crouching opposite the entrance to a large modern barn. If he could edge round the back of the building, he might be able to see what was going on.

Moving slowly he crept round the building. Unless this third side had an access point in it, he would be back at the front without success. As he turned the corner, he could see a small door halfway down the long wooden structure. Stumbling towards it, he grabbed the handle and pushed. It resisted so he shoved harder, and again, until finally it gave way and he staggered inside.

Chapter 23

It was a calculated risk when Graham emerged through the barn door but the armed response unit had not yet arrived. He waved to Mills indicating it was safe to follow him out. He knew that the reprimands would come later but now he needed his Chief Inspector to hear what Mills had to say. She was a brave young woman and appeared relatively unfazed by her ordeal.

'Just tell them what you told me,' he encouraged her.

'There's someone in the cold room – he went in with a gun and he hasn't come out. Tyler, he's the son of the man who owns this farm.'

'Where's the father?'

'Don't know – looking for his wife, Tyler said.'

'Right. We'll send the lads in as soon as they arrive.' The senior officer was patting her arm and ushering her away but she resisted.

'You won't get in. I've tried. I think it's locked.'

'They'll get in, don't you worry.'

The girl threw Graham a look that read: help me out here.

'Sir, young Harry Clark is still in there, he's chained up. Can we get him out first?'

There was a pause. 'I don't see why not, if there's time before the ARV arrives.'

Graham told Mills to stay close, while the men gathered round his boss. One went off, returning with a bolt cutter and the group moved off into the barn. They waited in silence until finally the doors were flung open wide and Harry appeared, supported by two uniformed officers. There was a cheer and he smiled wanly before collapsing onto the low wall outside the farmhouse. Graham led Mills over and they sat in a row as Harry regained his composure.

'I'll get you both out of here,' he said.

'But Tyler...' Harry began.

'Look, lad. You're the victim here. No way will you be allowed anywhere near, so sit here and I'll make the arrangements.'

Mills waited until Graham was out of earshot. 'D'you think he's still... you know... OK in there?'

Harry nodded. 'We'd have heard a shot if he'd done anything to himself.'

'You think?'

'But he's been in there a long time. He must be suffering from hypothermia by now.' He rubbed at a patch of dirt on his leg. 'I've got to get out of these clothes. I must stink.'

'I don't know,' joked Mills. 'The smell in there was so foul I can't smell anything now.'

They watched the comings and goings of the police until the distant sound of a siren announced the arrival of the armed response vehicle. It was quiet as it raced up the track but five blue lights were flashing on the roof. Everyone had turned to watch as it screeched to a halt behind the patrol cars.

Graham returned to tell them that they would have to move back while the response unit set up in the yard. He took Harry's arm and led them back into the field where the Chief Inspector asked about the location of the cold room and how the situation with Tyler had developed.

'How dangerous is he?' he asked Harry.

'Not at all, sir. The lad's frightened. He's scared of prison. It's something his dad always threatened him with.'

'Well his old man should know all about it. Half the family have been inside.'

'They won't hurt him, will they?' Mills asked.

'Depends on whether he resists or not,' Graham answered. 'That's if he's survived the temperature in there.'

'There's something I need to tell you.' Harry said with an air of importance. 'It's about Jamie Reed…'

'I know, lad. He's been found.'

'…I think he's in the cold room…'

'No, it's OK, lad. He's been found in Mallerstang.'

'But there's a body in there!'

No-one said a word. Mills tried to think of something but Graham broke the silence. 'I'd like to take these two out of here if that's all right, sir?'

'Yes, Patterson, a good idea. If there is a… something in there, our men will find it. Good work, officer. Good work.'

Graham ushered them down the track towards the patrol cars.

'It's OK,' said Mills. 'I've got my car down on the road. I can take Harry back if you want.'

'They'll need you to make a full statement as soon as possible. I'll take you back to your digs at the farm, Harry, to get cleaned up and have a cuppa,' Graham suggested.

'Then you'll be needed by our colleagues in Lancaster.'

Graham ushered them to his car. As he made a three-point turn, Mills saw police with rifles storming the barn. Harry was craning his neck as the car picked up speed down the track and they exchanged anxious glances.

Mills rang the laboratory from the farm while Harry was in the shower. She didn't give them a reason why she wasn't in except to say she had to go to Lancashire Police Headquarters. It sounded feasible enough. She ate toast made by Graham while she gave him a blow-by-blow account of what had happened that morning. He said little, apart from repeating that he wished he'd known that Harry had planned to visit Mildroke Farm.

'It's notorious with Lancashire CID apparently. The guy down there has been under suspicion for a long time. His name is Tony Earnshaw. His brother, Jack, is a known villain. He spends a lot of time with an old boy I know who receives stolen goods.'

Harry came in complaining the shower was cold but he looked much more presentable. He walked carefully before collapsing into a chair at the table. He demolished a pile of fresh toast, stopping only to drink cup after cup of strong tea. Finally, when Mills and Harry had convinced Graham they were fine, he suggested they move on to Lancaster.

Now she'd eaten, once settled in the back of the car, Mills felt weary. She listened to Harry and Graham discussing what had happened, tossing theories back and forth. Finally she must have dozed off because the next thing she was conscious of was the car rattling over rough ground. They appeared to be in the middle of nowhere.

'Where are we going?' she asked.

Graham didn't answer so she looked at Harry but he was slumped in his seat, fast asleep.

They were shaken about and bumped up and down before stopping short in front of a collection of farm buildings.

'Stay here,' Graham ordered, 'I won't be long.'

He jumped out, slamming the door before striding across the rough grass towards an old longhouse. Harry sat up and looked round.

'What's he come here for?' Mills asked.

He rubbed his eyes and scratched his head. 'I know this place. I've been here before with him. Did he say why we've come?'

Mills watched Graham hammering on a small front door. Minutes went by. He looked in their direction, peered through the windows then knocked again. Eventually someone responded and he disappeared inside. Mills looked at her phone – it was ten past three. The car was warm, too warm and she felt herself drifting off again.

When she woke, she shivered. It was beginning to get dark and, sitting upright to find her phone, she checked the time: nearly four. Harry was snoring gently in the front seat and Graham was still missing. It was time to find out what he was up to.

A gust of cold air caught the door and flung it back so far she struggled to catch it. She closed it carefully to avoid waking Harry, pulled her jacket tight and made her way through the rough ground to the cottage. There was a light in the room to the left of the door and she peered through the window. Graham was standing over a small man who was shrinking back in his chair. The blanket over his knees gave him a frail appearance. He seemed to be

275

remonstrating with Graham, who was inanimate.

Mills knocked on the door then peered into the illuminated room again. Graham had left and the wizened man was rubbing his face with wrinkled hands. The door opened.

'Mills?' Graham seemed surprised to see her.

'I wondered how much longer you would be?'

'I'm just chatting to my mate Foxy. He knows your friend Tyler's dad and uncle – don't you?' He had led her into the tiny room and addressed the question to the old man.

'Tell this young lady what you just said about this chap Jack Earnshaw,' he demanded.

The old man sighed and shuffled in his chair.

'Come on Foxy, don't be shy.'

He coughed. 'He sells stolen meat.'

'And where does the meat come from?'

'The farms over in the Dales mostly. It depends. He deals in lamb – it gets the best price.'

'Tell her how you came to know him.'

'I do a bit of work down the market.'

'Poacher,' whispered Graham, winking at Mills.

'Mr Patterson, as I said, I do a bit of work now 'n again in the market and 'e asks me if I want to help 'im. Now I admit I may not be a saint but I'm not going to double-cross my neighbours. I told 'im where to go.'

'But he was here, wasn't he?'

'I told 'im to get lost but he's a bully and 'e keeps on. I know better men than me who's mixed up in 'is racquet – 'e needs the vehicles, see? Farmers hereabouts let 'im use their trailers.'

'Why would they do that?' Graham asked.

'He makes 'em an offer they can't refuse – if you get my meaning.'

'Was he looking for a vehicle when he came here today?'

'I told you – I 'ave't seen 'im.'

'Mills, love, do us a favour. Call Lancaster CID, tell them I'm with someone who knows where Jack Earnshaw is hiding. Ask if I should bring him in?' He repeated the number several times. 'Have you got that, girl?'

'Yes.' Mills put the number in her phone as he recited it, and rang it straight away. 'Stop, stop there young 'un!' The old man's voice was almost a squeak.

Graham indicated to Mills to cancel the call. 'What's that Foxy? Did you want to tell me something?'

'OK, 'e *was* 'ere – *was* mind – but 'e was onto 'is brother. Telephoned 'im from 'ere. I 'eard 'im.'

'Would that be his brother in Liverpool?'

'Aye, I suppose, Left soon after. I reckon 'e's gone to stay with 'im, although...' he hesitated.

Graham took a step nearer the sofa, 'Yes?'

'... although 'e was told 'is other brother's lad were in 'ospital.'

Graham stepped forward to shake his hand. 'Thanks, mate. That's all I wanted to know.'

'You won't be telling them, will you?' he implored.

'You know me, Foxy.' He touched the side of his nose with a forefinger.

Graham led the way out into the hall. The old man followed, seeing them off the premises, before slamming the door behind them. Mills could only smile at the cool way Graham seemed to have handled the situation and told him so.

'...and by the way, there's no signal on my phone,' she

said with a laugh.

'I knew I could depend on you,' he replied. 'He's a pussy-cat at heart, old Foxy, he doesn't want any trouble. Now we'd better get in touch with Merseyside to let them know that Jack Earnshaw might be back on their patch. Then we'd better get you down to make your statements.'

'What about the hospital? He might go to see Tyler.'

'You think so? We can tell them when we get to Lancaster.'

On the way, Graham told Harry what the old man had said about Earnshaw.

'You mean Scouse?' Harry asked.

'Scouse?'

'That's what I called him – I never knew his name.'

'Well, whatever we call him, he's a nasty piece of work but strangely he's never been arrested for anything – unlike his brother in Liverpool.'

'That's why his prints from the mobile weren't on the database,' said Mills.

'Well, well, well,' chuckled Graham. 'Even if he's managed to escape detection before, they'll certainly be able to throw the book at him now.'

It was a long time before Harry was satisfied with his statement. Every time he re-read it, his memory was jogged and he asked to add another piece of information. He went through it one final time before signing the three pages of type-written script.

'Just one piece that needs clarification,' the sergeant said when she'd finished reading it. 'The body you thought you saw in the cold room…'

'I did see it – I'm sure it was Jamie Reed.'

'The thing is, Harry, Jamie's body was found in Mallerstang.'

'When?'

'Yesterday.'

'Monday? Well I saw it on Saturday night.'

'Would you wait for me to get a photo e-mailed through?'

Harry went back to the lobby to wait with Mills, who had finished before him.

'Graham's been chatting to CID. They're watching the hospital in case Tyler's father or uncle makes an appearance.'

'How is Tyler?'

'He was unconscious when they broke in and he was rushed to A&E at the Royal Infirmary. No further news yet.'

'He didn't shoot...'

'No, it was just the cold.'

Graham arrived with tea and biscuits for them and a few minutes later Harry was asked to go back to the office. They turned the computer monitor round to display the photograph – the body of the man that Harry had seen hanging in the cold room. He even recognised the jacket.

'Yes.' It was all he could bring himself to say. 'Yes.'

'Well, he was found yesterday in Mallerstang,' the sergeant said. 'We're obviously waiting for the pathologist's report but I've asked if there's any possibility that the body was moved recently.'

Back in the lobby, Mills, who was slumped against Graham's shoulder, looked up sleepily.

Graham grinned at Harry, 'The DI's just gone past. He said they've found Tyler's father, Tony Earnshaw, with a woman, making enquiries at A&E. Sounds like they'll be picking him up now.'

'So he went to see Tyler?' asked Mills, sitting up and pushing back her hair.

'Yes,' said Graham, 'I reckon he did.'

'I wonder if he knew he was risking arrest – he must have been worried about his son to go to the hospital,' Mills said.

'Hopefully he'll be sufficiently worried to admit to dealing in stolen livestock.' Graham studied the floor for a while. 'If Tyler doesn't survive his ordeal, you two will be the only other witnesses to give evidence against the Earnshaw brothers.'

'And Nina,' Mills added.

'Yes, and Sergeant Featherstone, I agree. But from what you told me, Harry, the only evidence you've got against him is for trading illegal meat, and that's inadmissible. They'll charge him with false imprisonment and they may be able to prove the meat in that cold room was stolen but anything else is without credibility.'

'What about The Fox?' asked Harry. 'He knows all about what Scouse was up to. Can't he be made to give evidence?'

Graham looked round quickly and moved closer. 'Don't you *ever* mention him to anyone, d'you hear? The only reason he talks to me is because he knows I'll keep him out of it. You say anything and I'll deny knowing him or having ever spoken to him and he'll do the same.' He stood up and smiled benignly. 'It's getting late. I think I'd better get you home.' He looked at his watch. 'I can take you back to the farm, Harry.' He turned to Mills. 'Where do you have to get to, lass?'

'Don't worry,' Harry said. 'There's plenty of room at the

farm. She can stay there tonight, can't you Mills? We can pick the cars up in the morning.'

As they left the building, Mills recognised the DI who'd been at Mildroke Farm in the car park, he was beckoning Graham over.

'Just heard that they're bringing one of the Earnshaw brothers in,' he called. 'Tony Earnshaw.'

'How's the lad?'

'His son? The same – he's on life support. It doesn't look good but at least his mother is with him now.'

They walked together to the car where Mills was waiting with Harry.

'I'll need to go over your report in detail with you – and you, Miss,' the DI said. 'You two are going to be important witnesses in the case.'

Mills had slept badly on the lumpy guest bed at the farm and was up early, waiting for Harry to appear in the freezing cold kitchen.

'There's no hot water,' she announced when he first came through the door.

'Is there any tea?' he asked, then filled the kettle and switched it on. 'The Rayburn's gone out, that's why.'

Mills waited until he'd made the tea and sat down at the table.

'Harry, the torch you took from the Land Rover...'

'Accidentally.'

'The torch you took *accidentally* was checked for fingerprints and DNA. The prints match those on Nina's phone which means Jack Earnshaw put the batteries into the torch you found in Jamie Reed's father's Land Rover.'

'So he *was* involved in his death. I knew I was right about seeing the body in that cold room. They must have moved it after I was chained up.'

'That's not all. The DNA matched a close relative in the Liverpool area – they must be able to check that out.'

'Yes, yes that's all fine but what you forget, Mills, is that none of this is admissible because of the way the evidence was obtained.'

'I know, but at least we should tell the DI in Lancaster.'
'I'm not sure…'

'Harry! You can't cover up what you've done. What I'm saying, Harry, is that we should tell them everything. Any tiny detail could be important – and if you won't, I will!'

Chapter 24

Mills led the way through the crowd of press photographers outside Carlisle police station. The discovery of Jamie Reed's body had been made public and Mills guessed it would be national news. Harry looked nervous as they sat waiting for the DCI. The swelling on his cheek was less obvious but there was a nasty yellow and purple bruise above his left eye and the eyelid was half closed. When he was finally called upstairs, Mills waited in the lobby for Nina. Graham had been very supportive when they phoned and he offered to take them up to Carlisle himself but he hadn't been able to stay for long.

Nina arrived in a flurry of anxiety, having learned from Graham about what had happened to them at Mildroke Farm. She insisted on hearing all about it but Mills had only reached the part where she went into the farmhouse, when they were both asked to join Harry in the DCI's office. He introduced himself as being in charge of the murder investigation.

'PC Clark has given me a briefing on the visit you made to see Jack Earnshaw, sergeant. I understand that you took some evidence away with you that we could have made use of if it had been recorded formally.'

Nina agreed that the prints on her phone had been less than adequately documented. Mills knew she wasn't back on duty at the time and waited to see what would happen next.

'I spoke to PC Patterson yesterday and he told me that you'd been helping with his investigation. It has certainly uncovered the extent of the Earnshaw brothers' criminal activities albeit in a rather unconventional manner. Dr Sanderson,' he said, turning to Mills, 'I understand you have been carrying out the forensics on some of the items that PC Clark has told me about?'

Mills waited.

'Well?' he asked, 'we don't have all day.'

'Oh, sorry.' She coughed and put on her lecturer's voice. 'We found connections between some of the items, sir. The batteries in the torch from the Land Rover had prints and DNA from the same person who handled Nina's... I mean Sergeant Featherstone's phone. He's connected to a known criminal.'

'Who?'

'A man in the Liverpool area.'

The DCI looked down at a folder on his desk. 'A man called Tony Earnshaw was picked up at the hospital visiting his son.' He paused to turn a page. 'He's Tyler Earnshaw's father. You heard what happened to his son – he's still in intensive care. Tony has been very helpful, he blames Jack for the state of his boy.' He placed his fingertips together as if in prayer. 'He owns Mildroke Farm and its associated abattoir and he has admitted that he deals in stolen meat.' The DCI looked at them over his spectacles. 'He has given a statement to the effect that his brother steals livestock with the aid of local farmers –

farmers who are put under considerable pressure to do so.' He sighed and looked down at the desk. 'We believe a farmer called Thomas Drysdale took his own life as a result of that pressure.' He finally took a deep breath and sat up straight. 'Anyway, the good news is that we now have an address in Liverpool where we expect to find this Jack Earnshaw and the local force will be picking him up as we speak.' He smiled at them and shut the folder.

'Sir,' interrupted Nina, 'The DNA match is with a sibling by the name of Atkins from Liverpool. The Merseyside police e-mailed through his details and are questioning him about a brother who moved into this area some years ago.'

'Do we think this sibling is Earnshaw?'

'Most likely, sir.'

'None of this evidence is very helpful if we can't use it in court. However, I'm sure it will be valuable when we interview him.' He looked up with a smile. 'Thank you all for your help. And I appreciate your honesty,' he said, turning to Harry, 'I'm sure you've learned a very valuable lesson from this experience.'

Nina drove them both to Mildroke Farm to collect their cars. On the way, Nina insisted they repeated everything that had happened.

'So we think Jack Earnshaw was organising the sheep rustling?' she asked.

'Definitely,' said Harry, 'Graham said The Fox admitted that much. He would pay farmers to use their vehicles so no-one would be suspicious if they saw them out and about.'

'The Fox?' Nina asked.

Harry continued, ignoring the question. 'So I believe Tom Drysdale's trailer was parked down on the lane, ready for the night's work, when along comes Len Meehan who nearly drives into it. The way Tom reacted, I think he was somehow responsible for Scouse, sorry, Jack Earnshaw, getting to hear that Jamie Reed was around.'

'What do you think happened to him?' Mills asked. 'You know Brenda reckoned the thread you gave us was from his jacket.'

'Well I found that in Tom's trailer.'

'So they put him in the trailer, dead or alive, and dumped the Land Rover.' Nina added.

'Yes, then took his body to the farm but had to move it when I saw it.'

'You were lucky they didn't kill *you*,' Mills said.

'I thought they were going to,' he admitted.

'All they need to do now,' said Nina, 'is show that the body was in the cold room at some stage to link the murder to the Earnshaws.'

Mills was anticipating that Jamie Reed's clothing would be sent to their laboratory, particularly since Brenda had such wide experience of textiles. So when she arrived early next morning, she was disappointed to hear that Brenda was definitely not going to be around for another couple of weeks. The rest of them were not in their boss's league. Mid-way through the afternoon, a call came from Lancaster asking if they could fast-track clothing from a murder case and she agreed, keeping her reservations to herself.

Glyn was unusually obliging when she broke the news to the staff.

'Donna can help me – it will be good experience and we need another member of staff trained, with Brenda being off sick.'

'Thanks Glyn, that's great. The pack should be arriving in the next couple of hours. I'll log the items so they'll be ready to start on first thing tomorrow morning.'

Meanwhile Mills settled down to write up a report on all the analyses related to the Earnshaw case, and the cold case, which *had* been carried out following strict procedures. It was gone six when she tidied her desk and went downstairs to receive the clothing that had been taken from Jamie Reed. The documentation described the body being found on moorland in Mallerstang. Cause of death was inconclusive but there was trauma to the head and bruising to the neck. It appeared that hypothermia was the most likely cause of death but the body had been moved, possibly several times before being found. The laboratory was asked to search for fibres, hairs, body fluids on the clothing and anything else that might identify where the corpse had been located prior to discovery.

Through the plastic packaging Mills could see the shooting jacket that Harry had described to her. It was a very distinctive tweed with orange and purple threads running through it. Mills sighed and carried the parcel carefully along the corridor to the clean room. There she unpacked each item in turn, labelled them and bagged them in double layers of plastic with detailed labelling. She signed all the paperwork and locked the door.

As usual, she was the last to leave the building. The traffic had quietened down and she had a good run back to Swaledale. There was nothing at home so, as she came through Richmond, she picked up a ready-meal and a bottle of wine. It had been a tough couple of days and she was looking forward to a hot bath and bed.

As soon as she'd opened her front door, Muriel, came out of the next cottage carrying a large bouquet of flowers.

'These came for you, love,' she called and passed them over the hedge. 'Aren't you the lucky one, eh?'

Mills thanked her and went inside to read the card but there was no message, just a dozen red roses looking a little frosted. She checked the answering machine but there were no calls. Whoever had sent them clearly wished to remain anonymous. As she put them in water, she hoped they were from Daryl but had a horrible feeling they might be from Harry. She put the vase in the kitchen, out of sight as she ate her lasagne in front of the television. After three glasses of wine she'd had enough but the local news had just started with the discovery of Jamie Reed's body. There was no mention of foul play and viewers would have assumed from the coverage that the young man had simply been caught out on the moors in bad weather.

Mills watched Glyn and Donna working efficiently on the clothing for the entire morning, waiting to catch them on their lunch break to ask how it was going.

'Nothing unexpected,' Glyn said as he munched his sandwich. He looked at Donna. 'What did we see?'

She finished a mouthful of yoghurt. 'There was straw, hay, animal faeces – probably sheep – sheep's wool and soil on the jacket and jeans. That's all.'

'Nothing unexpected,' Mills repeated.

'They were a bit stinky like,' Donna added, scraping the yoghurt pot to get the last bit out.

'Stinky?' Mills asked.

'Like a farmyard I suppose.'

'Not surprising if there were sheep faeces on the clothes

— and he lived on a farm,' offered Mills.

'There you are then,' Glyn said sharply. 'I said it was nothing.'

'Well, make a note of it anyway,' Mills said, to compensate for Glyn's acidity.

Mills popped out to buy a sandwich and ate it at her desk. She was disappointed with Glyn and Donna's report and felt sure that Brenda would have made more of the examination. The phone rang and a woman's voice asked for her by name.

'Yes, I'm Dr Sanderson.'

'It's about the Reed investigation. I'm from Lancashire CSI.'

'Oh yes?'

'I've been working on the crime scene at Mildroke Farm.'

'I know it.' Mills heart was beating fast.

'We found a piece of fabric that was caught on a hook in the cold room and my DCI says it may be a match to the clothing you're assessing.'

'Can you describe it?' She was holding her breath.

'It's wool, like a blanket. Sort of khaki — like an army uniform I would guess. Shall I send it over?'

'Yes, yes please.' Mills gave her the details and asked for it to be sent as soon as possible, knowing it would be the next day before she was likely to see it.

'One last thing,' she asked. 'What size is this piece of fabric?'

'About a couple of centimetres square.'

She ran to the laboratory and banged on the window. Glyn came to the other side of the door, looking irritated.

'Glyn, does the jacket have a tear anywhere — probably

near the neckline at the back?' Mills shouted through the glass.

He went back to join Donna at the bench and they both pored over the jacket. Mills waited. Finally he nodded and returned to the door.

'Yes, just under the collar there's a rip about an inch across.'

Mills went back to the office and let the information sink in. They would be able to confirm it as soon as the material arrived but she was sure it was proof the police needed that Jamie Reed's body had been in that cold room, just as Harry had said.

Nina had been asked to go to Carlisle to confirm that Jack Earnshaw was the man she'd spoken to at Mildroke Farm. She was given a coffee and asked to study the video recording of his first interview. She recognised him immediately but drank her coffee slowly, to see what he was going to say, if anything. The officer conducting the interview was good, very good, and she asked if she could stay to watch it all, saying it would be good experience to see a senior officer in action. They left her to it, telling her to let them know when she'd finished.

At first Earnshaw would say nothing but confirm his name. The charges against him were explained, starting with the taking of livestock and passing it to his brother to butcher and sell from an unlicensed abattoir. He denied it. The interviewer pointed out that his brother, Tony, had already admitted that Jack had talked him into setting up the abattoir on his farm, against his better judgement. Next the questioning turned to where the meat came from – clearly not Mildroke Farm, which held only a handful of sheep.

'Do you admit that you were dealing in stolen livestock?' he was asked.

The solicitor spoke briefly to his client. Earnshaw shook his head and sat looking stubbornly ahead.

'We know you used Tom Drysdale's trailer to collect livestock from farms in the area and that on the night of…' he referred to a file, '…in the early morning of the fourth of February, sheep were stolen from a farm close to Sedbergh using that trailer.'

Nina was wondering how they would make the jump to show that Earnshaw was involved in Jamie Reed's murder, if he wouldn't even admit the sheep rustling, and watched, impressed, at how smoothly the interviewing officer worked, probing without alienating Earnshaw. Finally giving up on getting any further with the line of questioning, he jumped to the next charge. At first there was the same lack of response.

'I'll ask you once more, can you tell me why you held one of our police officers against his will, Mr Earnshaw?'

When he didn't reply, the officer continued. 'He has given us a full statement and so has Dr Sanderson. Do you admit holding PC Clark against his will?'

Earnshaw's solicitor muttered something but Nina couldn't hear what was said.

'I suppose I'll have to.'

'Can you explain why you did so?'

No answer.

'Do you know the name Jamie Reed? He was a police officer.'

'No, never heard of him.'

'He was found murdered on Wild Boar Fell.'

Silence.

'He was wearing a very distinctive shooting jacket belonging to his father. Unusual tweed for a man's coat.'

He waited for a response but there was none.

'A piece of that jacket, ripped from the back, was found on a hook in your cold room.'

'Won't be the only coat sold.'

'Can you explain why it would have Jamie Reed's DNA on it?'

There was nothing from Earnshaw but even on the video Nina could see he was thinking fast.

'We can prove that Jamie Reed's body was in your cold store before it was found on the fell.'

At that stage the solicitor asked for a break to speak to his client and the tape stopped. Nina went to find the DI to ask if there had been a further interview. She was told that Earnshaw had asked to visit his nephew, who was on life support at the Royal Infirmary, insisting there were compassionate grounds for doing so, prior to any further questioning.

'He wants to see how bad the boy is.'

'He must be concerned,' Nina offered.

'Concerned? He wants to know whether he's fit to give evidence against him before he decides how to plead, we reckon.'

'Seriously?'

'Think about it – the boy and his father are the only witnesses to what really happened to Jamie Reed.'

On Friday afternoon Mills bought doughnuts to celebrate the successful conclusion of the Jamie Reed case. Jack Earnshaw had finally admitted guilt because of the overwhelming evidence against him, which included DNA on the official items of evidence that the laboratory had been presented with. The DI from Carlisle had rung especially to congratulate the laboratory on their good work, indicating that more would be coming in their direction.

Mills had suggested an outing to the pub after work but Glyn wanted to get home and Donna had a date with her new boyfriend. The doughnuts had been good but she was disappointed that Brenda hadn't been there to share their celebration. So she decided to ring her.

'Is there a problem?' Brenda asked when Mills called.

'No, quite the opposite.'

She explained how they'd tied up the cold case and the current investigation. Brenda sounded impressed. Mills asked about the treatment and Brenda gave a light-hearted response, typically glossing over the details. After a brief chat, she began to sound weary and Mills said she should go.

'I'm so glad everything is going so well,' Brenda said. 'I knew it would. By the way, did you get the flowers?'

'Flowers?' And then she realised where the red roses had come from.

'Yes, they're lovely. But why… ?'

'I said to the girl at the florist's that they're for a very special friend of mine and I let her decide what to send. I hope they're nice – they were very expensive.'

'They're lovely, Brenda. Thank you.'

Chapter 25

Mills was disappointed the flowers weren't from Daryl, as she had assumed. The weekend loomed, cold and empty and she decided to give him a call when she got home. The light on the answering machine was flashing in the darkness when she entered the cottage and once again she thought of Daryl, rushing to play the message before she'd even taken off her coat.

'Hi, Mills, it's Harry. Hope you don't mind but I thought I'd drop in on my way to the flat. There's something I want to tell you.'

Now what? Mills wondered irritably, as she deleted the message. She made a mug of tea and opened the junk mail, then made the call. It went to Daryl's voicemail – she put the phone down without leaving a message. Switching on the television she curled up on the sofa, waiting for the heating to take effect and making a mental note to get more logs at the weekend.

When she woke, the theme music from "Coronation Street" was playing. There was a loud knocking and she stumbled to the door half asleep. Harry was standing on the doorstep with a carrier bag.

'I passed the fish and chip van,' he explained. 'Thought you might fancy some?'

Mills had to smile, despite herself. 'Come in. D'you want a plate?'

'Do you?'

'Not really.'

They sat on the floor, eating from the paper, speaking only to praise the quality of the meal.

'Hope you don't mind me coming over,' Harry asked, when they'd finished and she'd given him a coffee.

Mills shrugged in an ambiguous way. In some respects his company was better than none. 'What was the news you wanted to tell me?'

'Oh that. Yes, well, I wanted you to know I'm transferring to Carlisle. I'm giving up the flat and moving over to be nearer the station. Graham asked if I could go to work with him.' He laughed. 'He says he needs to keep an eye on me.'

Well, that's probably true, thought Mills, and wondered if it was part of an arrangement to rehabilitate him after his various maverick acts.

'What's the latest on your Scouse?' she asked. 'I hear he's admitted guilt?'

'He admitted to everything, including the murder of Jamie Reed.'

'And Tyler?' Mills asked, knowing the news would probably be bad.

'Still on life support. His father has a difficult decision to make soon.'

'You mean to turn it off?'

Harry nodded.

'It's not surprising he's giving evidence against his brother, then.'

There was an awkward silence. Mills carried the mugs

into the kitchen.

'Nice red roses.' Harry called.

'Yes.' She wasn't going to tell him they were from Brenda, he could wonder.

'It's Jamie Reed's funeral Tuesday week,' Harry said when she was back in the room.

'Are you going?'

'Yes, Shelley asked if I would. You know she went out with him before…'

'Are you still… ?'

'Yes, that's one reason I agreed to being transferred. I know she's a bit younger than me but… well, you know.'

'She seems very nice, Harry.'

As he left, she gave him a friendly kiss on the cheek. 'Thanks for the fish and chips, Harry.' She said as she followed him out to the car. 'Keep in touch.'

She could hear the phone ringing but waited until he shut the car door before running inside. Too late. The answering machine had kicked in.

'Hi Mills. I saw your missed call. I don't know what you want but I thought I'd made myself clear last time you called. I'm sorry but I'm in a relationship now so please could you stop ringing, OK?'

Shocked that Daryl had made it sound as if she was stalking him, she quickly erased the message, removing his number from her call list and reaching for the wine bottle.

When she woke on Saturday morning, although it was still freezing cold, the sky was blue and the sun was shining. Mills was determined she would have a constructive weekend and not mope about feeling sorry for herself. She went into Leyburn first thing to stock up with food, buying fresh vegetables and meat to make something nourishing,